Hearsay

by

E. M. Tilstone

Copyright © Jan 2025 Sue Upton

All rights reserved. No part of this book may be reproduced in any form or by any electronic or mechanical means, including information storage and retrieval systems, without permission in writing from the author. The only exception is by a reviewer, who may quote short excerpts in a review.

This book is a work of fiction. Names, characters, places, and incidents either are products of the author's imagination or are used fictitiously. Any resemblance to actual persons, living or dead, events, or locales is entirely coincidental. Neither the author nor the publisher assumes any responsibility or liability whatsoever on behalf of the reader of this material. Any perceived slight of any individual or organisation is unintentional.

First Published Jan 2025
by
Budding Authors Assistant
www.help2publish.co.uk

Cover design by Deb Griffiths

ISBN: 9781917128100

To Annalie and Deb,
with love.

The Game of Chess is not merely an idle amusement; several very valuable qualities of the mind, useful in the course of human life, are to be acquired and strengthened by it, so as to become habits ready on all occasions.

Benjamin Franklin, "The Morals of Chess" published in 1786.

Marie-Antoinette was a victim of circumstance. In her youth, she was a pawn on the diplomatic chessboard of Europe.

Britannica

*Now I ain't sure that time does heal,
Maybe dulls 'til we don't feel,
Forget don't always mean forgive.
Hearsay…*

Gary Fletcher

From the song 'Hearsay', track 4 on Gary Fletcher's album 'River Keeps Flowing'. See Hearsay (youtube.com).

PROLOGUE

PARIS 1818

FLORENCE

Sitting in the deep shadows, cradling a piece of wood, Florence observed the little knicks and cuts her father made. Every so often he would raise his head, grey hair falling across his weather-worn face, hold it to the light pushing through the thick window glass, grunt and then bend his head to study the piece yet again and scrape the tiniest of slivers to ensure perfection.

This was the final piece to be crafted. The red king. Shavings as thin as a cat's whiskers floated through the dust-filled air, landing on the battle-scarred bench below. There had been many battles over the years, Florence reflected. Battles with people, with the absinthe, with the demons that would possess her father. All of which had brought them nowhere.

Chess sets carved by Gabriel Blanchard were highly prized by the bourgeoisie of Paris. He was hailed as an artist and yet where did his wealth go? Florence knew only too well. Into the sewers, into the pockets of grasping, selfish brothel madams, into the chattels of self-loathing that her father carried with him like a hangman's rope. Once a set had been sold her beloved papa would disappear for days and days. She had followed him once and only once as the sights and sounds had turned her stomach. She had retched into the already overflowing filth of the cobbled streets. The shame and shock came bubbling through her lips as green bile. Gnarled hands, tiny child hands, rough bloody hands had grasped at her skirts as she heaved. Leave me be, she had shrieked. They had shrunk back into the shadows as she had straightened her spine; not a weak woman as they had supposed but a wild cat spitting into the wind.

Never again did she follow Gabriel, knowing she couldn't change the man. Instead, she changed herself. While he was out with legs spread below a whore or folded over a bar with a gut full of absinthe, Florence spent hours whittling and carving; turning the lathe, her booted feet guiding the pedal; sanding and polishing; varnishing and waxing until the different coloured hues shone.

And when it was necessary, which was becoming more frequent as her father's skills deteriorated, she remade the chess pieces he had damaged. At night with only the glow of a tallow candle to light her progress and in secret so he never knew the truth.

If someone ever questioned her, she would reply, 'Hearsay. It is not true. Only Gabriel Blanchard can weave the magic of the chess.'

Chapter One

CHRISTMAS 1984

LUC

The smell of unwashed bodies pervaded her senses, yet all noise was cut off by the voices of Bob Geldof and his band of merry men and women trying to feed the world. Luc screwed her eyes shut and then blinking them open the sight of tightly packed human beings made her want to close them again. Her head ached and the aroma of garlic breath from the man next to her turned her stomach. No sleep, too much wine and God knows what else brought her to this.

The train shuddered to a stop and without anything to hold onto Luc slammed into an elderly woman wearing a fluffy pink coat and a bright emerald hat. Luc held up her hands as an apology, the woman sniffed and turned away. No one spoke. No one reacted. *No one ever speaks to anyone on the Tube, people think you're crazy,* Luc thought to herself, lifting her eyes to the adverts above the window.

Luc found herself sucked out onto the platform along with a sea of other London folk. Her canvas holdall became entangled between her jeans-clad legs, and she almost fell as the tide dragged her along to the escalators.

Stand on the right, walk to the left. Constant rules. Do this, do that. Don't eat with your mouth full and don't get drunk. Her father's voice played in her head along with Midge Ure as though he was inside her Sony Walkman. *What would he say to me dancing on the tables last night and nearly getting arrested?* A smile licked her dry lips, cracking the delicate skin as she saw her father remonstrating in a fantasy courtroom—informing a judge that his wayward daughter ought to be locked up. *She's twenty-four and needs to learn some manners. Throw away the key. She's useless just like her mother.*

It had been like that since her mother had left them. Abandoned at the age of eight by a woman who didn't care. Nothing she ever did was good enough for her father. Having aged before his time, bitter and lost and too weak to look after a child, he handed Luc over to his sister to look after.

Now she was going back up north for Christmas—back to a place she had called home once. Her aunt always trying to see the good in everyone, attempting to repair the cracks in the father-daughter relationship by inviting them both to stay. *Well, she can try,* Luc thought, *but I won't hold my breath.*

Scanning the enormous board of lists of places where she didn't want to go, and others she was desperate to get to, made her head begin to pound. Luc dropped her heavy bag near to a litter bin, the only space she could find, and squatted on the bulging mass. The next train was due to arrive at platform 11 in half an hour, but as always was late. Hugging her shoulder bag—*you can't trust anyone*—Luc found her eyes becoming heavy.

The cassette came to a sudden halt. Just in time for Luc to hear the announcement. Pulling her headphones away from permed curls she registered there were just five minutes before her train departed.

She scrambled to her feet, grabbed her holdall and staggered towards platform 11. They were always the

1984, Luc

furthest away. *Ticket please—yes, it's here—thank you. Merry Christmas—you too,* and she was onto the platform running now. *Flippin' First Class—mostly empty.* A porter, with festive holly pinned to his cap, hustled her on board, slamming the door before lifting a silver whistle to his lips.

Luc found herself back in a world of bodies squashed together. Everyone going home for Christmas it seemed. Everyone in the corridor looking drained and hungover just like her. *I wish I'd driven now.* Her little Hillman Imp remained parked outside the red brick block where her bijoux studio flat nestled on the 5th floor—no lift. Camden Town—home for the last couple of years since university. Sighing, Luc slid down the wall landing onto her holdall, wrapped her arms around her legs and slept.

She was woken, at intervals, by several other passengers pushing past her to leave at random stations and finally, around Peterborough, managed to get a seat near to a squealing family of four, all of whom wore tinsel around their bobble hats. She had no option then but to stay awake until arriving at Leeds.

Dragging her bag through the barrier, shoulders drooping, Luc entered a hurrying, scurrying mass of humanity. A brass band pumped out carols while children became detached from parents to run to gaze up at the Christmas tree in the main concourse. Luc scanned the crowds while being swept along the river of people. A voice rose above cries of *hellos* and *haven't you grown* and sullen faced teenagers turning away from sloppy kisses.

'Lucretia! We're over here, darling!'

Luc raised her head and saw her Auntie Alice hopping from one leg to the other. Her arms windmilling high above blonde bouffant hair, solid with hairspray; rather OTT and blissfully unaware of it. Finally, Luc plonked her bag in front of Alice and Hugh Sydenham to be embraced firstly by a huge furry beast and a haze of perfume and then a shag pile carpet smelling of wet dog. Peeling herself away from her Uncle Hugh in his favourite sheepskin coat and Fedora hat, she found herself grinning at the two of them.

You can't be miserable with Hugh and Alice around, she thought to herself. 'Thank you for coming to meet me. Did you manage to park? I was going to get a taxi.'

Hugh waved a gloved hand in her direction. 'Don't you worry about that, my girl. I have my own special parking space.' He tapped a finger against his nose and winked. 'I'll take that, shall I?' he asked, shouldering her bag like a sack of spuds. 'Good to see you, love.'

Alice took her arm and purposefully marched her towards the exit. 'We've just got time for a drink before we're due at the party.'

'I don't have to come, do I?' She just wanted to curl up in front of the television—Raiders of the Lost Ark was on and she was in love with Harrison Ford.

'Of course you do. They want to hear about your new job. I'm so proud of you.'

Luc grunted. 'It's only an admin job. Nothing special.'

'But it's an auction house. A step in the right direction.'

'Hardly!' Luc shivered as the icy Yorkshire wind caught her breath.

Alice harumphed and shepherded her across the road. Neither spoke until Hugh turned down a side street, not far from the station, where an antiquated mustard-coloured Rover was parked on double yellow lines. He ushered them into the car, insisting Luc sat in the front and after falling into the driving seat threw a parking ticket onto her lap.

Luc suppressed a laugh. Hugh wasn't fazed. 'I like to keep them in a job, you know!' he chortled, and with the engine roaring, they set off.

1984, Luc

The house was in darkness apart from red, blue and green twinkling lights in the bay window, when Hugh pulled onto the narrow driveway. The combined smell of recent baking and lavender furniture polish reached Luc on entering the glass porch and the tightness in her stomach dissipated. Her aunt and uncle bustled off to the kitchen at the end of the hall, throwing coats onto the hall chair.

'How about a G and T, darling?'

Luc hung her coat and scarf on the newel post, throwing a reply in the affirmative and made her way down the hall. Catching sight of her appearance in the oval hall mirror, an ostentatious kind of thing, she paused. Moss green eyes stared back at her, sultry grey and silver above with black kohl framing them. Her gaze travelled to her hair—dyed maroon and permed into a froth of curls. Twisting her head, her eyes still focused on the mirror she admired the back of her head shaved to a soft velvet.

A ghost of a face appeared in the glass, accompanied by a mournful, 'Good evening, Lucretia.'

Luc stepped back. 'Hello,' she said coldly. 'I didn't think you would be bothered to come.'

'My sister invited me. Thought I would be lonely at Christmas. Seeing as my own daughter won't visit me.'

Luc pursed her lips and took a deep breath. 'Well, you know why that is, don't you, Dad?'

Before he could reply, two glasses were thrust between them. Slices of lemon topped by bright paper parasols bobbed in a sea of ice.

'Come along into the front room, you two. We've got the gas on, nice bit of warmth to defrost us all,' Alice said, gently guiding them into a room saved for special occasions. 'Be nice to her, Ralph,' she added.

'There's nothing wrong with me, Alice,' Luc's father

said seating himself on one of the armchairs flanking the fake marble fireplace.

'Now, Ralph, you promised me,' Alice said, perching on the opposite armchair and crossing her legs. 'It's Christmas and you said you were not going to be like Scrooge.'

Ralph Stourton glowered. 'I didn't say that. I said...'

'Well, whatever you said, I'm saying you need to be nice to each other. Life's too short for disagreements.'

Throughout this exchange, Luc had hovered by the door, gulping her drink. Now, she said, 'I'll be nice if he is.'

Ralph snorted and then slowly nodded. 'That's all I want. For me to see my only daughter at Christmas.'

'Right. I'll drink to that,' Alice said, taking a sip before patting her hair. 'Now run along sweetheart and put a frock on for the party, there's a dear.'

Luc grimaced before turning and leaving the room. Hugh was coming down the stairs puffing and wheezing as she came out. 'Your bag's in your room, princess.'

She thanked him and went to climb the stairs. Hugh added, 'Don't worry about Ralph, love. It'll be all right.'

'I hope so, Uncle Hugh. I just wish he treated me like an adult.'

'It's hard for us oldies to do that sometimes.' With that he pecked her cheek and lumbered into the front room.

Luc took the stairs two at a time and went into her old bedroom. Posters still adorned the yellow striped wallpaper. The bed was made up with a garish turquoise bedspread and a black and white panda sat propped on the white nylon headboard. She sighed as she pulled her bag onto the bed and dived into it to find something suitable for the party. Soon the bed and floor were covered with clothing and Luc was ready. *A party could be*

1984, Luc

good fun, she thought, *Harrison Ford will have to wait.*

The final adornment was a pendant strung on black ribbon. Before placing it around her neck, Luc held it in her palm. A piece of carved red wood, the one thing Isobel Stourton-Hurt had given her. Her mother had told her it was bloodwood and held magical powers. This was just one link back to the woman who was once always there and then one day was gone.

Why? Luc asked herself for the millionth time. *Why would mum go out of my life and never contact me? Perhaps 1985 is the time to face my own demons. Perhaps it is time to discover what happened to her and why she left so I can move on with my own life.*

Standing, Luc lifted the pendant over her head. Magic or not, it was intricately carved, and the wood shone a dark red, the colour of blood. Checking herself in the mirror on the pine dressing table and squirting Opium on her neck and wrists, she thought she looked okay, but someone had different ideas.

Luc swept down the narrow stairs to be met with…

'You're not seriously going out like that, are you?'

Luc swallowed. *I won't rise to his goading.* She sidled away towards the front door and turned to face her father; a lean man, eaten up by self-hate, guilt and bitterness.

'What's wrong with how I look, Dad?'

'That skirt hardly covers your shame. More like a pelmet,' he sneered.

'I'm a grown woman. I can choose what I wear. Everyone in London's wearing skirts this short.'

'I hardly think Mrs Thatcher would wear that cheap tat,' he scoffed, reaching for his trilby and scarf. The discussion was over. Luc's joy at going out, even though it was to the house of friends of her aunt and uncle, all middle-aged and boring, evaporated. The air between them was ice. Luc wanted to scream and shout, to cut through the wall her father had built around himself since her mother had left them. Instead, she silently took her coat and shrugged it on.

Aunt Alice bustled past her—a vision in green and cream—leaving a cloud of Chanel No 5 in her wake. 'Ooh, you look lovely, my dear. That colour really suits you.'

'Thank you, Auntie.' A glint of warmth flared momentarily.

The door opened and a rosy face appeared. 'It's already icy out here. I've had to defrost the car and get the engine running. It's lovely and cosy in there now.' Uncle Hugh's words heated the cold hall and the three of them followed him out.

The party, held at The Old Vicarage, was vibrant and fun, if you were of a certain age. Luc knocked back a third mulled wine, hoping it would brighten the endless chatter by decrepit middle-aged people. She was the youngest person there and fed up with obnoxious old men breathing over her, complimenting her outfit; their eyes travelling up and down her body as they spoke. She was running out of excuses for walking away—the loo, another drink, food. Now she was wedged between the drinks table and a group of people all laughing at the most awful jokes.

Luc was stretching out her hand for another drink—anything rather than the cheap mulled wine—when a voice interrupted her. 'I love what you're wearing tonight…'

Before the voice could finish, Luc told it in no uncertain terms *to just bloody well go and boil their head!* Grabbing the nearest bottle, she marched out to the hall, pushing past the melee of wrinkles and TCP and stumbled to the stairs. *Where now? I can't stay here. I'm going to die.*

Weaving her way upwards, the thick velvety carpet

1984, Luc

cushioning her feet, Luc scanned the summit for a hideaway. Nowhere to hide. Settling herself on the top step and leaning against the wall, she relaxed, the bottle still in her hand. *What is this anyway?* she thought, glancing at the label. *1960—a good year. I was born! Chateau Lafite Rothschild—sounds posh.*

'Perhaps I can help.' The voice from the drinks table floated up the stairs. A dark-haired man was holding up a corkscrew and two glasses. 'Do you mind if I join you? I feel out of my depth with these old age pensioners.'

Luc relented, nodded and the man climbed the stairs. Finally, he stopped a few steps below her and flopped down. 'I decided not to boil my own head. If that's okay with you.'

Luc mumbled an apology and in silence handed him the bottle. He in turn gave her the glasses.

'Good choice. Very expensive jollop this,' he said reading the label. Luc watched as he plunged the corkscrew into the cork and pulled it out with a resounding gloop. She held up the glasses, the crystal catching the lights of the Christmas tree nestled below them in the wood-panelled room and he poured out equal measures.

Silence reigned while they savoured the wine.

'I'm sorry again for… well you know… what I said earlier,' Luc said.

'No worries at all. I'm Adam, by the way.'

'I'm Luc… Lucretia… but I prefer Luc…' Her words trailed away, and she took another gulp of wine.

'Do you come here often?' Adam asked and then catching her eye, grinned. 'Sorry. I know. What a corny line.'

Luc smiled back. 'Not if I can help it. What about you?'

'I try not to but as I grew up here, I...' he tailed off, looking guilty.

She stared at him and gulped. 'You're Adam Woodruffe?'

'Yes, that's right. Pleased to meet you.' He tossed his head; glossy black hair shook back into place. He wore a shirt with a fine pink stripe and a matching tie, smart black trousers and shoes polished to a mirror shine. All of which, thought Luc, spoke quality.

'I'm so sorry for before. I should have recognised you.' Luc found herself brushing her fingers through her own hair and coughed. 'Erm... yes... well... I'd better get going. Gosh, is that the time?' Suddenly the power of speech vanished and not knowing what to do next she drained her glass and stood up.

'You don't have to go, do you?' Adam's voice was soft. 'Have another glass. We can sit somewhere else. We don't have to be on the stairs.' He rose and stepped down to the hallway below.

Luc tried to glide down the stairs but finished up catching her foot on a stair rod. Nearly dropping her glass, she grabbed at the rail knocking a picture from the wall. It bounced from step to step, landing in front of Adam's feet.

'Shit! I'm so sorry.' Luc went to pick up the picture, nearly colliding with Adam's head as he bent to retrieve it. She finished up sitting on the bottom step, red-faced and trembling.

'No harm done. Dad hates this picture anyway.' He turned it to show a little boy in a sailor suit with a poodle and grinned. Placing the picture and the wine bottle on a table covered with holly and candles, he then held out his hand to Luc. 'Come on. Let's find some coffee.'

Luc shrugged his hand away then followed him through the hall to a large, empty kitchen. While she watched him fill a kettle and lift two mugs out of a

1984, Luc

cupboard before spooning coffee granules into each one, she thought back to their last encounter. He was sixth form, she just a second year. *And I was scrawny with braces. No wonder he pushed past me in the corridor knocking all my books out of my arms. All the girls were in love with Adam Woodruffe. He won't remember me.*

Adam handed her a mug and they took a seat opposite each other at the marble-topped table. Luc cupped the mug in her hands and sipped, burning her lips and tongue in the process. Adam did the same and they both glanced at each other.

'I always seem to do that,' Adam admitted. 'Just too hasty I suppose.'

They drank in silence until Adam spoke again. 'I was admiring your necklace earlier; you know when I had to boil my head and stuff.' He smiled.

Luc wrapped her fingers protectively around her pendant.

'My mother gave it to me, before she left.'

'Left? You mean…'

'No, she's not dead. Well, I don't think she is. She left when I was about eight.'

'Sorry to hear that. You must miss her.'

Luc didn't want to share her mother with this man so just inclined her head.

'I didn't mean to intrude. I'm sorry. You don't have to show me. I understand.' Adam drank some more of his coffee.

Luc held out the pendant. 'It's okay. It's just an old chess piece, a pawn, I think. Nothing special, really.'

Chapter Two

1917

EDMUND

'I got matches. We could use two of 'em.' A tiny flame lit up the boy's face. Beyond, on the silver horizon, streaks of orange danced like the devil, mocking them.

'The lads are getting plenty tonight.'

'Glad we're back 'ere,' Brad said leaning across to light Ed's fresh cigarette.

An ammunition box made a crude table between them—a chess board laid out—each of the men and women in their rightful place on the board. Except for two. One white, one dark red.

'Matches won't stand up by themselves,' Ed observed, drawing smoke into his chest. 'They need support.'

Both men sat in silence, each one blocking out the blasts and explosions from faraway. Each one with their own noises burning into their brains. Each one reliving the squalid trench. Edmund desperately tried to think of summer fields of wheat, the blossom on spring trees.

'Buttons, mate.'

1917, Edmund

Ed narrowed his eyes at the interruption by the young lad before him. A candle flame lit up the wisps of bum fluff tickling a sharp chin, ghostly blue eyes that had seen more than any nineteen-year-old should ever have.

Brad went on. 'Buttons, I got some in me greatcoat. Hold on.' He fumbled in a pocket and drew out an envelope, the seal ripped, and the paper torn. Brad thrust it back into his pocket, muttering under his breath, 'letter from Ma.' Then two solid discs presented themselves. Brad placed them on the board, drew out two matches and lay one down. A pocket-knife soon joined them.

Before Ed could stop him, Brad grasped the knife, flicked out the blade and sunk it into his outstretched thumb. Red pearls necklaced the skin and Ed watched in horror as his companion slid his now bloody thumb over and around one of the matches.

'Mate, what are you doing?' Ed stuttered.

'Well, I was thinking about the colour of these pieces. Blood red. So, I thought let's try that to colour 'em. These others are just white so we can leave 'em be.' He smeared the match, rubbing in the redness.

'My dad said the whites are oak. The reds are bloodwood. He said when they're cut down, you know, they bleed red sap. Like they're dying.'

Ed couldn't take his eyes off the blood and the wood. Two becoming one. He had seen so much blood in the trenches. And now the very life force of this soldier was being added to his old chess set. 'Blood will have blood,' he murmured.

'Wha' d'ya say?' Brad was now rasping a hole in the button after slicing off the match head.

'Shakespeare… Macbeth… men have so much blood in them,' continued Ed mesmerised.

'Too right, mate. I've seen enough to last me a lifetime.'

Hearsay

Brad continued with his craft. 'Yer got yourself a dud 'ere. Why d'yer buy a set that's not all there?'

Ed shifted slightly in his seat, embarrassed to tell this newcomer, that he had given the white pawn to his mother before leaving for the shores of France to prove to her he would return. He knew she would cherish it until he came back to the farm in Shropshire. He had thought his girl, Myrtle would do the same when he presented her with the red pawn. But her reaction had been very different. He remained silent, hugging his memories to himself.

They both instinctively ducked as a shell exploded far to the east. Too far away for them but far too close for the men in the mud. Screams rent the air as the two men looked at each other with blank faces. Two very different men, neither having siblings, both a similar age, except their lives before the war couldn't have been more different.

Brad had been brought up in a basement flat beneath a grand Georgian house in Leeds, his widowed mother was housekeeper to the wealthy gentleman above. Brad had never known his father, never had a figure to look up to, on how to behave as a man should. His mother had tried so hard, tried to *'bring 'im up proper, like'*. His fine features, skin as pale as milk, watery blue eyes topped off by hair of straw had led many a school friend to trust him to then be manipulated and controlled to do his bidding.

Edmund, on the other hand, had led the life of open fields, sunshine, sticklebacks in the stream. With hazel eyes and sandy hair, he had the look of a schoolboy, yet he was strong and attuned to hard graft. A son of a farmer faced hardship each and every day, nevertheless, his parents, Sidney Cruso, and Eirene Field Cruso had produced a child with the sun in his heart and a smile for all.

1917, Edmund

Now, Ed scratched his chin, rough and ready to be razored. The knife Brad was plying to his craft brought images of the cutthroat blade his father would strop against the leather band, the smell of the creamy froth applied to his face.

''ow's that?' Brad held up two grey bone buttons, the four holes now melded into one. A sly smile broached his face. 'I 'acked 'em off a corpse.'

'Not one of ours?'

'Fritz. He won't be needing 'em. A souvenir, like.'

The next part of the operation was delicate. Brad placed the naked match into the hole and taking up the white candle, pulling off its dress of lacy wax, he dropped a couple of fat globules into the hole. In the cold air it dried quickly. Then without any emotion, he squeezed his thumb dripping his human dye into the remaining wet wax, stirred it with the bloodied match and then stood it in the hole of the second button.

'There yer go,' he announced proudly, adding them to the already assembled armies on the chess board. 'Two soldiers for yer. A bit o' me and a bit o' Fritz.'

Ed didn't know what to say. He swallowed. And nodded. He could feel Brad's eyes burning into his soul.

'Thanks. By the way, my name's Edmund, Edmund Cruso.'

'Bradley 'urt at your service.'

'Shall we have a game?'

'Dunno how to, chum. Never learned.'

They both laughed. Their breath making the candle flame dance between them.

'I'll show you,' said Edmund, always wanting to please. 'Let's start with the names.'

Chapter Three

1917

EDMUND

On arrival at their accommodation for the night, Edmund handed out letters and packages to the men. It lifted their spirits and for a time they could all feel the love from home. Before handing a letter to Brad, Edmund sniffed the envelope. 'You're a dark horse, Brad. A perfumed letter from a sweetheart perhaps.' Behind him, Art and Crabbe chuckled.

Brad scowled. 'Give it 'ere. It's nowt to do wi' yer.' Edmund pursed his lips and threw the letter at him accompanied by jeers from the others.

He found a space away from the rest of the platoon. It wasn't easy. They were squashed into a barn with hay bales as bedding and a couple of cows for company. The odour of both filled him with a painful joy—pain of missing home and joy for the homely smell. The farm. The cattle. Mum and Dad. *I won't think of them just yet. I have things to do first.*

He hunkered down in the corner, a gap in the

1917, Edmund

planking lending him a little morning light on the pages of his notebook. Pulling out the pencil as thin as a cornstalk from the spine, he turned to a page entitled **1917**. **"Jan: Arrived Etaples"** being the first entry, his finger followed his journey down through other dated entries including **letter from Mother, letter from Myrtle, pass, guard, bathe** to a space at the bottom. Licking the lead he added in **August 16—Night march**. And then returning the pencil he turned the pages to the back, checking his accounts. *Not much to show for all the hours spent in the trenches*, he mused. He turned back to the flyleaf where he had affixed a stamp just by its corner. He would read mother's letter and write a reply. Snoring from the other side of the piled hay reminded him he must sleep. *Another march tomorrow, no tonight—it's already tomorrow. I can't sleep until…*

'Private Cruso?'

Edmund stared up at the gaunt face of his sergeant. 'Sarge?'

'I need you to do something for me.'

Edmund sighed. He began to stand but the sergeant raised his two hands and pushed down on the air between them. 'No, lad. This can wait. Keep an eye on young Hurt will you. I know you've been playing chess with him and befriended him, but I don't trust that Bradley Hurt.'

'Why? What's he done, Sarge?'

Sergeant Frost sucked in air through lips protruding from under a blanket of a moustache. 'Nowt, yet… nowt. It's my gut. Can't put my finger on it like… something not right about him.'

Edmund nodded. 'All right, sarge. I'll watch him for you. But I think you're barking up the wrong tree if you know what I mean. He's a good lad. We get on like a house on fire.'

Frost lifted one hand to stroke his moustache like

someone would pet a dog. In fact, in Edmund's eyes, Frost looked a bit like one of the old farm dogs back home. Currant black eyes, sharp, ready to pounce on any unsuspecting mice. Or soldiers.

'If you ever want to make corporal, then you know what to do.' With that he turned smartly and returned to the gloom of the barn.

Edmund thought, *I hate this. I hate all of this. We're fighting against the enemy not each other. Hurt's a bit strange but harmless.*

Edmund returned to his notebook sliding out two envelopes. The one with Myrtle's childish round lettering he held for a moment before shoving it into his pocket to read another time, when he felt stronger to deal with the rejection. He slit open the second envelope with his penknife.

My dear Edmund,

I hope this finds you well. I wanted to tell you that I have taken steps to ensure your safety. I put the pawn you gave me, in an old metal soap tin and buried it in Top Field beneath one of them circles – yes, they came again, just like last year. Flora had told me they were magic and gave me a little prayer to say. I don't know if it will help – I felt very peculiar while I sat in the field. I will do anything to bring you home again.

Dad's doing well but he's very forgetful. He falls asleep and doesn't recognise me when I wake him for his tea. The doctor says

1917, Edmund

he's getting senile.

We'll be starting the harvest soon. The spring wheat is turning golden now. I wish you could see it. We desperately need some good weather. I have some girls from the WLA coming over to help us as there aren't many of you young lads left in the village.

Anyway, I'll love you and leave you. I hope you're eating enough and keeping dry. I heard there had been a lot of rain in France. I'm knitting you some socks so will send them soon.

All the best.

Mum xx

Edmund read the letter several times before folding it and returning it to its onion skin envelope, shaking his head in disbelief at his mother's actions. *She means well and if it helps her to keep going then that's fine. When I do get back it'll be like looking for a needle in a haystack. Burying my chess pawn inside a soap tin in an enormous field? What was she thinking?*

'Get some sleep, Cruso,' the sergeant barked. 'Long march ahead of us.'

Edmund settled down, his head on his pack and dreamed of running through golden fields with a dog whose face turned into the sergeant's whenever it barked.

Chapter Four

1985

LUC

Luc's feet ached. She had been standing for hours, showing people to their seats or handing out glossy brochures. The Hyde Park Auction House was a very prestigious place to work but they didn't always look after their junior employees. A woman was striding towards her, her face sharp, eyes narrowed.

'Luc, could you please stay on for a little longer. I know it's been a long day, but Effie has had to leave— she felt faint. Probably due to the pregnancy, I don't know. She's hardly showing yet. Anyway, they've said you will get paid double time if you can stay until eight this evening.'

Luc grimaced. She had a date with Adam around eight. But the money would be useful, and he would understand if she was a little late. 'Yes, that's fine, Grace. But can I please have a break now. I need the loo, and my rumbling stomach is distracting the buyers.'

Grace Fine relented. 'Yes, of course. Take 45 minutes but be back prompt at 5.30.'

1985, Luc

Luc nodded and walked away towards the back room before Grace changed her mind.

Finally, after grabbing her bag, Luc escaped into the London streets. On the way to the burger place she thought she had better phone Adam, but each telephone box she passed was either occupied or broken. *Not to worry*, she thought to herself. *He'll have to cope with me being late, again!*

They had met up a few times after the Christmas party and each time she had been late and each time he had chosen the venue and activity. He would speak about his job and very little else and never seemed particularly interested in what Luc was doing. Back in Leeds, as a young teenager, she had watched him from afar, quite starstruck with his good looks; never to be noticed by the popular, intelligent sixth former who was now something high up in the city at a merchant bank.

As Luc entered the burger bar, she thought this was not the sort of place Adam would frequent. She laughed to herself as she took a seat, and a waitress appeared. The order was taken, and Luc relaxed. Checking her watch, she didn't have long before going back, but the food arrived quickly, and she shovelled it down. Sipping a black coffee, Luc contemplated her life. 24 years old, living in a studio flat in Camden with very few prospects. But at least she had a toe through the door of a good auction house. Her dream was to work in an art gallery, be amongst beautiful art and design. Perhaps the Tate one day. But for the time being, this was a stepping-stone. And she had met some interesting people. One buyer from earlier that day suddenly came to mind.

A very dapper gentleman—a smart expensive-looking suit, a bright shirt of turquoise stripes, a tie to match and a green handkerchief blossoming from his top pocket. He had made a comment about her name badge.

'Luc Stourton-Hurt. An interesting name,' the man had murmured.

Thinking he meant her first name, as many people would often look quizzically at her when she said her name was Luc, she patiently explained her name was Lucretia after an aunt from hundreds of years ago.

The man nodded and then said, 'Lucretia is a very nice name, but I meant your surname. Hurt. I used to know someone of that name a lifetime ago.' And for a moment his eyes fixed on a spot to the side of Luc before he glanced back at her and smiled. 'Yes, a lifetime ago.'

Luc had picked up a European accent while the man was speaking and asked him where he had come from. The man explained he lived in Paris and had flown over specially for one of the lots in the auction.

Now, sitting in the burger bar, Luc remembered the man's name. *Maurice Smith. Not a very French-sounding name,* she reflected. *But an interesting man, nonetheless.*

Leaving the café, she raced back to the auction house and arrived with Grace Fine, her line manager, just checking her watch. Her eyebrows shot up as Luc entered but she remained silent.

Luc placed her bag in her locker, checked her appearance and then made her way to the main room where the next auction was about to begin. She guided the buyers to their seats and was pleased to see Maurice Smith taking his seat near the front.

The auctioneer was very skilled in getting the best prices for the articles and many went way over their expected valuation. Luc stood at the side of the rows of seats ready to help anyone with their bids, but everyone seemed to be seasoned buyers. The sale finally reached the last hour and the miscellaneous section. Various items

1985, Luc

went under the hammer. Nothing of interest to Luc but then two chess sets were displayed one after the other and her hand instinctively went to her throat where her pendant usually lay but today, she hadn't worn it. Only simple jewellery was permitted for the stewards.

The two sets easily went above their estimate, exquisitely carved figures—black and white pieces on large decorative boards. And then a third set was brought out. Small, compared to the others. Simple, unlike the others. Red and white, different in every way to the two that came before.

The auctioneer announced, 'A set, believed to have been crafted by Gabriel Blanchard in the early nineteenth century. Bloodwood and oak. I would like to start the bidding at one thousand pounds sterling.'

Luc looked again at the set. Bloodwood? Like hers. She found herself walking slowly towards the front to take a better look. *It can't be,* she thought to herself. That is too much of a coincidence. But there it was, a chess set laid on a red and white chequered board. It certainly looked like her piece but at a thousand pounds Luc told herself it couldn't have been where her piece had originated from.

A voice called out, 'Yes please.' Luc turned to see the Frenchman she had spoken to earlier had raised his hand.

Luc moved across to stand against a wall near to the row where Maurice Smith sat. A strange feeling wormed itself into her stomach. She put it down to tiredness, but feelings of expectation and exhilaration flickered through her.

'Thank you, Mister Smith. We have our first bid.' The auctioneer turned her head to observe her audience.

A voice came from the back of the auditorium. '1200.'

Maurice threw back, '1500!'

Hearsay

Like a tennis match, Maurice and the other bidder batted the price back and forth, until finally, Maurice called out, '5000 pounds.' Luc held her breath, willing the sale to go through.

'Sir, do you wish to make a bid? No? Going once, going twice, go…'

'6000!' It was the voice from the back. Luc craned her neck to see who else was bidding. A grey-faced, grey-haired businessman.

No reply came. People shifted and sighed and fell silent.

Once again, the auctioneer asked Mr Smith. Luc saw him shake his head as the gavel crashed down on the mahogany lectern. And then the audience was clapping as the auctioneer announced that was the final lot of the night and could buyers make their way to the main desk to pay for their purchases.

Luc wanted to speak to Maurice to ask about the chess but before she could get near him, she found herself lost behind the throng of people leaving. She was asked directions to the desk so many times she wanted to hold up a placard with a large arrow. The last few streamed through the main swing doors and Luc and Grace Fine along with the other stewards shooed out any malingerers.

A silence fell on the foyer and an ache came to Luc's chest. Once again, as in all times of distress her hand strayed to her throat. The pendant wasn't there but the action gave her calm. Maurice Smith had left. She couldn't ask him anything. Luc's shoulders drooped and she let her head hang as she turned towards the stewards' room to collect her bag. Noticing the time was almost eight she contemplated she might just make it to see Adam if she went now.

Outside it was dark and the March air was cool after

1985, Luc

being in the warmth of the auction house. It wasn't far to the tube, and she set off turning right onto the pavement and promptly collided with a figure standing near to a black cab. Looking up to apologise she saw it was the Frenchman.

'Ah, bonsoir mademoiselle. I would like to speak with you for a moment.' Luc glanced once more at her watch and her movement did not go unnoticed.

'I will only take a second of your time, Lucretia Stourton-Hurt. Please take this.' He held out a card which Luc took. He continued. 'Please phone my art gallery in Paris. I think you would enjoy working there.'

He nodded before climbing into the taxi. The driver pulled out to join the traffic leaving Luc staring at the red lights fading away down the street. A sudden cold breeze whipped her legs, and she came to. *Adam! Oh my God! I must go.* She pushed the card into her coat pocket and sprinted towards the tube station.

Ten minutes later she arrived at Oxford Circus and after scurrying along the crowded pavement passing Top Shop and Etam she turned away from the madness of Oxford Street and made her way up Winsley Street.

A fusion of plant life and fairy lights and the steady beat of music met her, but no Adam. Simon Le Bon was pumping out Hungry Like the Wolf while people spilled out onto the pavement from the busy wine bar. Perhaps he was inside.

The bar was dimly lit, candles in wine bottles, a chalk board announcing the cocktail of the day. *Perhaps a Tequila Sunrise would be nice*, Luc thought, weaving through the crowd of city bankers with their Filofaxes and talking loudly into black bricks. A mass of bubbly curls crossed Luc's path, and she stopped dead, admiring the girl's scarlet leather jacket with bat wings. Her shoulders caught Luc as she carried on her way, *sharp enough to gouge your eye out,* thought Luc.

'Luc. Hello!' It was Adam propped nonchalantly against a purple velvet stool, a leather Filofax in one hand. He leaned forward and kissed her on the cheek.

'Hi.' Luc's stomach did a funny tilt, and it wasn't tiredness this time. 'Look, I'm sorry I'm late…' She tailed off and took a large glass of white wine from him.

'Sorry, I can't hear you… I got you this.'

Luc took a gulp of the golden liquid. 'Not quite tequila, but this will do. Thanks.'

'What did you say?'

'Nothing.' She took another mouthful. 'I really need to sit down before I expire,' she shouted into his ear. Adam bobbed his head, rose, and steered her towards a table at the back of the restaurant. It was quieter and the music more mellow. He placed an open bottle of wine and his glass on the table.

'Did you have a good journey?' Luc asked.

'Yeah. Tube was busy, as always. Arrived early…' he broke off and looked at her.

'Sorry about that. I had to work late.'

'I'm almost getting used to it.' His tight smile didn't bring any light to his eyes. His tone seemed easy, but she could tell from the tension etched on his face he was unimpressed about having to wait again. While she slurped some more wine, Adam tapped his fingers on the table, his eyes constantly straying to his closed Filofax. Luc swallowed, trying not to feel undermined and unimportant.

Adam took her silence to be an opening for him to talk about his day and to boast about the big deals he had made. Drinking distracted her from getting bored with his

1985, Luc

description of bonds and shares, hedge funds and stocks, dollars and yen. Refilling her glass, her mind began to wander, her focus becoming fuzzier, and she forgot to look interested. *Why do I put up with people who don't care about me? Adam's not really interested in me and the feeling's becoming mutual.*

Adam was smiling at her, and this time his whole face lit up. And once again, Luc found herself floundering. He was so gorgeous and rich; she would be stupid to not give him a chance, yet a little voice in her head reminded her to value herself. *Looks and money aren't everything,* she mused.

'How's your job going?' Adam asked. Finally, he was showing an interest, yet his tone was of resignation not caring. Wanting to go up in this man's estimations Luc went into detail about the auction house. Since studying at university and gaining a degree in the arts and events management, she had been trying to gain employment doing just that but to no avail. She had taken the job hoping it would lead to her developing her skills but most of the time, she was a dogsbody. She didn't tell Adam all of this, wanting to impress him. Instead, she told him of today's auction, where she had been a steward, and how she had met this man, Maurice Smith. Adam nodded in all the right places, but his eyes told a different story. He clearly looked unimpressed to Luc. She was reluctant to tell him about the chess set. Her heart told her to leave that as a secret. Then remembering what Maurice had said earlier she reached into her pocket and drew out the business card.

'He gave me his card before he left and said he had an opening at his gallery in Paris. That would be amazing wouldn't it, Adam?' Luc said eagerly, looking across the table, hopeful as a small child on Christmas day.

In answer Adam snorted. 'Like that's going to

happen. He fancies you. He's just chatting you up!' Taking the card, he glanced at it and then threw it back at Luc.

Luc's excitement dissipated into a small 'Oh' and she looked down at her glass. Feeling squashed by his comments she took a mouthful of wine, giving her time to disseminate her feelings. Perhaps Adam's right, but it was nice to think someone was interested in offering her a good job. After all, Adam had more experience, and she could be quite naïve when it came to business and careers.

'Well, I'd better get going.' Adam drained his wineglass.

'So soon? I thought we could…'

'I'm sorry, Luc. I don't think this is working. You're very nice but…' he trailed off. 'Obviously, you can stay and finish the wine. I'll see you around.'

Before Luc could say anything, he was gone. Glancing around the room, she was aware of a heat spreading across her cheeks and coughed before plastering a big smile across her face. *Oh well, that's it then. Another one bites the dust. I should be the one walking out though. Auntie Alice would have called him a cad. Me, I think he's not worth spending any more time thinking about.*

She held her glass aloft towards where he had exited. 'Cheers Adam,' she said aloud. And in her head—*you've done me a favour. I don't need a man to make me whole, especially one so arrogant as you.* Lowering the glass to the table, she muttered, 'And I don't need this drink either.'

If there is someone out there to share my life with, I want to have someone who will respect me for who I am, someone who I can trust. And then a grainy black and white image of two people on their wedding day came to her. *Bradley and Elspeth Hurt—Grandad and Granny. They had a wonderful loving relationship. I want that too, one day.*

Luc stretched. It had been a very long day, and she

1985, Luc

still had to get home. She rose from her seat and reaching for her bag, noticed the discarded business card on the table. *Perhaps Adam was right after all. The man hadn't been serious about a job. Anyway, I can't go to Paris—that would be ridiculous.* Luc turned away and left the crowded bar.

Chapter Five

1985

LUC

The next few weeks went by, with Luc learning more about the work of an auction house. She didn't know enough about antiques to do any valuations, but she was finding that the job was interesting, and she was becoming more aware of the history behind some of the items. Provenance was key, she learned, if you wanted to prove that something was what it purported to be. Luc found herself spending more time wandering around antique shops and old bookshops, enjoying the smell of old books and the feel of the paper. *If you could bottle this smell, you could make a fortune,* she thought to herself.

As a teenager, Luc had loved visiting the school library—the middle-aged librarian was always pleased to see her and often tasked her with things to do after school. Labelling books, adding on dust covers to the new books, returning books to the correct shelves.

Visiting book and antique shops brought a sense of place to Luc, a sense of her own mortality. After Adam Woodruffe had walked out on her she had thrown herself

1985, Luc

into her work and in trying to find her own identity. She spent many times pondering on what it was that made us who we are. The sadness of not knowing where her mother was weighed upon her shoulders more and more. Luc knew that the only way to find out more about her mother, was to talk to her father and that meant she would have to make amends. *But was it all too late for that?*

One evening after another long day of stewarding at an auction, Luc decided to look at some old photo albums. She pulled open her wardrobe door and was presented with shoe boxes toppled over like a collapsed tower of Jenga; shoes tied up with bags and belts; metal coat hangers just about holding clothing and right at the back a couple of albums.

Climbing onto her dilapidated sofa and sitting cross-legged she pulled one of the books onto her lap. Another fragile link to her mother. Isobel hadn't taken much with her when she abandoned them and what was left behind, her father, Ralph, had chucked out. Luc had thought she was loved by both her parents, remembered happy family times, brought up to believe that life was good. And yet, it obviously wasn't. When there are untruths swirling within a family no one remembers things as they really were. We remember what we want to remember, our perception being different. Were her own memories the same as what her family had experienced?

Photos held in place with clear triangles, flattened memories now incarcerated within grey card of Luc as a child on stilts next to her mum; in front of a wigwam with her favourite doll; with her father on a park bench. Some had hand-written additions of dates and names. Memories were there in black and white—proof positive that they occurred. But was it the image that was the memory, or vice versa? She had loved that doll and remembered trying to sleep in the wigwam one night, until the rain poured down and she had to go inside. She had been determined to walk on the stilts and then she fell off and never went on them again. And her father, her beloved father, turned horrid almost overnight when her mother left them. He became the man where nothing was ever right.

And yet, there were moments where he was disarmed, and his shield of anger was removed. These were the moments Luc cherished. When they talked—properly—and laughed—properly. He would tell of his younger life with her mum going to dances and concerts. How they would dance down the streets under the moon and hold hands under the lamplight outside her family home.

Luc wanted that with someone. She had met various men over the years, but no one was ever quite right. Her grandparents had a very close relationship when she was growing up. They had met during the first world war. An image lay on the grey card, of the two of them on their wedding day, both smiling, gazing into each other's eyes. No writing below this one, after all everyone knew who they were.

But old photos were not enough. Luc wanted proof. The only way forward to discover more about her family and especially her mum, she would have to go and talk to her father.

Two weeks later, and Luc was still feeling low. She had decided to put off returning to Leeds and to confronting her dad about her mum. It was how she had spent the last few years: not facing up to reality; always finding something else to fill her time rather than seeing her dad. *He was never there for me so why should I put him first?* She had been afraid that he would tell her bad news about

1985, Luc

her mum but also, she couldn't cope with the accusations thrown at her, just like at Christmas. He implied that it was her fault that her mother, his wife, Isobel had walked out on them and that was too much to bear for Luc.

Having a rare day off, she decided to spend the time seeing the sights in London to lighten her mood. Visiting the Victoria and Albert Museum was always a highlight for her, and she almost skipped around the exhibitions.

The time passed far too quickly for Luc, and she eventually made her way out of the main entrance, her head full of history and culture, fashion and ceramics. *A day just for me and building my knowledge of antiques,* she mused as she wandered along.

Her mind overflowing with the many sights she had observed in the museum, Luc's body walked in automatic mode until someone laden with expensive designer shopping bags barged into her. No apology and Luc bristled with indignation. Pausing to watch the woman stumble on her way in her high heels and Dior suit Luc looked around to get her bearings. She didn't recognise the street, just a few shops and cafes yet somehow, she had stopped outside an old bookshop.

Needing a moment to compose herself, Luc ventured inside. That comforting smell of old paper hit her nostrils immediately and her stress dissipated. Checking her watch against the card with the opening hours, she saw she had an hour or so before it closed.

There were just three other people in the shop, a shop assistant sitting behind a desk and two others, a man in his fifties or so and an elderly woman, their noses deep into the books they held open. A hushed space to breathe and to read. Luc strolled around the many heaving shelves, stroking the spines, occasionally taking one out to read the blurb or the first page and then returning them back in exactly the spot they had originated from.

One spine of a thin leather-bound book, shiny as eggshell, red as blood, stood out from the others. Absentmindedly, Luc went to push it back in and then noticed a tiny gold emblem at the bottom of the spine. A chess piece. She pulled it from its space and saw it was all in French, not a language she knew well. Opening the cover carefully, Luc gently turned the first few pages. She drew back a breath—there on the page before her was her chess piece. Fumbling to bring out her pendant to compare the two she almost dropped the book.

Needing more light to see, she took herself to the shop window and then placed her pawn against its twin. It was an exact copy. Her mind raced. What was the name of the maker of the chess set the French art dealer had bought in the auction? She turned back to the frontispiece

L'histoire des Jeux d'echecs Blanchard par M. Flaubert.

Blanchard. That was it, I'm sure of it. Then my pawn could be part of a set like the one he bought. She blanched, thinking of what a set would cost if she could find the rest of the pieces and sell it. *Wow!*

'May I be of help?' said a voice from behind.

It was the shop assistant, a man in his forties with jet black hair and wearing a plain white shirt and blue jeans. He repeated her question and grinned.

'An interesting book. French, I believe. Do you speak the language?' the man asked.

Luc shook her head. 'A little bit of O level French but that's about it, I'm afraid.'

'May I?' he asked, holding his hand out. Taking the book, he turned to the opening page and scanned the page. 'This seems to be an introduction—I think someone has pasted this bit in. Look.' He showed Luc where the

1985, Luc

edges of the extra bit were curling away from the original. Then he read aloud, translating as he went:

'"The chess set belonged to Michel Flaubert, a prominent and highly respected statesman. He took ownership of the Blanchard set following the death of his father, Victor, and kept it untouched as it had been since the day it was made. Victor Flaubert had ordered the set to be made for his wife but before she could play, she died giving birth to a daughter. Unfortunately, the child did not survive either. In his grief he vowed no one would touch the pieces again.

The Blanchard set went missing from the home of Michel Flaubert in 1854, believed to have been stolen in a burglary as jewellery and silver ornaments were also taken. Nothing was ever found, and the culprit was never discovered."'

'Goodness, how sad?' announced Luc.

'Yes, it is. An interesting story, nonetheless. Would you like to purchase it?'

'Yes please,' Luc said quickly.

An impatient cough came from the reception desk and Luc turned to see another customer standing at the desk.

'I won't be a minute.' And with that he strolled over to the counter.

Luc leafed through the book—distant memories of French lessons with the dreaded Miss Jolly—a name that Luc and her friends had always seen as being ironic. She was far from that! A few words came back to her. She murmured the title quietly to herself, L'histoire des Jeux d'echecs Blanchard par M. Flaubert, enjoying the sounds of the words but frustrated with her own pronunciation. She worked out the title was something like: The Story of the Blanchard Chess Sets by M. Flaubert.

Hearsay

What did the assistant say about M. Flaubert? The chess set had belonged to Michel Flaubert, and the set had never been played and then it was stolen. Luc turned to the first page, but it overwhelmed her. *I'm going to need some help if I want to find out more about my chess piece.*

Luc made her way to the counter and while the assistant placed the book inside a paper bag, several thoughts and questions came to her. Who could help her further with the translation? What did all this mean—why would her mum have given her this one chess piece—a red pawn and where was the rest of the set?

'Good luck,' called the man as she left the shop. 'I hope you find the meaning behind it all.'

Throwing back a thank you, Luc hurried out onto the street, her mind full of ideas and plans.

Chapter Six

1918

EDMUND

Edmund packed away the chess pieces into their wooden case, wiped spots of mud from the polished marquetry surface before placing it in his kitbag. *A diamond in a pile of shit,* he thought. A piece of home, a gift from his father and the last link to Myrtle.

Of course, she had wanted a real diamond.

Beside him in the dugout, Brad was stomping around. With every action of throwing things into his bag he grunted. Under his breath, he muttered a series of expletives.

'You'll be all right. You won't be alone,' Edmund said crouching to check on a brew. The water was coming to a rolling boil; he filled two tin mugs and passed one to Brad.

He took it, still complaining. 'That bloody man. That fuckin' tree!' He gulped some coffee down and then swore again. 'You trying to kill me? That's friggin' 'ot!'

Edmund tutted. 'That'll be the boiling water.' He chuckled. Brad grimaced.

'Think you're funny, do yer?'

Hearsay

'Hey. What's the matter?' Crabbe asked, ducking to miss the corrugated roof as he entered. In answer, Bradley Hurt shoved the coffee mug into his chest, spilling the contents across his uniform jacket and pushed past him sniping.

'I'm going to see Sarge. I'm not rostered for that bloody tree until next week.'

'He'll get short shrift from him. Stupid bugger!' Crabbe said, testing the coffee before glugging it back.

Brad returned with a face as black as thunder. 'I blame you, Corporal Cruso.' He spat the words at Edmund. 'You fuckin' goody two shoes. Sucking up to Sarge, telling on me about the supplies. I only took a couple o' bits to replace my rations.'

Fed up with Brad's attitude and constant complaining, Edmund stormed back at him. 'That's enough from you, Hurt! We're in this together. We're fighting the Hun not each other.'

'Exactly!' replied Brad. 'So why didn't you speak up for me? Fine friend, you are!'

A deep Welsh voice came from the shadowy depths of a recess in the trench wall. 'I quite like being in the tree. I feel special you know.' A red glow and a puff of smoke reminded them of Art's presence.

'Look, Pencil, me ole mate. It's all right for you. There's nothing of yer. Yer ma never fed yer.' Crabbe's laugh was throaty, and he began to cough and splutter. 'Me, on the other 'and, has to squeeze this gorgeous specimen of muscle and manliness inside the trunk.' Crabbe began to parade around the tight space, knocking into Brad who shoved him away.

Art threw back his head and roared, 'You're no more muscleman than me. Your chest is like one of me dad's pigeons.'

Edmund checked his watch. 'It's time gentlemen. Brad and I need cover to get across to the tree. Once we're

1918, Edmund

in, you'll see our lantern go out.'

'Yes, Corporal.'

'Brad, are you ready?' Edmund asked.

Like a spoilt child, Brad said nothing.

'Private Hurt, if you don't answer me, I will take steps to have you court marshalled for subordination and refusing to follow orders. What do you say?'

Brad shouted back. 'Aye, Corporal Cruso I'm ready.' The voice was strong and polite, but the glint in his eyes warned Edmund not to trust him fully.

The four of them trudged through the communication trench to the front line where Art and Crabbe made ready, mounted the fire steps and took up position against the barrier of sandbags. Brad and Edmund climbed over the parapet, slid under the barbed wire taking a different path to the route they had used before. They were surrounded by desolation, a place of death and fire; the oak a twisted, burnt-out husk stood proud from this.

Arriving at the fake tree, Brad insisted Edmund went first up the rope ladder. 'I'll watch yer back, mate. No hard feelings, hey?' Edmund nodded and shimmied up, wrinkling his nose against the pungent, earthy aroma. Taking his place on the seat, he glanced down and gave Brad a thumbs up. Brad then extinguished the light and closed the hatch.

Edmund still marvelled at the ingenuity of the artists and engineers who had crafted this from wrinkled iron, painted to look like bark exactly like the original burnt-out tree that had stood there before. For a moment or two while his fingers sought the periscope, an image of the old oak tree in the woods near his home flashed before him and yet again he saw Myrtle flinging the innocent red pawn into the leaf mould and ferns growing at the base beneath their initials scratched into the bark.

In the darkness, his fingers, encased in leather gloves, grasped the metal and he lifted it to his eyes, blind to the outside world due to the metal protective wall. The diamond mesh covering the viewing hole above his head came into focus as he moved his eyes until he could clearly see into the German trenches. A bird's eye view, just like the two cooing doves that had watched the two lovers fight over what made a love token.

Myrtle's voice now echoed within his mind. Disappointment within her tone. 'I don't want a stupid bit of wood!'

'But it's a love token,' Edmund had explained.

'A diamond is a love token,' she snorted.

'You know I would if I could. I have no money put by.'

He knew she was the one, this firebrand of a girl. His world had tipped that first time he saw her. She, on the other hand, needed convincing.

Stepping gingerly towards her, Edmund reached out to stroke her cheek, to lift her chin, her eyes to his. 'I'm sorry I can't give you a diamond ring, but I will one day, when I make my fortune. Then I'll shower you with diamonds and rubies and pearls. I promise.'

Myrtle had glared back at him and then her features softened. 'I'm sorry. I don't want to fight—heaven knows there'll be enough of that over there.' She waved an arm towards that unknown, far-off land, not knowing which direction it was. 'But I need you to show me how much you really love me. I think we're best off not waiting for each other.

'I love you, Myrtle. I don't want this to end. I'll write,' Edmund said, his voice husky with desperation.

'I don't know, Edmund. I'll think about it. I can't wait for ever. I'll write and let you know.'

1918, Edmund

Now, inside the oak tree, just a few yards from the enemy trench, that one letter from Myrtle crackled in his pocket. Ignoring its call Edmund jotted down notes on the pad hanging from a string and continued to watch unobserved, like an owl at night.

Chapter Seven

1985

LUC

Luc stared up at the huge iron legs of the Eiffel Tower and felt diminished in size by the enormous edifice. The sun was warm for a spring day and an ice cream purchased from a little cart painted in raspberry pink and mint green, made her feel summer wasn't too far away. At this moment in time, she felt free and yet unsure of what lay ahead. *Have I always been insecure or is it this vibrant city flashing past making me feel so insignificant?* Her thoughts wrapped around her as she licked the strawberry ice.

A family, the mother looking hot and bothered, approached. The father asked for directions in school-boy French, struggling with the words and adding in gestures and mime to aid his questions. When Luc replied in English the relief on his face was palpable. She pointed to the ticket office; they thanked her and moved on. The youngest child waved and as she turned, Luc saw tiny white wings attached to her back with elastic. The fluffy, feathery edging gave the impression of her flying as she skipped along finally catching up with her father. He

1985, Luc

caught hold of her and swung her up so she could fly higher in the Paris sunshine.

Luc wended her way through the mass of tourists joggling for positions for the best photographs: couples entwining, children giggling, families arguing, all trying to squeeze the Eiffel Tower into their camera lens. As she finished nibbling at the cone, she spied an empty space on one of the benches and made for it. It was good to finally sit down, her feet aching from new court shoes, purchased specially for today. Removing her jacket and crossing one leg over the other she arranged her pencil skirt to cover her knees. Luc was glad she had dropped off her suitcase at the hotel and just had her shoulder bag.

A letter, sent to her via the auction house, had brought her here and she now took it out and read it again. An offer of a job interview with Maurice Smith, the art dealer she had met at the auction at the beginning of March. Adam's mocking voice came to her then and she pushed it away, telling herself she had been right all along, and yet a gentle inner voice reminded her to take care.

Green ink spread across the paper like rampant ivy. The lettering looped freely. Whoever had written this felt no pain or anguish, they had love in their heart; Luc could see that.

My dear Lucretia,

I have a proposal for you. I was very impressed by your professional attitude in London and would like you to come for an interview. There is an opening at my gallery, and I think you would be the perfect fit.

Enclosed is a plane ticket and details of an hotel I have booked for you. Please contact my office as soon as possible for further instructions.

Regards
M. Smith

Luc folded the letter and then took out the book she had purchased from the bookshop in London—the story of Florence Blanchard, the craftswoman who had helped make the chess set. She had managed to work out some of the French using a dictionary but was floundering. By coming to Paris, she hoped someone might help her with the understanding behind Florence's story. Luc turned to the first page once again and began to follow the lines with her finger.

A shadow fell on the gravel before her. Luc looked up shading her eyes. A man in his late twenties was staring intently down at her. He coughed, shielding his mouth and then pushed his glasses back up onto the bridge of his nose.

'Yes? Can I help you?'

'I have been asked to come and meet with you.' His English was thickened by a French accent, like honey drizzled on a croissant. Lucretia smiled sardonically. *An interesting chat up line*, she thought. *The French will try anything.*

'I don't think so,' she said, her smile beginning to wane. 'I think you have the wrong person.' Luc stuffed the letter and the book into her bag, pulling the strap across

1985, Luc

her shoulder as she rose to leave.

'Excuse me, mademoiselle. One moment of your time, please.'

Luc paused. 'Do you want money? Is that it?' She stepped away from the man—*yes, he looked harmless but that is how they suck you in.*

'Your name please… it is Lucretia Stourton-Hurt?'

'Yes. That's me. How did you…?'

'I'm sorry for the confusion. Maurice Smith asked me to come and take you to him.'

Luc could feel her throat constrict and when she tried to answer her words just died.

'Please… it is not far.' He pointed away to his left and Luc's eyes travelled along his finger to a café with colourful metal tables strewn across the path. People drinking coffee, smoking, sunning themselves.

She wasn't convinced. 'And you are?' she croaked.

The man's sandy hair flopped over one spectacled eye, and he pushed it back. 'I am Scott.' With that he turned and made his way across to the café.

And that's all the explanation you're going to get, Luc. She followed him trying to keep up with his lolloping, easy stride but it was difficult in high heels on gravel and then cobblestones. Nearing the tables, she could make out amongst the other patrons a silver haired man sitting alone. The man wore a dark blue suit, a daffodil yellow tie and matching handkerchief frothing out of his top pocket. He was reading a British newspaper and occasionally put out his hand to grasp a coffee cup and raise it to his mouth. *He looks like the man I met in London,* Luc thought. Scott whispered in the man's ear then sat down.

Unaware of her immediate surroundings, Luc didn't see the wrought iron leg of a chair until her foot made contact and she went sprawling. People at the table began to shout in French and gesticulate wildly at her. A waiter bustled over and helped her up, attempting to dust her down, but she pulled away preferring to do it herself.

Apologising to the lady whose chair she had collided with, Luc glanced across at the table she had been aiming for. It was empty. The man had gone. So had Scott. Arriving at the table she fell onto one of the chairs, still warm from its previous occupant and rubbed her ankle.

A waiter appeared at her elbow. 'Mademoiselle—you would like coffee? Yes?' He busied himself with the cup and saucer drained of liquid and a plate sporting cake crumbs and was about to place the newspaper under his arm when Luc noticed the crossword on the folded-back page. The answers inked in a lurid green.

'May I?' She gestured to the paper. With understanding he laid it back in front of her and before he could leave, she added, 'Yes, coffee please. Black, no sugar. Thank you.'

Ignoring the growing pain in her ankle, Luc took out the letter once again, smoothed it flat and compared the writing. The crossword was all in capitals, but it could well be the same hand. Her thoughts in turmoil, Luc hardly noticed the waiter return until the aroma of the coffee beckoned her.

Where did they go? If he wanted me to come all this way to then vanish, why did he invite me in the first place? When she had contacted Mr Smith's office, she had been told to be at the Eiffel Tower on April 2nd and to wait near the ticket office. *Why did I ever come here? He is leading me on a merry dance, and I don't feel like dancing.*

Luc sipped at the scalding coffee, feeling her limbs loosen a little. *I suppose there are worse places to be,* she thought. Her ankle throbbed and she raised her leg on the empty chair opposite her. *I may as well rest here for a while. I can't*

1985, Luc

follow them with my ankle like this and I have no idea where they went. I just have the gallery address. Luc picked up the paper and turned to the front cover—world disasters, financial problems, a lost child. The following pages just the same. An article about an auction being held in Paris was on page 12. Colourful images of the artwork going up for sale covered the page and there in the margin in loopy green ink was a message.

181 Rue Volnay. Maurice

An address. Did he want her to go there? Unsure of what the next step was, she tested her ankle on the ground gingerly putting some weight onto it. *Not too bad*, she thought. The rest had helped. She found some francs, dropped them into the small plastic plate where the receipt resided and stood. She would get a taxi.

Hailing a cab, Luc was soon speeding through the narrow streets, some packed tightly with people, others empty of life, until the driver pulled up outside huge gates with a lattice pattern worked in iron. Through the criss-crosses she could make out a courtyard where a fountain of glittering water danced around a stone nymph in the sun. Smooth cobblestones led to a polished black door, chaperoned by tall thin windows either side. Luc pushed open the gate and stepped in. The sound of traffic was hushed as she hobbled (her ankle was beginning to throb again) to the door and hammered the brass door knocker. A moment of silence and then a blackbird took up a song in a nearby tree.

A sudden movement to her right caught her gaze—a curtain twitching and a glimpse of an auburn-haired girl. A shy smile and then she was gone.

Luc waited but no one came. *I am not being ignored again. I will not be treated like this.*

Hearsay

She thumped the door and shouted hello and bonjour through the letter box. The words echoed and died. Finally, footsteps arrived on the other side and the door glided open. Scott beckoned her in.

'My sincere apologies. Maurice was resting—he easily tires these days. Come.'

Luc stumbled over the threshold and Scott grasped her hand to steady her.

'I'm all right thank you,' she spat, pushing him away. Her patience was wearing thin, she was sweating from the warmth of the day, and her ankle needed rest. Scott pulled away like he had been burnt by hot coals. He spread raised hands in an unspoken apology.

'Maurice is in the salon to your right. I shall bring coffee.' With that he strode across the broad hallway and through an open doorway which seemed to lead to a kitchen. Luc just glimpsed gleaming stainless-steel cabinets before the door slammed shut.

She pushed out pent up air, raised her head and shuffled to the door on her right. A voice from within answered her knock straightaway. Entering a light high-ceilinged room with windows overlooking the courtyard, Luc's love of art took over and she stopped to admire the mouldings and fireplace. Baroque, yet the furniture was very much of the 1960s. Recognising a Picasso and a Van Gogh on the wall either side of the fireplace, Luc swallowed a gasp. Cheap imitations. Just like this man who presumes I would want to work for him after all of this. Maurice was holding his arms wide to greet her, but she sidestepped him.

'Of course, I understand. You don't know me. Yet I feel I know you so well, Lucretia.' His voice held an accent familiar to Luc and tainted with a cadence of someone who has lived part of their life in France.

1985, Luc

Luc, unsure of what to say to this, murmured. 'I am here for the interview for the job at the gallery.'

Maurice Smith nodded before settling himself on a low-slung leather chair and gestured for Luc to sit. He began to speak when the door was flung open.

'Coffee and I thought a little cognac might do us all good.' Scott swept in carrying a heavily laden tray. Placing it on a glass coffee table he added, 'Oh and biscuits to sweeten the mood. Voila!'

He gestured to the small figure behind him, and Luc saw the little girl she had glimpsed through the window, carrying a plate of biscuits cut into the form of animals. Scott went to pour the coffee.

'Papa?'

He turned. She held out the plate to him. 'Please take it from me. It is heavy.'

Luc was surprised—the girl's English was perfect.

Maurice leaned forwards and took the plate from her. 'Lucretia, may I introduce my grandson, Scott Smith and his daughter, Sophia.'

'We've met, but thank you for the clarification,' Luc demurred.

Scott and Sophia offered around cups and glasses, plates and napkins. Luc found herself softening to these strangers. The little girl, dressed in purple jeans and a cerise T shirt with LOVE emblazoned on the front, was now sitting next to Maurice delicately licking the icing off her biscuit before popping it into her mouth. He in turn had demolished two and was reaching hopefully for a third when Scott knocked his arm away. 'You know what the doctor said. You must be careful with your diet.'

'Oh, pish-posh. I am 86 years old—and a little bit of sugar isn't going to kill me off.' He slugged back his cognac. 'And this is medicinal; French doctors swear by it.' He winked at Luc, grabbing a biscuit before Scott could stop him.

Scott shook his head. 'Well, I suppose two world wars couldn't kill you off. You might make a century, but you need to be careful.' He sipped at his own coffee and then began, 'Lucretia.'

She had decided through all of this to ask why she had been invited, whether this was the interview and why they had walked off at the Eiffel Tower Cafe. 'Scott.' She began at the same time and broke off. His intent stare just like before, unnerved her. Luc began a different tack. 'Maurice—'

The elderly man held up his hand. 'It is time for some explanations.' He turned to Sophia. 'Now run along, cherie. Mimi will find you something to do. We grown-ups need to talk.' The little girl obediently jumped off the chair and skipped out of the room.

'I apologise for abandoning you at the café. My grandson is very protective of me, and I had felt rather ill sitting in the sun. That is why we left. However, I must admit, I was keen to see how determined you would be in finding us or would you give up. I needed to know you were the right person.' Luc stared at him, about to protest but Maurice held a finger to his lips. 'I am so sorry you hurt yourself. Yes, you deserve an explanation. There is much to share with you Lucretia, and you too, Scott. You don't know it all and perhaps you won't fully understand why I did those things I am about to tell you. But the past is the past and I can't change any of it.'

Luc glanced from one face to the other. Nothing made any sense.

Maurice continued. 'There is no job interview.' At this admission, Luc stared at him, slivers of ice slipping down her spine.

1985, Luc

'I'm sorry for deceiving you but I wanted to see you after all these years. It was finally the right time to make amends. Lucretia, I knew your grandfather, Bradley Hurt, and I believe he tried to kill me in the Great War.'

Chapter Eight

1985

MAURICE

Luc went to remonstrate but Maurice resumed. 'I need to tell you a story. Hopefully that will help you to understand why I invited you here, Luc.' He turned to Scott. 'There is much you don't know about my past, and it is the right time to share this with you, Scott. I hope you too will understand.'

Scott glanced across at Luc and they both nodded for Maurice to continue.

'Before I left for France, my father gave me his old chess set. He told me he had purchased it in Paris at the 1889 Paris Exposition when the Eiffel Tower was first opened to the public. My romantic side took over and I gave my mother the white pawn and Myrtle the red pawn, so that we all knew that I would return. Daft idea, I know, but at the time I would have done anything to stay alive; so many had given their lives before me.' He turned to Luc once again. 'I taught your grandad how to play chess. He crafted two new pawns to replace the others.' A vision of Brad Hurt adding his own blood to the matchstick and wax to make it red suddenly returned to Maurice. He winced

1985, Maurice

at the image and returned to the present.

'You may remember I was trying to purchase a chess set in London when we first met.' Luc nodded. 'It wasn't mine but was very similar. At the last minute I decided not to spend my money on a set that wasn't the right one.'

'Anyway, let me tell you more about my time in France. We had a difficult time in the trenches. It was hell on Earth. We lay cocooned in our muddy haven, Bradley Hurt and I, terrified by the fire and damnation spinning around us. We had fought and lost. Interlopers in No Man's Land—one of us bloodied, one dying—side by side with our comrades' corpses in the darkness.

Weeping came from my right, probably from another hole in the ground and then a plaintive voice called for their mother. Shivering, I pulled my knees to my chest, wrapped my hands around my ears and let out a silent scream.

Amid the battle, the four of us had thrown ourselves into this putrid, sticky mud. The whistle had blown, and as one we had all gone over the top. Earth and stones, from what had once been ploughed and tended by French farmers, flew into the smoky air as shells exploded into the furrows and clods. As I shifted position to ease my shoulder, in my confused state, I saw the once golden stems of wheat reaching up to the sky, their heads tight with grain. I could smell the leather soap on the tack and hear the clink of metal as our horse shook its head free from buzzing flies, while it waited for me to walk on, back down the field. The skitter of field mice and the flutter of gulls and I was, just for a moment, transported to the fields of Shropshire. The solitary oak tree proud in its own majesty, where Dad would circumnavigate the horses and plough around its far-reaching roots. And for a moment I was at peace. *Is this dying? Is this the moment my soul leaves this Earth?*

'Are you there?'

Hearsay

God was calling me. I didn't reply. I wanted this picture to remain with me. I didn't want to die. The voice came again. This time the familiar harsh tone roused me from my dream.

'Brad? Is that you?'

'Who else would it be, me ole mate?'

'I thought I was dead.'

Brad snorted. 'These others are. They've copped it right enough.'

I strained scratchy eyes, seemingly the only dry part of my body, towards his voice. 'I don't think I can move, and I've gone deaf. I can't hear any guns.'

'You daft bugger. You're not deaf. The Hun have stopped firing.'

'Why?'

'Same as us. Shovelling up their dead.'

I swallowed and found my throat was also dry. The liquid mud swirled around me, sucking at already saturated khaki. This sea of blackness broke waves against my face as something dragged itself to lie next to me. I felt hot breath on my cheek.

'That's what I'm going to do.' Brad's voice pierced my hearing.

'You just need to take their red disc. The orderlies will collect the bodies.'

'Stop giving orders, you shit! I'm sick of you!'

I twisted my neck to stare at him. Was he having me on? I had been made corporal a few months before, yet surely, we were still friends.

I started to laugh. It was a joke. 'We're still mates. I just want you to help me back to the trench, first. I need to get to the doc.'

'I'll get you to the doc, Corporal, friggin' Cruso.' Spittle flew from his mouth. 'Then you'll go home to your

1985, Maurice

lovely girl and your friggin' farm.' Pure hatred poured out of his lips at me, like bullets smacking into me. 'You're not going home if I can't. I'm sick of your whinging.' His voice changed to a petulant whine. 'Does she love me? Will she marry me? You and your stupid Myrtle and your friggin' chess bits. You don't deserve her.'

I began to shake. The cold had entered my bloodstream numbing my brain. Brad had taken leave of his senses. Screwing my eyes shut, I prayed then for help. I knew I wasn't going to last long in this place.

Opening my eyes, I dragged myself away from Brad grabbing at lumps of earth. I could just about move my arms with the weight of my wet tunic. From somewhere a hidden strength, a desire to live perhaps, took over. I managed to reach the edge of the crater before I felt rough hands pulling at me. Suddenly he had me by the throat, ripping off my identity discs with one hand and pummelling my face with his other. I tried to pull him off, but he was too strong. I saw him raise his fist once again and then only blackness.

I awoke to see white eyes staring into my very soul. Then a torrent of German poured from the lips below and I was dragged out of the crater. Another man appeared then and between them they hauled me through No Man's Land to a trench and tipped me into the abyss. I landed in a heap on wooden duckboards where I heaved with pain, spewing up mud and bile.

I don't remember much of that time, fortunately. I was held in a POW camp, I believe, until the end of the war. I didn't know who or what I was. The Germans were waiting for me to die, I think. Yet I survived.

After a horrendous journey on a steamship, trains and an old bus, I found myself in heaven. An old pile of a place it was, nestled in the Bedfordshire countryside. A big old house, belonging to a lord, was now a hospital for the military.

I enjoyed pottering around the wards, chatting to the other chaps, sometimes reading to them, or sharing a fag on the terrace. Some days I would go out and help with the gardens. This place had orchards, vegetable gardens and sweeping lawns. My body healed yet my mind would not.

I could name the different plants and trees, even knowing the Latin. How my brain remembered that but not my name, and who I was, lay beyond me. They had set up an operating theatre upstairs and performed surgical procedures. Orderlies would struggle with carrying the men on stretchers up the elegant staircase. I was physically strong so often helped them. I loved to imagine the portraits that had obviously hung there for centuries; hooks remained, and shadowy rectangles survived, the pictures having been hidden away in storage.

Many of us came and went, but I stayed. I had no family, or no one wanted to know I existed. I was quite content, but I couldn't stay there for ever. There were three wards set out in the most beautiful rooms you can imagine; most of the decorations hidden behind hessian, bookshelves in the library lay bare. Yet, lying in my bed I would just stare up at the painted ceiling, the gold scrolling, and ornate carvings. Perhaps that was where my interest in art began. I would dream of what this house looked like in its heyday before it was full of sick men. I imagined the balls, and the carriages bringing lords and ladies in velvet and silk, organza and diamonds. Each guest would glitter in the candlelight and swirl around the floor to a string quartet.

One wet day, I wandered into the drawing room, rain lashing against the glass in the tall casement windows:

1985, Maurice

frames rattling against the wind. A fire burned in the grate, and several men had set up camp close by enjoying the warmth. Some just sat staring into the flames, others writing furiously or reading while one man stood alone like a sentry at a dugout. Going over to him I saw he was pulling at his fingers one by one and murmuring.

'You all right, Jem?' I asked, my voice gentle so as not to startle him.

'This little piggy stayed at home,' the man replied.

I nodded and said, 'Jem, there's a box of stuff on the table. Donated by the local scout group. Do you want to take a look? There might be some books in there. I could read to you if you want.'

Jem stopped his rhyme and stared at me, then stared across at the box. 'This little piggy had roast beef.' He began to pull at his fingers once again.

I was about to try again when a couple of orderlies arrived. 'Right, come on Jem. Time for your treatment, lad.' The older of the two men took Jem's arm and steered him towards the door, but Jem became fractious, arms flailing, and the nursery rhyme became louder and even more shrill.

'Don't make any fuss now, it'll make you feel better,' the younger medical orderly said.

'Be careful with him,' I shouted at their backs as they hustled him out. The room had become agitated, anxious voices rose. A woman entered. Starched apron rustling as she came across the parquet floor. Stopping to chat and calm each man in turn, she was able to settle everyone back to their tasks.

'Come along now, don't you be worrying about him.' Her Yorkshire burr soothing in my ear. 'Let's take a look at what those lovely boys have brought, shall we?' She bustled me over to the box and pulled back the flaps.

Hearsay

'Will I finish up like Jem?' I asked.

Matron had taken out a couple of books and held them mid-air like statuary before she spoke. 'Let's not dwell on what might happen after your treatment. Jem's not in a good place at the moment and hasn't been since the Front. But you're well, aren't you? The doctor just wants to help you remember.'

'I don't know if I want to remember. I'm quite happy being Maurice Smith and working as a gardener here.'

'The war's over. You can't stay here indefinitely, Maurice. What about your family? Don't you want to see them?' While she spoke, she was removing more books and small boxes and placing them in piles on the table.

'I don't think I have a family. If I did, they would have asked about me, wouldn't they?'

'Well, we're going to try again with the pictures in the newspaper. Some men have been recognised through that. Losing your identity discs wasn't a good idea.' She placed an old shoe box next to the pile of books.

'I didn't lose them.' I pulled the box over and began to lift the lid.

'No dear, of course you didn't.'

Her head whipped around as a voice at the door called out, 'Matron, you're needed on the telephone.' A young nurse hovered there and then was gone.

Matron turned back to me saying, 'I must go. Your first electric shock treatment is booked for three o'clock this afternoon. Please be on time.' As she walked to the door, she called out, 'Come on boys, have a look at the things on the table. I want to see everyone doing something now. Good for the brain, you know.' She strode off leaving me with my hands placed firmly on the shoe box.

I was contemplating on what she had said, unaware

1985, Maurice

that a couple of the lads were now standing beside me and were rootling through the books and boxes. Their muttering brought me out of my reverie. They took away a set of dominoes and another three chaps took their place at the table. Tiddlywinks, cards, dice, a book on growing roses were soon whisked away.

'What's in there, mate?'

I looked up to see a young fellow with one eye sheathed in gauze and cloth, his other eye the colour of bluebells. He repeated his question nodding at the box still under my palms. I answered him by grasping the lid and lifting it off.

'A board of some kind and various bits of wood,' I said holding up one shaped like a horse.

'Ah, chess. That's grand. Do you play?'

'Not sure, mate. Happy to learn,' I said.

'That's grand,' the man repeated. 'I'll teach you if you want.'

We began to clear the table of the debris, but a loud gong interrupted us. 'Let's do this after lunch, shall we?'

'Right you are,' I said. 'I'm Maurice by the way.'

'Fynn. James Fynn, but everyone calls me Sharky.' We shook hands. 'Your first lesson starts at two this afternoon, then.'

Following a substantial lunch, I was standing at one of the windows when Sharky arrived. The sun had come out now and I was admiring the curlicues of the railings that ran around the paving slabs outside, spiders rebuilding their webs, jewelled with raindrops. Life goes on, I thought. You just need to keep on going. I must have stood there for a while because on turning I saw he was setting out the board and wooden figures. Some of creamy coloured oak and the others of ebony.

Sitting down opposite Sharky, I saw the flimsy card

was covered in brown and beige squares. I reached across and grasped one of the smaller pieces, a black one, all now standing to attention in front of taller, oddly shaped pieces.

'That's a pawn, that is.' Sharky put his hand out for me to return it.

'Myrtle,' I said.

'What's that, old chap?'

'Myrtle. The pawn.' I looked up at him. 'The wrong colour. She's red.'

Sharky frowned, his one visible eyebrow angling down, and his lips twisted. I grabbed another one, the light oak. 'Mother.'

'Blimey. I've got a right one here.' Sharky whistled through his teeth. 'What the…' he stopped short as I dragged my hand across the board, the pieces hitting the floor like bullets ricocheting off a tank. I pulled a pencil from my jacket pocket and began to write across the squares. Myrtle – Mother – Father – farm – field – Brad – Edmund Cruso – 266421.

I sat back and looked around me dazed. A crowd had gathered. Sharky was on his feet. Whispers became words and then became shouts of 'Maurice' and 'You all right?' and 'Blimey, he's finally cracked'.

The crowd parted to allow the formidable figure of Matron to sail through like a stately galleon, her white sail of an apron and white frilly headdress stark against the khaki uniforms. Arriving to face me at the other side of the table she raised her hands and clapped them smartly to call a halt on the noise. As though a sergeant major had barked at the troops, each man fell silent. I stared up into her smouldering eyes. She must have seen my expression, my tears and her face softened, her eyes shone. 'Maurice? What is it? What have you been up to?'

1985, Maurice

'I'm not Maurice. I'm Edmund.' My words came out of my mouth and then my brain caught up with them. 'I'm not Maurice Smith,' I repeated. 'My name is Edmund Field Cruso.' My tongue and lips savoured the names like a lost taste. I repeated it over and over again, until the men around me began to also repeat my name. Their chant soared up to the gold mouldings and the rosy, fat cherubs above our heads. My heart seemed to rise with them until a strident clapping and a single word.

'Gentlemen!'

Again, a hush descended. Matron's voice advanced over the chess board, gentle yet assertive. 'Maurice... I mean... Edmund. That's marvellous. Shall we go somewhere more private?'

I searched her face. She doesn't believe me, I thought. She's being kind. She doesn't understand. I have to make them understand. Tears poured from my eyes; words kept coming. I scrabbled around on the floor searching for two pawns. Rocking back on my heels, I held them up for all to see. 'I gave the white pawn to my mother and the red one to Myrtle. I love Myrtle. I'm going to marry Myrtle. She threw it away, but she still loves me.' My remembrances stalled as my mind tried to work that one out. 'I think.'

'A diamond would have been better, mate.' A jocular voice emanated from the circle of men and laughter chorused.

'Yeah, mate. My Elsie wanted a gold band. You should try that next time when you woo a girl.' Sniggers and snide remarks joined in before Matron shouted for them to hold their tongues. Somehow, she was now at my side.

'Come on now. Let's go and have a nice cup of tea and you can tell me all about it.' She took my arm and helped me up. I was still clutching the black and white pawns. On skirting the table, I paused and pulled the board to my chest. Then I allowed myself to be taken from the room.'

Abruptly, Maurice stopped and sat back in his chair, breathing heavily. Luc and Scott were staring at him, and he could see they were upset by his story. He, on the other hand, was experiencing a lightness, a freedom that he hadn't felt since walking in the fields of his family's Shropshire farm. He waited for the bombardment of questions to begin. Finally, he was ready to open up about his life and his past.

Chapter Nine

LUC

Luc didn't know how to respond to this saga. *This is a crazy house and Maurice Smith is an imposter. He probably isn't even an art dealer,* she thought. Instinctively, she gathered her bag to her and stood. 'I don't know why you have told me this. My grandfather was Bradley Hurt, but I've never heard of Edmund Cruso. You told me your name was Maurice Smith and now I don't know what to believe. I don't know what sort of stunt you two mad men are playing here but I don't want to be a party to it.' She edged towards the door, keeping her eyes on the astonished duo sitting around the coffee table.

'Please, my dear. I am sorry for the confused tale. I didn't know the best way to tell you. Please sit down again. I will explain further if you just give me the chance.' Maurice had shakily risen to his feet and was waiting for her to decide what to do. Then almost as an afterthought, he added, 'I'm not mad.'

'I'm sorry, I don't know who you are. You leave me at the Eiffel Tower after I hurt my ankle and made me come and find you. You say you knew my grandfather, Bradley Hurt and then you make out he tried to kill you,'

Luc replied calmly, but accompanied by a screaming voice inside her head. *My grandad was a good man, a kind, gentle man. He wouldn't hurt anyone.*

The inner voice took over and a torrent of words gushed from her now. 'Bradley Hurt was a brave soldier in the war and worked hard all his life. Either you knew a different man or you're lying.' Her pride in being invited to Paris for a job interview had been eaten away by the acid of failure. Another mess-up in her life. Another time of trusting the wrong person. Her voice rose to a whine with her discomfiture. 'You enticed me here under some pretence of a job interview. I don't know who you are. In fact, I don't know anyone called Cruso or Smith.' Even with disappointment and frustration flowing though her veins, she reflected on this and added, 'Well, I know lots of Smiths, but not you. I don't know you.' Luc pointed across the room at Maurice and Scott, before turning her back on them. She went to grab the door handle but on hearing Scott now speak she paused and turned her head.

Scott had jumped to his feet. 'Wait, Lucretia. I'm sorry too. So, you're saying, Maurice, that your name is Edmund Cruso. That doesn't make any sense.' He removed his glasses, as though to make it all clearer. He stared myopically at the old man and then across at Luc. Carefully putting his glasses back on, he said to her. 'I don't know what he's talking about either, Luc. Please wait. Give him a chance and I'm sure he will explain why he's asked you to come here today and why he dragged you around half of Paris.' Scott paused and then looking down at his feet, added, 'I apologise for my part in that. I hope your ankle isn't too painful.'

Luc removed her hand from the brass doorknob but stayed put, her heart drumming at her ribs. 'All right, I will give you both a chance to explain.' She turned to face

Luc

them again, suddenly tired from all the conflict. Her voice was calmer when she spoke again. 'I would like to know someone who knew my Grandad during the war and hopefully I can prove his innocence. I remember him as a good man.'

'Thank you. I really appreciate you letting me explain and I understand your reticence. In fact, I commend you for it.' Maurice sat back down, with Scott following suit. Shifting a little in his chair the old man crossed his legs and smoothed the fabric of his trouser leg. 'Please sit down, Lucretia.'

Looking to her left and right she saw matching upright chairs with velvet cushioning, on either side of the door. Wanting to be ready for a quick escape if the need arose, she perched on one, still hugging her bag to her chest.

Maurice strummed his fingers on the arm of his seat, seeming to collect his thoughts. Then in a strident tone, he said. 'I know you both have many questions for me. Some of which I am unable to answer, yet. Anyway, I discovered my name had been given to me in the POW camp. Perhaps someone was a fan of Maurice Chevalier.' He smiled at this. 'I don't know. Perhaps they thought everyone in England was called Smith.' He chuckled then. 'I don't know,' he repeated, shaking his head, smile fading. 'I just knew I was once Edmund Cruso and he no longer existed, and no one cared.'

Luc began to soften. 'I'm sure someone cared. You mentioned your mother, and someone called Myrtle. Did they try to find you?'

'I don't know. Many things happened after the war. Too much to tell you it all today.'

'Please tell me about my grandfather,' Luc asked. 'I remember very little of him. Granny said he was a rogue and a liar, but I only saw the man who gave me sweets and comics, who pushed me on the swing, who taught me how to ride a bike. I was about nine or ten when he died.'

'Then that is the man you must remember. The man I knew was very different, but I saw him in extraordinary circumstances.'

'Then tell me about the man you knew,' Luc urged.

'Well, I met Bradley Hurt in 1917 in the trenches in France. I joined his platoon, only nineteen myself. Just around twenty men with various skills. He was slightly older than me and more of a Jack the Lad. I remember the first time we met was over the chess set. I taught him how to play and he showed me how to keep my rifle clean and oiled. He was a good fellow in many ways, a real joker and a good comrade to begin with.'

'To begin with? What happened to change all of that?' asked Luc, leaning forward, elbows resting on her knees.

'As I said, the war changed us all, but I think Brad had a chip on his shoulder. It wasn't things he said, it was those eyes of his. That face, the face of an angel got us into a few bars and brothels.'

Scott snorted derisively.

'Hey, don't knock it. We were a long way from home under what you now call stress. You could get a hot meal too if you were lucky. I would chat to the girls while Brad went upstairs, I didn't want all that fumbling with a tart, I just missed being around women. To tell you the truth I wasn't very good at chatting them up. Myrtle had told me in no uncertain terms she didn't want to be with me, so I lost all confidence, not that I was very confident in the first place, unlike Brad. He could charm the birds out of the trees. He was always trying to hook me up with someone, but I wasn't interested.

Anyway, I had told him all about Myrtle and the farm

Luc

and the beautiful Shropshire countryside. In turn he told me about Leeds and growing up. He never knew his real father, but his stepdad was a miner and used to hit Brad with his belt, telling him he was a waste of space and that his poncy looks would get him battered.

I suppose he wanted to prove he was a man. Brad got into a gang who, according to him, carried out robberies and he started carrying a weapon, either a kitchen knife or an old revolver from the Boer war, his stepdad kept in his sock drawer.'

Luc couldn't believe what he was saying. This can't be the same man. 'Are you telling me my grandfather was a criminal?'

Maurice raised both hands as though protecting himself from an enemy. 'At the time, I didn't believe a lot of it myself. I thought it was all part of the Bradley Hurt act he adopted trying to be superior.'

'Superior?' Scott threw back. 'He was a thief!'

'No, you don't understand. I'd led a very sheltered life in a little sleepy village. The most exciting thing that happened there was when a haystack caught on fire from a bolt of lightning.' He shuffled himself to the edge of his chair and slowly rose muttering as he straightened his back.

'Are you all right, Maurice?' asked Luc with concern.

'I'm fine. Getting old is not the greatest thing but some of those men never saw past their twentieth birthday so I won't complain.' Closing the curtains against the twilight, he muttered to himself.

Maurice pottered around turning on table lamps and a bulbous, metallic floor light. Luc rubbed her arms as though cold, yet it was the cold of despair slipping into her mind as she tried to process all of what she had been told. She never really knew Bradley Hurt. She saw him through a child's eyes of unconditional love. And now she pondered on what she really did know about him. The snippets she had heard, the arguments and silences held within the house. The odd name being tossed into the air like a grenade to cause an explosive reaction. The times when Granny would complain about her limbs aching and the dark bruises on her arms. Then in contrast, words of love and murmurings from the yard when her grandparents sat out on their wooden bench with glasses of beer, holding hands and watching the stars flicker and twist.

Was that love or hate? What did that surface of loving words hide deep below? Was it like the rich chocolate left until last as no one wanted it, yet it looked delicious? And then surreptitiously opening the box, when no one was around, to sink your teeth into the creamy chocolate to discover a fat nut encased within. Luc hated nuts. She would spit it out back into the plastic tray and close the lid, hoping someone else would get the blame.

Maurice returned to his seat, helping himself to the last biscuit on the plate. Luc smiled at this. I hope there's a nut inside there, she thought and then reproached herself. *I must give him a chance; I said I would.* Her eyes caught her watch—it was getting late, yet she needed some more answers. She decided to change tack and asked, 'Your family, your mother and Myrtle? The pawns?' With shaking fingers, she checked her pendant was still at her throat. 'Why didn't you go back? Why didn't you go and see the woman you loved?'

Maurice strummed his fingers on the arm of his seat, seeming to contemplate these questions and then turned to Luc.

'I know you both have many questions for me, and I can give you *some* answers, but even I don't know

Luc

everything that happened in the past. One thing I do know is my chess set is up for sale at a Paris auction later this week. A rare set: it should fetch a good sum.'

'I don't understand. I'm impressed of course; you will make a lot of money by selling it, but what happened to Myrtle? And your parents?'

'All in good time, my dear. There is more to tell, but not today. I am buying the chess set back. I am already very wealthy, as you can see,' he said waving his arm around. Then with difficulty rose again from his seat. Scott went to help him, but he was firmly told by a raised palm not to aid this proud old man.

Maurice walked stiffly across to one of the paintings, the Picasso, 'I saw you looking at this earlier, my dear. You were trying to work out things about me. I understand. I would have done the same in your shoes. This is the real deal.' He chuckled. 'This was my first acquisition.'

'Why did you sell the chess set in the first place, Maurice?' Scott asked.

'There hangs a tale,' Maurice answered. 'The same old thing that causes so much sadness in this world. I was poor. I had no money when I was let go.'

'Let go? From what?' Luc was becoming enthralled by this man's story, yet she needed answers.

'From the hospital, of course.'

A coldness cloaked Luce. 'You said you gave away two chess pieces. Tell me again who you gave them to?'

Maurice returned to his chair. He poured himself another cognac and leaned back.

'I gave one pawn to my mother—Eirene Field Cruso—she had the white one. The red pawn, I gave to my sweetheart Myrtle Johnson. I promised I would return from the war. We would all be reunited. The chess set would be complete again.'

Hearsay

Unhooking her necklace, Luc stood and went across to Maurice. 'My mother gave me this before she left. Is this your pawn?' She dangled the pendant before dropping the blood-red chess pawn onto Maurice's outstretched hand. He didn't even blink. It was as though he was expecting this.

Tears rolled down his face. 'Hello, my old mate,' he whispered. 'Good to see you again.'

'Do you know what happened to the white pawn?' Scott asked.

'Oh yes. Yes, I do.' Maurice didn't elaborate further; he was studying the pawn in his hand.

Chapter Ten

MAURICE

'I will go back to my time in the hospital so you can understand some of the things I did,' Maurice said. Luc took a seat close to him, wanting to understand this man and his story, wanting to know more about her own history. Scott handed her a glass of cognac which she held tightly against her chest and then he returned to his chair opposite Maurice.

'Matron's office was a cosy affair,' Maurice began. 'A fire burned merrily in the cast iron grate; a dog stretched out on the rug warming its belly. A solid mahogany desk took up most of the space with neatly stacked bundles of folders and papers, a brass inkwell and pen and a heavy metal stamping implement. Pictures in silver frames adorned the mantelpiece flanking a wooden domed clock. Two easy chairs stood either side of the fire, and the dog, a black and white spaniel, with ears fanned out wide, opened an eye as I took my seat. Matron placed a tray of tea things on a low table before sitting down.

She leaned forward and poured the tea—milk first, then two sugars for me (good for shock) and then black treacly liquid.

Hearsay

'A good strong cuppa heals us all in so many ways,' she murmured handing me the tea. I was still hugging the chessboard and pieces to my chest and was loathe to let go of them.

'I wish it was that easy,' I muttered.

'Come on now. This is not like you. You're always so positive for the others.'

'Not like me!' I retorted. 'Who am I? Am I Maurice or Edmund? Am I a man or a mouse? A friend or a fiend?'

'You're a good man and we need to establish all of that so you can move on with your life. Drink your tea.' She was still holding out the cup, blue and white forget-me-nots dancing around the rim.

Sighing, I balanced the board on my knees and slipped the two pawns into my breast pocket. I took the proffered tea and drank. The liquid burned my lips and throat and for a moment or two I held the pain of the heat to tell myself this was really happening. The tick, tick, tick of the clock and the crackle of the logs splitting, and I was back in our kitchen at home.

'Tell me about your family, Edmund.' Matron's distant voice accompanied me as I strolled through our family home. I described the kitchen with the range and the dresser, the front room with its lacy antimacassars and porcelain figurines. My bedroom, with the candlewick bedspread and eiderdown and a shelf of books and tin soldiers. My mother out in the back garden beating an aging oriental rug, the dust and dog hairs hazing around her. My father in the barn feeding the horses, checking on their straw bed, clucking at the hens and eyeballing Moriarty, the rooster, who stood astride the hen house, his domain.

'And what do you do on the farm?' Matron's gentle questioning brought me to a field.

Maurice

'Dad taught me how to plough and to lead the horses in a straight line. It was hard work. The first time we got stuck on every furrow. Jess and Bolt straining as I held the wooden handles to guide them and pushed with all my might. We did it though. Seeing that crop grow green and then gold was most satisfying.'

'And Myrtle?'

I was back with Matron again. I drained my cup. It was cold. Like the coldness I felt when Myrtle had thrown the red pawn into the forest floor.

'She was my first and only love.'

'Do you want us to contact her? And your family of course.'

'I don't know. This is all too much to take in.'

The door flew open abruptly. 'Ah, there you are. Matron, what are you doing having a cosy chat when you know Maurice is due for his treatment? I thought you kept a tight ship here.' The solid figure of Doctor Price stood on the threshold.

Matron remained seated, observing the intruder. 'And you also know Doctor Price that you should knock before entering my office. Edmund and I are having a private discussion away from prying eyes and ears.'

The doctor harumphed. 'Sorry about that, Cress. You know how it is.' Matron tutted and then smiled.

I looked from one to the other and then back, my head a pendulum swinging, my mind putting two and two together. Cressida Stevens and Doctor Price?—well I suppose they're only human.

I coughed, reminding them I was still there. Both sets of eyes swivelled towards me. In reply, I held up the chessboard.

The doctor asked if he could take a proper look, and I nodded. Pulling out Matron's chair from her desk, he sat and began to read aloud the scrawled handwriting. 'Oak tree… leaves… conkers… field.' Pausing he looked up at me, his greying moustache like a separate entity as he moved his jaw while in thought.

'I don't think this lot adds up to much, old boy. You like being outside, it's the autumn, you've been raking up the leaves.' I was about to interrupt when he raised his hand to me. 'But these names do show that your memory of something is coming back. We could still try the electric shock treatment to just bump up these memories.'

'With all due respect, Doctor Price, I don't think that will help in this instance,' Matron said.

'My dear girl, which of us is the expert here?'

'I am not your "dear girl".' Matron stood, her full five-foot three quivering. 'Please be so good as to leave my office now and delay your treatment until another day. I know what is good for my boys and I will deem when Edmund is fit to see you.' She strode to the door, pulling it open and waiting for the doctor to leave.

For a moment or two, I thought he wasn't going to go. Then with another harumph, the man rose, his frame dwarfing the slight woman and he strode out of the room.

'Sorry about that, Edmund. Now where were we?' As she spoke, she took the chessboard from the desk and handed it back to me before sitting back down. Pouring more tea for both of us, she finally leaned back. 'He's not that bad once you get to know him. All bark and no bite, just like Sixpence here. Soft as butter really.' Hearing his name the dog's eyes opened, thumped his tail once, twice and then resumed sleeping.

I drank some tea, memories coming now. 'We've got two farm dogs. Two black labs. Dad takes them out shooting for rabbits. Several hens, a few cows and pigs and twenty-five acres make up our farm. Oh, and a couple of cats, kittens too.'

Maurice

'Do you remember where the farm is?'

'Shropshire,' I replied without thinking. My answer surprised me. I hadn't said that for a while. 'The most beautiful county there is,' I added.

'England's green and pleasant land.'

'William Blake.'

'Yes, that's right.' Matron beamed at him. 'You're doing so well. Are you ready to talk about Myrtle?'

'Not yet.'

'What about Brad?'

'Who?'

'His name is in one of your chess squares.'

Exhaustion washed over me then. I didn't want to remember any more.

Being the expert nurse, she was, Matron recognised I had done enough for one day. 'I think you need some fresh air or perhaps a rest out in the autumn sun. Let's talk again later.' She held up her watch, a small gold ornate brooch, not the usual standard issue. 'My goodness!' she exclaimed. 'I need to accompany Doctor Owsley on his rounds.' She stood, smoothing down her uniform. I also stood. Our discussion was at an end, and I walked out into the corridor along to the main hall and onto the terrace beyond.

Just a few weeks later, as I let myself in through the back door of the farmhouse in Bounds End, the sun was hovering above the far hedges of Top Field, readying itself to slowly drop beyond the horizon. I had taken a train to the town of Ashfield and then walked up the hill to the village. I had asked the authorities to not inform my family. I wanted it to be a surprise. I think I was more surprised by what I discovered.

I filled the kettle and placed it on the range to boil, (a habit that lurked within my psyche) took the brown teapot

Hearsay

from the shelf near the sink and added tea leaves. A cup and saucer were draining on the wooden rack, so I placed them on the table. The cloth was blue and yellow checks—I remembered my mother ironing it on the day I went off to France. I touched its crisp folds creating ridges across the table like a mountain range overseeing a flat valley, the sugar bowl and milk jug, with their lacy covers, flattening the peaks.

I let the tea mash for a full three minutes before straining it into the delicate cup. Adding milk and two heaped teaspoons of sugar I had a sudden image of the tin mugs with bitter camp coffee I had endured in the mud of France. I sat and savoured the first proper taste of home.

It hadn't changed much—the village, the farm, this kitchen. Still clothes drying over the range on the high ceiling rails. Still Dad's boots, caked with soil, by the back door. And yet everything was different. What had once been a vibrant colourful village was now sepia; the war leaching the very colour out of the place, out of the people.

I wondered where mother was as I sipped my tea. I glanced across at the familiar grandfather clock, its roof grazing the beams above. She's probably feeding the chickens or checking on the cattle. What will she say when she sees me?

'Bradley, is that you?' A small wavering voice came from the passageway beyond the kitchen door. A figure appeared. 'Bradley, you're back early.'

Feeling strange at hearing this name I stood and went to greet the shadow of a man who now stood before me. 'Dad, it's me, Edmund. I've come home.'

He stopped then. 'Edmund?' He rolled the word around in his mouth as though tasting something unsavoury. 'I knew an Edmund once.'

Maurice

I reached out to grasp his arm. He pulled away, shaking his head and my heart cracked. I tried again. 'That's me, Edmund. I'm your son…' My voice trailed away as the words fell against a stony face.

'No. Edmund is dead. He's gone. He was a coward.'

My heart splintered there and then. What had they been told? All this time I had been trying to remember my life, had been banged up in a POW camp not knowing who I was. And now some of my memories were returning I find that my father, my dear beloved father didn't remember me. His mind had finally given over to senility.

Before I could explain, Dad shuffled over to the range and shook the kettle. The water sloshed back and forth, and he placed it on the hot plate, saying, 'Right young Bradley let's have a brew. The ladies will be back from their shopping expedition soon.'

My mind couldn't take in all this. Bradley… ladies… shopping? What was happening?

'Dad?'

He turned and a smile split his face. 'Yes, son.'

A flicker of hope nudged my heart for a second. It was all an act, he was joking. Thank God.

I smiled back. Same old Dad. Winding me up. The kettle sang out and he turned to fill the pot. 'Now then, Bradley, I know you like yours strong, so I'll leave it for a bit.' The muttering continued. A sudden pain knifed my eyes, and a tear slid down my cheek. For some reason, my father knew Bradley and thought he was his son. Another thought hit me—to whom was he referring? Which ladies?

'Dad, remind me who's gone shopping and why. I'd forgotten they were doing that.' Whoever they are, I thought.

Dad sat in his wing-backed armchair by the fire. Blew

Hearsay

on his steaming drink and ended my life.

'Myrtle and Mum. They'll be back soon. Only nipped off to Stafford on the train. They probably didn't tell you. It's a surprise they said. Looking at wedding dresses they said.'

'My Myrtle?' I responded.

My dad grinned, showing a graveyard of teeth. 'Of course, your Myrtle. Your girl. You're a lucky man, Bradley.'

Anger ripped through me then and my voice rose. 'No Dad! She's my girl. I'm Edmund.' Dad placed his cup on the hearth and then looked directly into my eyes.

'No, Bradley. Edmund is dead. You told us he left you for dead in a mudhole. The coward! Missing in action. Dead and gone.' Tears rolled down his sunken cheeks. 'You're my son now.'

I couldn't stay there. I couldn't face anyone. I was a ghost to them all. My mother wouldn't believe all of this. 'What did Mum say about all this?'

'She was very sad. Edmund will always be perfect in her eyes. But now with the baby on the way and the wedding and what have you, Eirene is busy and happy once again.' He nodded to himself, his eyes misting over.

'A baby? When?'

'Goodness me, Bradley, is it that shell shock getting to you again? You'll be a father before the year's out.'

That conniving, manipulative so-called friend of mine has taken over my life; I was truly angry now. The man I taught how to play chess had lied to my father; Sidney Cruso, the man who had given me the chess set in the first place. Chess. Something else my brain had rubbed out and then suddenly pencilled back in. My chess set.

'Where's the chess set?' I asked trying to calm my voice.

Maurice

My father shook his head and muttered, 'I dunno, lad.'

I began to pace around the kitchen searching for the chess set. He can have Myrtle—they were two of a kind. He can have Dad too—he's lost to me too. Mum? She was the one I wanted to see but I didn't want her to be upset all over again. She was happy looking forward to the birth of a child. Not her grandchild but the closest she'd get to one. Myrtle, having no family, would thrive on her help. No, I can't do that to her.

I found it in the front room, inside the glass cabinet where mum showed off her display of heirlooms—silver dishes and porcelain cups. There it was—the wooden inlaid box—a bit battered but the colours still stood proud. Taking it into my hands like a lost love, I thought again about my lost love, Myrtle, who would never be touched by these hands again. Yet, I can have this. This is mine.

Returning to the kitchen and my father I decided to take on the persona for a moment. 'Right then, Dad. I'll get off. Got some things to see to in the village. Tell Mum and Myrtle I'll be back soon, to see the dress.' I moved across to the door to the outside world.

My father chortled then. 'You will have your little joke. You know it's bad luck to see the dress before the big day. See you later, son.' He pulled a newspaper onto his lap and was reading intently when I closed the back door behind me.

Anger kept me warm on the long walk back to the station. I took it at a full march, and it brought me early for the train. It was deserted apart from a porter and a couple of people stamping their feet and rubbing their hands. The clock above them announced the time, just a quarter of an hour for the cold to seep into my bones. I found a bench and unlaced my kit bag. The box sat squarely on top of folded clothes. I thought I was going home. Funny that! Where is home? At that precise moment I had no idea.

Placing the box on my knees I marvelled at how the box, even with dents and knocks, had retained its beauty. My fingers traced the squares—red, white, red, white. I had never thought about it before but now I began to conjure up an image of a craftsman making this, lovingly fitting the pieces together, sanding and polishing until it shone cherry red and pure white. The edging was of interlocking diamond shapes, black and white and red, bordered by a thin line of red encompassing the whole of the perimeter of the board once opened flat.

I released the catch and opened the lid revealing the pieces lolling in their scarlet velvet hollows, like open graves before being covered by earth and cinders.

Running my finger across the ridges of the pawns until I reached the makeshift pieces fashioned out of matchsticks and German coat buttons. Bradley's blood stained one. I took it out and as it lay in the palm of my hand—his blood in my hand—I vowed, grinding my teeth, I would not let the bastard get away with this treachery. I lobbed his two pawns into the valley between the two platforms, to be crushed by a train.

So… the pawns had not been returned to the set. Perhaps no one cared. Perhaps as I didn't return, they threw them away, but why not make up the set? My head throbbed.

A bluster of smoke heralded the train pulling into the opposite platform and ripped me from my reverie of the past. I closed the box, placed it back in my kit bag and checked the station clock. The train should be here soon. The war would have been over by that first Christmas if

Maurice

the Germans had to use our trains, I mused. Passengers were gathering before me now, each looking hopefully to their right. The train took its leave with more clouds of smoke, a distant whistle by a hidden porter and it was away. Off up the line towards Shrewsbury.

Several people had alighted—some struggling with cases and trunks, others with briefcases. As the smoke whispered around them, I could make out two women—one grey haired, the other with luxuriant brown hair tumbling down her back. Hair that I had twisted in my fingers so many times. Neither looked my way; both focused on another familiar figure lifting a hat box and several bags. Bradley Hurt. And he certainly does hurt people, I thought.

I should have shouted across at them. I should have run across the bridge and punched him. My body was too weak. I just stared.

Mother straightened her hat, the little black straw hat she kept for church and glanced across towards me. There was no sign of recognition—her eyesight had never been good. I pulled the tip of my trilby further down my face. And when I looked up the three of them had gone.

I stared across the void at my past and as the train pulled in, I met my future.

Rose.

Chapter Eleven

LUC

Luc yawned. It had been a long day and the ormolu clock on the mantelpiece was about to strike the eleventh hour.

'I'm so sorry but I must go back to my hotel,' she said stifling another yawn.

Maurice nodded sagely. 'Yes, my dear. There is a lot to take in. I forget that this is so new to you both. I have lived with it all for so long it is imprinted on my skin.'

Luc glanced across at the old man, in the pooling light from a nearby table lamp, the shadows had lengthened in his cheeks giving him a hollow ancient look. She found herself warming to this stranger who had been part of her life within the shadows of time.

'I'll walk you back to your hotel,' announced Scott, jumping to his feet.

Luc smiled bleakly. 'But it's miles. I'll take a cab.' She strolled to the door, pulling on her jacket and hitching up her shoulder bag.

Scott held the door open for her and snorted. 'It's literally two minutes around the corner. I'll get my jacket.'

Maurice called across the room, 'We thought you should be close. I hope you don't mind.'

Luc

Luc shrugged. 'Perhaps we can talk tomorrow, Maurice, before I fly back to London?'

'Yes. A good idea. Let's say 11 or 12. Yes 12 at Le Grand Véfour for lunch. Bon nuit cherie.' He gave a little wave.

Luc raised a hesitant hand and returned the wave. 'Bon nuit.'

Scott was waiting at the front door and ushered her out into the courtyard and the street beyond.

They walked in silence until they reached the end of the block, Luc mulling over an extraordinary day; Scott, with hands pushed into pockets of his linen jacket, striding beside her.

'He's a good man,' Scott said, turning to Luc. They had stopped to cross the road, a busy thoroughfare with no gaps between any of the cars.

She sighed. 'I thought my grandad was a good man. Now, I'm not so sure.'

A lull in the traffic and suddenly Scott grabbed her hand and pulled her across the road. Cars hooted and flashed at their recklessness, but they were soon making their way past plate glass windows, vibrant and bright, full of Easter promises. Luc, breathless from their mad dash, realised Scott was still holding her hand. Taking it from him, she caught his sideways glance in the lamplight and then looked away at the window display. The mannequins, enrobed in feathers and fur, watched them from their pedestals. Pausing to catch her breath, Luc watched as a giant Easter egg in the centre of the display burst open, showering confetti over a carpet of spring flowers where bunnies and chicks gambolled after foil covered eggs. For a moment she was transfixed, a child-like joy rushing through her.

'How can you tell?' Scott asked.

Hearsay

Luc glanced up at the man beside her. 'Sorry. What?'

'How can you tell if someone is good?' Scott urged, pushing his glasses higher on the bridge of his nose.

'A gut feeling, I suppose. Getting to know someone, spending time with them.' Her eyes wavered between Scott and the Easter offerings.

'What about me?' Scott insisted. 'Do you think I'm a good person?'

Luc finally turned away from the chicks and the eggs. 'I don't know you. First impressions don't always have longevity. I didn't trust you when you appeared at the Eiffel Tower and to begin with at the house.' She grinned.

'And now?'

'The jury's out at the moment.' Luc chuckled.

Scott rubbed his jaw. 'My daughter thinks I'm a good person.'

'Hearsay, I'm afraid.'

'Objection, your honour.' Scott grinned back. 'Lots of people think I'm kind, even my boss likes me…'

'More hearsay,' Luc interrupted. They both laughed.

They fell more comfortably in step now. 'So, what do you do?' asked Luc. At his look of confusion she added, 'What's your job?'

'Ah, yes,' he began. 'I'm a journalist, freelance.'

'That must be very interesting.'

'Yes, it is but it does mean I have to be away from Sophia for long periods of time.'

'Your daughter is very sweet,' Luc said, glancing at Scott. 'She seems to be very fond of you and Maurice.'

Scott grinned and then announced, 'And here we are. The Ritz Hotel.'

Even though Luc had dropped off her suitcase earlier, not knowing Paris, she hadn't realised they had arrived. 'Gosh, you weren't joking when you said it wasn't

Luc

far. If I had known, it would have saved a lot of faffing around at the Eiffel Tower and falling over.'

'But you wouldn't have seen our beautiful city. How is your ankle feeling now?' Scott's voice was full of concern.

'It's fine.' Luc had forgotten all about her injury but now at the mention of it her ankle complained with a twinge of pain. 'But I think I'll better go and get some sleep and take some paracetamol.'

'Good idea,' Scott agreed. 'I will pick you up at 8 tomorrow.'

'But Maurice said 12. Lunch somewhere.'

'Maurice wants you to fall in love.'

Luc blinked several times at this admission.

Scott grinned, a little colour coming to his cheeks, 'He wants you to fall in love with Paris. I'm to show you a little piece of heaven tomorrow.' With that he spun on his heels and waved goodbye.

The next morning, while checking her handbag for her passport and cash, Luc pulled out the slim red book, the story of the Blanchard chess set. With everything that had happened the day before, she had completely forgotten to ask Scott or Maurice about it. She quickly stuffed it back in her bag; she would show it to them later that day. A quick check in the mirror, a quick comb to her permed hair and a lick of lipstick and she was ready for the day.

Arriving in the hotel lobby at precisely 8 o'clock, Luc saw that Scott was already there, his long legs stretched out in front of him, reading Le Monde.

'Bonjour, Scott,' she said, stopping in front of him.

He lowered the paper and looked up into her eyes. 'Bonjour, Luc. Ca va?'

Hearsay

'I'm good thank you. How are you?'

'Tres bien, merci.' After folding the newspaper and placing it on a side table, Scott leapt up. 'And your ankle? Did you sleep well?'

Luc nodded but she hadn't slept well, and it wasn't her ankle that had kept her awake. Images of her grandad, Bradley Hurt and Maurice Smith fighting under the Eiffel Tower on a giant chessboard helped and hindered by chess pieces that came alive, had finally brought her to give up on sleep around 5am. She had watched French television, a British sit-com dubbed with strange sounding voices, until nodding off and being woken by her alarm clock at 7.30.

'Come, the sun is out, and Paris is waiting for you. You need some sustenance as we have a lot to do. Let's go.' Scott guided her to the open doors and out onto the street.

They were soon in La Place de la Concorde, cars bowling along, people ambling or rushing to wherever they needed to be. Work or play, Luc couldn't tell as everyone seemed to be dressed for a fashion show. She felt quite dowdy in her jeans and T shirt. Yesterday she had dressed up for a non-existent interview. Now, she wanted to relax and breathe. Scott was sporting bright blue shoes, pale blue chinos and a crisp white T shirt, a nonchalant navy and white striped jumper looped around his shoulders. His blonde hair bobbed as he walked and every so often, he would sweep it back from his forehead. Luc found herself surreptitiously casting her eyes sideways. He was a handsome man, a few years older than her and she knew he wouldn't be attracted to her, anyway there were other things that were at stake here and of course he was married with a child. Falling in love was not an option. It would just complicate things. She must stay focused.

Luc

They paused by a café with glittering brass railings and tiny round tables. Scott strolled through the open glass doors after guiding Luc before him. Smoke hovered in clouds above tables where clients rustled newspapers and sipped from miniscule shiny gold cups.

They were shown to an empty table. 'Chocolat et croissant, s'il vous plait,' Scott said, holding up two fingers.

Luc stayed silent, frustrated as yet another man decided for her, until a bowl of steaming hot chocolate and a warm croissant arrived. She watched as Scott broke off a bit of the flaky pastry, dipping it into the thick chocolate before popping it into his mouth. Luc followed suit and soon found that little bit of heaven he had promised her. She relented. Perhaps he made the right choice.

'Good? Yes?' Scott was asking. Luc nodded, her mouth still full of pastry and chocolate.

The morning flew by with a stroll through Jardin des Tuileries where Scott divulged that his parents were visiting his brother in Florida and that his divorce had just gone through. He explained he was living with Maurice until the financial settlement was arranged and that Sophia lived part of the week with him and the rest of the time with his ex-wife.

'Your daughter is a sweetheart,' Luc ventured as they approached the Louvre.

'She is, but her mother spoils her.'

Luc waited for Scott to continue, but he seemed reluctant to add more.

'We just have time to see the exquisite Mona Lisa.' Scott was already making his way towards the main entrance of the Louvre.

Luc, following him, checked her watch. 'Could we

look at some of the other paintings? I'm not too bothered about old Mona, to be honest.'

For a moment, Scott looked like he had been slapped, then his eyes lit up and a broad smile came to his lips.

'I have to say, it's not very big and not that impressive. It's all a lot of hype for the tourists.' He laughed. 'It's probably a fake anyway.'

Chapter Twelve

MAURICE

Maurice was waiting for them, studying a book while sipping from a wine glass.

'Sorry we're late,' Scott said sitting down. 'We lost track of time in the Louvre.'

Luc added her apology and Maurice waved it away. 'Ah, my old stomping ground.' He didn't elaborate any further, just snapped his book shut and placed it in a slimline leather briefcase beside his chair.

'How are you, my dear?' Maurice asked, lacing his fingers on the table mat. He wore a dark grey suit, a bright orange shirt and amber coloured tie nestled between the wide lapels.

'I'm very good, thank you. Scott has been showing me Paris.'

'Are you falling in love?' Maurice winked at Scott who seemed to suddenly find his folded napkin very interesting.

'With Paris, yes,' she said smiling. 'It is a beautiful city.'

'I am so pleased. Now what would you like to eat?'

Hearsay

The food came, was eaten and then plates cleared away. And throughout, just small talk about Paris: the weather, the food, anything but the things Maurice had divulged the night before. It wasn't until coffee arrived with their desserts that the old man began to speak.

'Last night, I threw you both a little I think, and I am sorry for doing that. I have so much to tell you, but also very little as there is so much that I still don't know.'

Luc and Scott continued to eat their respective sweets, neither of them wanting to interrupt.

'For a long time, I have wanted to find out what really happened after I left. I feel that my mother's death may have been caused by Bradley Hurt.' Luc gasped at this. Maurice continued, 'I can't prove anything though and perhaps it is too far in the past to do anything. Anyway, I moved on with my life, literally away from Bounds End on a train and met my sweet girl, Rosemary.

Rose was the glue that stuck my heart back together. Later, she kept our family together in just the same way, through her love and tenderness, her joy of life and her unbound belief that everything will be all right. But I was just like a smashed cup put back together, there were tiny chips that were lost forever—Mum, Dad and Myrtle. I carried those wherever I went.

Rose was a teacher of French then and we decided to move to Paris. We were married after only a few weeks of meeting. I had very few skills; there wasn't much call for a farmer in Paris. I grabbed any job that came along while Rose taught in a school and kept food in the larder.

After the war everyone was re-inventing themselves. I could become Maurice Smith and not be Edmund Cruso any longer. No one cared what I had done in a past life. Then, I fell into the art life when Rose introduced me to Pierre who was working at the Louvre. I started as a

Maurice

janitor and held many jobs there and as I learned more about the paintings I wanted to know more. I began night school studying history of art.

The one true sadness that blighted our lives was that Rose and I couldn't have children. Once the anguish began to fade, well at least become a pain that could be tolerated, we investigated adoption.

After the Great War, there were many people who were struggling. Wives had lost husbands; children had lost fathers. We adopted two beautiful children, both from English families who were unable to look after them. They became our life, our absolute joy. Rose was a wonderful mother and…' Maurice came to a sudden stand-still in his recapturing of the past.

Luc could see he was tiring. She leaned over and patted his arm. 'You can tell us this another time, Maurice.'

Scott agreed. 'Grandma was a lovely person, a *good* person.' He glanced at Luc as he emphasised the word 'good', and she nodded.

'I wish I had met Rose.'

'Yes, cherie, I wish you had.' Maurice wiped a tear from his eyes. 'Yes, we can talk more about this another time. Today, though, I need to ask you both to do something for me.'

Scott asked, 'Maurice, how can we help?'

The old man sat up straighter in his chair. 'I want you both to visit Bounds End and Ashfield to find out what happened. What happened to my family and to Myrtle. I went back briefly in the thirties and saw my parents' graves. I saw Bobby, my childhood friend's name on the war memorial. That shook me, I can tell you. My name wasn't there so I assumed people thought I was still alive, but then why did no one care enough about finding me?'

Reflecting on this statement, Maurice paused. Then after gulping back his coffee, cold now after sifting through his memories, he said, 'I knew that Edmund Cruso had died in the war, and I was reborn as Maurice Smith. I had been given a second chance, a second life perhaps. Would you do that for me? Will you go back and find out what really happened to my family. Please?'

Luc nodded and said, 'Yes and if it's okay with you I would like to find out more about my own family.'

Scott added, 'I would be very happy to accompany Luc.'

'That settles it. Thank you for trusting me. Now let's pay and get Lucretia to the airport.'

Chapter Thirteen

LUC

A few days later, Luc and Scott, found themselves in a quiet bistro in Covent Garden. Luc played with the stem of her almost empty glass and glanced about her. Check tablecloths, plastic fruit hanging from the ceiling and a haze of cigarette smoke from the back of the room. The candle in the Mateus bottle sitting between them was new, but the green glass shrouded in layers of wax, like a Victorian crinoline, told of many evenings spent between friends and lovers. With this thought, Luc smiled.

'Where are you staying, Scott?'

'Just a small hotel—nothing too flash. Maurice wanted me to stay at The Grosvenor House—his favourite place but it's a bit pompous for me.'

'Maurice could afford to stay anywhere, I suppose?'

Scott smiled. 'Do you want another? He said I had to treat you well.'

'Well, I'd better enjoy myself if he's paying.' She laughed while Scott caught the eye of the waitress and ordered a bottle of wine.

The wine and then the food arrived, and they were

silent for a while. Luc was mopping up the steak juices with a chip when Scott began talking.

'I'm going to be here for about a week. I have some errands to run for Maurice, but they won't take long. Saville Row to collect new suits, Harrods to collect bits and pieces. That sort of thing. Anyway, we will have plenty of time to travel up to Shropshire like we agreed and explore the area. Dig around a bit. Find that missing pawn.'

'If it wants to be found,' joked Luc.

Scott placing his steak knife down, lifted a hand to cup his chin. He stared intently at her. 'What do you mean by that?'

Luc breathed out. 'I don't know. Just a funny feeling. Mum said there were special powers in the chess piece.'

Across the table, Scott frowned, then a sparkle appeared in his eyes. 'Really?'

Luc went to reply and saw Scott's mouth twitch. She smiled back. 'I don't know what to think. All I know is my pendant holds a special meaning for me as it belonged to my mum.' She sighed and cast her eyes down.

Scott reached across and took her hand. 'I'm sorry you don't know where she is. It must be awful not seeing her.' He gazed at her, his spectacles making his eyes larger.

Thrown by this caring gesture, she removed her hand from his grasp and lifted her wine glass. She wasn't ready to tell Scott about her mother, her inner voice reminded Luc to hold forth.

Instead, she spoke about the wood of the chess piece. She began, her voice becoming low and mystical. 'The bloodwood tree comes from Madagascar. When it's cut down, it bleeds red sap. The indigenous people stored it in the waterways ready until the ships arrived to transport the wood to far-off places like China. The water runs

Luc

blood red.' Luc held up her glass, swirling the contents in the bowl. She paused and rivulets of wine ran down. 'The legs, I believe they call this.' Scott nodded.

'The bloodwood sap can heal medical problems that affect the legs, stomach and eyes. It can even cure malaria.' Luc sipped her wine. 'The tannin in the grape is the same chemical that is in the wood. The lifeblood of both the vine and the tree.'

Luc leaned back in the chair. 'Coffee?' she asked, grinning. The mood was lightened.

Scott nodded. 'Is that all true?' he asked, leaning forward.

'Cross my heart and hope to die.'

'You don't need to do that,' Scott's eyebrows knitted showing concern.

Luc chuckled. 'You're French—you won't understand. Suffice to say I am telling the truth.'

'I'm not French.' It was Scott's turn to smile now.

'Sure, you are. Maurice married a French woman.'

'No, Rose was English. Remember he said they couldn't have children so turned to adoption. After the war my father's birth parents couldn't care for him and his sister. They came to Maurice and Rose while still very young. My mother was also English, working in France in the fifties. I was born in France and have a French passport, and of course I speak the language, but I don't know if I'm truly French.'

Luc pulled her bag onto her lap. 'Scott, I wonder if you can help me with something?' She drew the red book about the Blanchard family from her bag and gave it to Scott.

'What is this?' he asked.

'I found it in a bookshop here in London, before I came over to Paris. With everything else going on I kept forgetting to show it to Maurice. I need help with the translation. Please look inside—you will see my pendant in there.'

Scott turned the pages until the image of the red pawn appeared. Glancing across at Luc, he murmured, 'This is Maurice's chess set… the one he wants to buy at the Paris auction. This is incredible, Luc. Yes, of course I can translate it for you. Maurice would love to see this, I'm sure.'

A waiter bustled over, removing their plates, interrupting the conversation. Coffee was ordered and brought to the table. And then Scott began to read aloud the story in English.

'"Sitting in the deep shadows, cradling a piece of wood, Florence observed the little knicks and cuts her father made. Every so often he would raise his head, grey hair falling across his weather-worn face, hold it to the light pushing through the thick window glass, grunt and then bend his head to study the piece yet again and scrape the tiniest of slivers to ensure perfection.

This was the final piece to be crafted. The red king. Shavings as thin as a cat's whiskers floated through the dust-filled air, landing on the battle-scarred bench below. There had been many battles over the years, Florence reflected. Battles with people, with the absinthe, with the demons that would possess her father. All of which had brought them nowhere."'

Scott paused and looked at Luc. 'This is fascinating.'

Luc just smiled. Florence Blanchard and her father were beginning to take shape in her imagination.

'May I borrow this please, Luc. I will write down the translation, but it will take time. Will you trust me with it? I promise to take care of it for you.'

Luc

She nodded. Instantly she knew she could trust this man and not just with the book but perhaps with her heart too.

Two days later, Luc's little Hillman Imp nosed its way past a pub and several houses fronted by neat gardens and held in by wrought iron gates. A chapel to the right and a village hall to the left and they arrived at a crossroads and another pub and a petrol station.

'Where to now?' Luc's eyes scanned right and left. A tractor chugged by, followed by three impatient cars. This was a traffic jam in Shropshire!

Studying a map from Maurice, he replied, 'Right and then first right.'

Both Luc and Scott had struggled deciphering the map earlier before setting off—it wasn't to any kind of scale plus there were several green-inked annotations added to the original pencil strokes.

Top Field (crop circle 1910). Lovers' Lane (I know that place well!!). The Firs (Myrtle threw pawn away) The Rock Hole (good for climbing and falling off!).

'There must still be people here who knew Maurice,' Scott suggested. 'He went to the local school, up near the church… I think.' He broke off turning the map. 'It could be miles away though according to this.'

'We could try a local pub—we've passed two already—ask around.'

'I like the sound of that,' agreed Scott. 'Though I'm not keen on warm beer. This is it. Pull over, Luc.'

The houses on their left had petered out and to their right stood a substantial, red-bricked farmhouse. Luc could make out barns with black corrugated iron, doming over untidy stacks of straw and hay.

Hearsay

She parked the car by a high bank of spring green and stepped out. A thin breeze caressed her face, and she ran her fingers through her hair, still tightly curled from the perm. They crossed over to get a better look. From their first vantage point, the ground floor of the house had been obscured by tall fat shrubs. Now, on closer inspection, they could see the windows, blind to life on the outside, were covered with rough planking and rusting nails. The front door, once a cherry red, was mottled and peeling.

Scott swung the metal garden gate open, and they strolled up a gravel path, flanked on the left side by rampant briars, rose bushes with bronze hips and withered leaves and on their right standing majestic in what had once been lawn, now a collection of meadow grass, daisies and dandelions, was a monkey puzzle tree.

Luc raised the square brass knocker and banged it down three times. Echoing through the house, the sounds gradually died away.

'Oh well. We tried. Maurice was wrong, there's no one here.' Scott had already begun to walk back towards the gate when Luc shushed him. She closed her eyes, blocking out the daylight to concentrate on listening. There had been a sound from within—only slight but someone or something was there. She could feel a presence.

Scott was standing next to her when she finally opened her eyes, and she stepped back in surprise, almost slipping off the doorstep. He raised one eyebrow and both hands, palms uppermost. 'Really? There's no one there.'

Luc, determined not to let go, knocked again, and called through the brass letterbox. 'Hello, is anyone there? Maurice asked us to call.'

The words bounced around for a second and vanished into the shadows. No reply came. No movement. Nothing.

Luc

'We'll come back. Maurice Smith…' and then remembering, '…Edmund Cruso sent us,' she shouted up at a bedroom window. 'We need to know what happened.' A spit of rain caught her eye, and she blinked. 'I know you're listening,' she whispered.

Climbing into the car, fat splotches of water hit their backs, the car interior, their ankles. They sat and watched the rain dribble down the glass, until a fog of condensation hid all from view. Luc started up the engine. It coughed a couple of times before firing up. Turning on the lights and wipers, she murmured, 'We could try the church. They'll have records. The graveyard might show up something too.'

'I don't know about you, but I don't fancy wandering around graves in this.'

'True. Okay, let's go back to one of those pubs we passed. We could grab a sandwich and wait for the storm to pass.'

'Just what I was going to suggest,' Scott said. 'You never know, someone might remember the Cruso family.'

After dodging bullets of rain and hail, they entered the busy pub and after ordering some sandwiches, they took their drinks to a secluded table near the fireplace. Luc sipped her lager and lime, leaned back on the velour covered bench and took in her surroundings. Dark wood tables held various drinks in half-empty, half-full scenarios; rosy faced people chatted and laughed; dried flower arrangements and shiny horse brasses finishing off the typical village pub. Even the old chaps propping up the bar were the archetypal image. And through the low windows sharp rods of rain hit the car park and tubs of spring flowers.

Scott dived into his rucksack, pulled out a grey shoebox and laid it on the table. 'This belongs to Maurice.'

Hearsay

He removed the lid revealing a mass of paper and card, some torn, others neatly cut. Each one held scribbles of ink, mostly green. There were drawings, maps, plans and photos all squashed in alongside a dark red card folded in two.

'Some people keep diaries, others neat notebooks. Not Maurice, it seems. This is how his memories have come to him. Haphazard, in snippets. Some are dated, others are not.'

'A bit like the worst jigsaw puzzle ever. And I hate jigsaws!' Luc felt deflated. How were they going to make any sense of all of this?

The arrival of piled up plates interrupted them, and Luc moved the box to the bench beside her. The food kept them quiet for a few minutes. A thought came to her and swallowing quickly she started. 'We need to try and organise this into sections.'

'Right,' said Scott. 'Let's start with this. Every jigsaw has a picture to work from.' He now unfolded the board, and Luc could see by the chequered brown and cream squares it was a chess board. He passed it across to her and she could see writing on some of the squares.

Running her fingers over the haphazard handwriting, Luc said, 'Is this the one from the hospital? The one that helped with his memory?'

Scott nodded. 'While he was convalescing in a medical hospital after the war. Do you remember he said the nurse was furious with him for covering the board with scribble. He told me later she used to write sums on the back of her starched apron as she couldn't remember the formula for a lot of the medication. So, they came to a deal that he could keep the board as, she admitted, it might help him remember, and he wouldn't tell the doctor about her secret sums.'

Luc

Luc laughed and then read the words aloud like an incantation. 'Conkers, leaves, Bobby, soap tin…' She looked up into Scott's eyes. 'This is incredible,' mused Luc. 'Still, I can't think why a soap tin is important to him.'

'His mother buried the white pawn in a soap tin in a field,' Scott explained. 'The answers are in the box—the puzzle pieces.' Scott laughed at this. Luc glared at him.

'We need some space to spread all of this out. We can't do it here. What do you suggest?'

'We also need more time, don't we?'

Luc had a thought. 'Why can't Maurice sort all this out? And what are we trying to find out anyway? I can't just go off and do his silly detective work.'

Scott nodded. 'I know. I've asked him that many times. He just shrugs his shoulders and tells me to find out for myself. Anyway, one thing he has agreed to do is record himself reminiscing. I've shown him how to use the cassette recorder and the mic. We can then listen to it when we have time.'

'Perhaps Maurice finds it too upsetting to delve into the past.'

'Possibly but don't forget he wants to find the missing white pawn,' Scott responded. 'It would be worth a lot of money complete.'

'I don't think money is the only thing he's interested in here.'

'Would you like to see the dessert menu?' A disembodied voice came from their left.

Luc blinked. She was so far into the discussion she had quite forgotten for a moment where they were. In unison, they both shook their heads. 'A cup of tea, please,' Luc said, and Scott asked for a coffee.

The waitress cleared the plates and empty glasses while Scott disappeared off to find the toilet. 'Have you lived here long?' Luc asked the girl.

'I was born here.'

'Do you know the Cruso family?'

'Don't know that name, sorry.' She went to leave, clutching the plates in one hand and the glasses in the other.

'How about Hurt? They had the farm up near the new school.'

'Not sure. Sorry.'

Luc sighed. 'Don't worry. Thank you.'

The waitress rushed off, almost colliding with Scott as he returned to his seat.

The tea and coffee were delivered by an older woman, her hair in a bun, silver woven throughout.

'I'm impressed,' announced Scott, pushing down the plunger of the little cafetiere and poured the black liquid into his cup. 'Real coffee in this backwater of a place.'

'You haven't tasted it yet,' Luc smiled at him over her teacup. 'It could be made of acorns.' The aroma told her otherwise.

Scott took a mouthful, swallowed and smiled. 'Very good. Even Maurice would approve.'

Both quiet while they sipped their drinks; Luc studying the box of paper while Scott stared out of the window. Twisting her head to do the same, she saw the rain had dissipated leaving tulips with drooping heads nodding in a gentle breeze; sky still tinged with gun-metal grey.

She turned back. Scott was studying her. Their eyes caught for a moment before they both looked away.

'Luc?' He cleared his throat.

'Hmmm?' Luc pretended to be reading the chess board.

'Luc, I feel… we…'

Luc

'Yes, I feel we should…' She stopped. She had got this wrong so many times before. 'Sorry, what? What do you feel?'

'Erm… I feel we need more time to do this. Don't you?' His hand gestured towards the box and board.

A lump of disappointment slid down Luc's throat. *He's only interested in Maurice and finding the pawn for him. Not me, at all. Why do I lay myself open to this? A good-looking French, no, an English man, interested in me! What was I thinking?*

'Luc? Are you okay?'

Unable to form a sentence, she nodded. Busying herself with returning the board to the box, closing it firmly gave her time to think. *I can walk away from all of this. I can keep my red pawn and my identity, my life, my… I don't care about the war. I know my family. I know my grandfather lied, but it's all in the past now. Why help these strangers who broke into my life? And yet…*

'I… I… need the loo,' Luc said rising from her seat. She didn't look back ploughing on through the other patrons of the pub, not knowing where she was making for. Following signs, she found herself in the ladies and shut herself into a vacant cubicle. Shrugging her jeans and knickers down she perched on the dark wood seat. *My life isn't exactly exciting. My job isn't going anywhere. I've never taken risks. No! I'll get hurt. I can't do that all again. Yet, I've entrusted Scott with the book. Was I right to do that?* Her mind flew back and forth—the pros and the cons of what to do, until she screwed her eyes tight to block out the voices in her head.

How was it, that going for a wee can stimulate the brain to work? Because as she washed her hands, Luc came to a decision. She marched back to Scott, ready to tell him. The table was empty, the box gone. Pursing her lips, pushing out pent up air, she looked around for a shock of blond hair. Nothing.

Hearsay

We haven't paid and he's just gone. Bloody typical. I begin to trust someone, and they walk out on me. At the bar, she pulled out several notes from her purse, but the barman waved it away. 'Y' man's paid, love.'

Luc thanked him. *My man? My man? He is definitely not my man!* She stumbled out to the car park to find Scott leaning nonchalantly against the little Imp. His face lit up at her approach.

'Sorry, I just needed some air. I told the waitress to tell you.'

'Well, she didn't, did she?' Luc knew her voice was coming out like that of a fractious teenager, but she needed to offload some frustration.

'Have I upset you or something?'

In answer, she unlocked the car, got in and slammed the door, her heart thudding against her ribs. Automatically, she twisted the key in the ignition and waited for the little Imp to fire up, yet it refused to do so. Knocking on the passenger side window made her glance across to see Scott's face peering intently at her. Turning off the engine, Luc stretched across to unlock the door.

A damp smell rose around them; their breath fogging up the glass. Luc tapped her fingers on the steering wheel.

'I should have waited. I would have done if I'd known you were going to be so angry. I just needed to clear my head. So much to think about.' Scott turned to her. 'I'm sorry.'

Luc slumped. 'I'm sorry too. I find it difficult to trust people after Mum left.'

Scott remained silent, the air thickening around them.

'My mum walked out on us when I was a child. My dad gave me up to my aunt and uncle—he didn't want me. They looked after me until university and I've made my own way ever since. I don't need anyone in my life.' She

Luc

glanced across to see Scott looking back at her. 'Meeting you, though, has given me hope, that there are nice people, even good people, in the world. You and Maurice have been so kind to me. I've always mistrusted hearsay. I'd like to know more about my past because it might help me to shape my future.'

'I don't know if we can help you find your past, Luc. I don't know if I can offer you what you're looking for, but I'm happy to learn alongside you. And if on the way we become… friends that's a bonus.' Scott's brow creased and dropping his gaze, he dropped his tone. 'I hope we are friends. I hope I can depend on you just like you can depend on me.'

'You can. Let's do this together and see what happens.' Luc stretched out a hand and he took it.

In their fogged-up world, they both jumped, letting go of each other's hand, as hail rattled harshly against the roof. Luc started up the car, (this time it began first time) wiping her sleeve across the window and turning the heater to boost. Pellets of ice bounced off the bonnet, pummelling the little car.

'Where to?' She asked her passenger hoping he would suggest somewhere warm and dry.

He didn't.

Well, it would be dry, at least, she thought as she turned out onto the road towards the church.

Chapter Fourteen

MAURICE

Maurice sat at his desk, overlooking the garden; a neat rectangle of green, edged with sculptured box and Greek statues at each corner and entrance. A miniature facsimile of Wrest Park, where the hospital had been incorporated during the Great War but without the long sweeping lawns and the straight expanse of water running through the middle.

Mimi, his housekeeper, had brought in a tray of coffee and biscuits and now there were no more excuses, he had to delve into those shadows in the recesses of his mind.

Switching on the cassette recorder and pressing down the record button, he began to speak, to remember.

'It wasn't until the thirties that I walked up the high street of Bounds End once again.

I had returned to England to take a look at some possible premises for a shop with a flat above. We had decided to return to London as there was unrest in Europe and Rose's father was unwell. We needed a change.

I phoned Rose from a telephone box outside King's Cross station. She kept saying to slow down. I couldn't

Maurice

help it; I was so excited. I had found the perfect place in Camden. I had put a down payment already and would come home the next day to start packing.

I didn't know what to do with myself. I so wanted to be with Rose and the children at that moment, to hug them all, to begin our next chapter together. Yet, the past pulled me back to the high street of Bounds End, standing under the old conker tree, sticky buds forming on outstretched branches. Would the children collect the conkers like I did with my friends? Would they harden them in the oven and pickle them in vinegar? Would they be proud to have a niner and then watch their shiny brown conker explode as it took a direct hit; listen to the taunts as they sadly picked up the pieces?

I continued through the village, past the road leading to the farm, I wasn't ready to see Mum and Dad yet. Dad who had lost his mind and Mum who had a new family to look after. They didn't need me. Over the years I had written so many letters to them, each one I had screwed up and thrown into the hearth to die in flames. None of them ever posted, none of them ever read. They were better off without me, and I had a new life now as Maurice Smith.

I walked on, finally coming to the war memorial where I paused to check out the rollcall of names, some men I knew, some I didn't. Now just names and yet each one told a story.

And there I saw Bobby's name amongst so many others I knew from school, each one bringing memories of football and rugger, of algebra and equations. My chest tightened. I crouched and traced the lettering with my index finger, to prove to myself I wasn't seeing things. I knew Bobby had been killed but this made it all real. In a dream I turned away and stumbled on along the footpath.

Hearsay

So many gone. So much waste. Not really knowing where to go I stopped at the bottom of the sloping path towards the church and decided to find solace there.

I paused for a moment to breathe in the air, clean and crisp in my throat and saw once again the gouges in the sandstone wall allegedly made by Cromwell's archers as they sharpened their arrows. Bobby and I often recreated that scene with our own home-made bows and arrows. And in that moment, I saw my friend once again—his hair tufting from sleep, slurps of jam on his cheek shouting with innocent joy as he raised his bow aloft and aimed at a grassy hassock inside the churchyard. And the shouts from a woman at the church entrance, shaking out her feather duster, to clear off or she would tan their hide and no mistake.

Bobby and I had been choristers there. Mum would scrub my face clean at home and then again with spit on a hankie before I set foot in the vestry. Now I entered the coolness of the church; familiar smells of lilies and lavender furniture polish hitting my senses as my eyes accustomed to the light. Having walked down the main aisle I took my old seat in the choir stalls. Prayer and hymn books laid ready for youthful hands to cradle them. Yet so many hands would never hold a prayer book again or sing a descant that rose up to heaven and the angels; Bobby amongst them.

We enlisted on the same day, he a Pioneer, I a private in the Shropshire Yeomanry. We lost touch. He travelled to Salonika and while shoring up a bridge he got it. Mother told me in one of her letters. I burnt that one. With the flame I lit a woodbine and toasted my old friend, Bobby, with a tot of rum. Bradley had been there with me; always there by my side scowling and muttering. So different from Bobby who always had a kind word and a cheeky grin.

Maurice

Bobby and his girl and Myrtle and I would go to the dances in the church hall. We loved to dance the waltz even though I had two left feet. Sometimes we did a bit of square dancing too. My dozy-doe and my skips weren't up to much and Myrtle often bore bruised shins as I turned the wrong way and kicked her. Those days were long gone, that life a distant memory.

Peace fell upon me sitting there in the church, and I murmured the Lords' Prayer for the first time in years. Light shone through a window puddling reds, blues and gold across the carpet and onto the cross on the altar. I had never been very religious, and the war stripped me of many long-held beliefs, yet at that moment I believed God was there with me. Tears stung my eyes, sharp as thorns. The innocence of youth torn down, the waste of so many lives. My life had been lost too. Taken by a so-called friend, Bradley Hurt, robbing me of my dignity, my family, my future. What had he told them? Did they think I had been killed? A sudden thought came to me. If that was the case, then why was my name not on the war memorial? Did they think I was still alive? If so, why hadn't they looked for me?

Rousing myself from maudlin nostalgia, I took my leave. Outside the spring sunshine lightened my load and I took off towards the Rock Hole. A good walk would clear my head. Reaching the gate at the opposite end of the graveyard from whence I had come there were fresh graves, wooden crosses marking the spot. I stopped and glanced along the row, wondering if I recognised any names.

A light suddenly extinguished within my mind and the plastered over cracks in my heart fractured once again. Cruso. Eirene Field Cruso and Sidney Cruso. I stepped gingerly around the other graves and knelt to read the stone slab. This wasn't recent. This was a few years old with weeds nestling around the edges.

Leaning back on my heels, I read the words. My mother had passed away in 1922 joining my father in heaven who died in 1920. They would be forever together.

An old shrimp paste jar held a single daffodil, its stem broken off near the bloom and the petals ragged as though someone had found it by the roadside. Someone who thought it would bring joy to the memory of the two people who had died never knowing I was still alive.

'I'm here now,' I whispered to the cold stone. 'I have a family. You would love them so much, just as I do.' Tears splashed on my bent knees, and I uncurled and sat back against another grave behind me. I told them of Rose and of the children. I told them of my plans for an art gallery in London.

And I begged for their forgiveness, for not coming back. I wasn't a coward on the battlefield—I was the coward who couldn't face them.

The tears came thick and fast now as I sobbed all the pain and regret away. My chest, a hollowed-out tree trunk, nothing left within it. Eyes raw, peeled bare, a heart splintered once again. I ran from that place; past the old black and white houses down the track, running like the whole German army were after me. The wind whipping my face, briars scratching my skin. My heart pumped new life back into my lungs and as I reached the Rock Hole with my shoes sliding on a sandy patch, I skittered to a stop.

A shout from behind made me turn and two young lads on bikes roared past me. Their legs stretched out away from their pedals, hollering in absolute joy, their bikes sliding, shimmying, skimming down to the floor of the quarry and then onwards and out to the far fields.

Maurice

I took their exuberance, snatching it from the breeze they left behind in their wake, and held it tight in my heart. I have been given a life, I thought, I must keep this feeling within me and live. I could live in the past and regret my decisions but there was no going back now. I had a past, present and a future with Rose and the children. I wanted them to enjoy life in the countryside, the freedom that Bobby and I had had. The exhilaration of riding your bikes, fishing for sticklebacks, conker fights and so much more.

I walked on through the rocky enclave, the raw, red sandstone hacked back where blocks had been hewn to build the village church. Ivy and brambles tumbled, tree roots clinging, boulders nestled. A blackbird gave song and accompanied me as I turned right. In the field to my left a grey tractor chugged along with gulls diving down to search for loose seeds and worms uncovered in the turned earth.

Once I came to the road, as though an invisible string pulled me, I eventually found myself outside our farm. Not ours anymore though. With Mum and Dad gone, who had it now? I wondered. Brad and Myrtle weren't farmers. Brad was a petty thief from Leeds and Myrtle had never wanted that kind of life.

The place looked quiet, the yard empty. I wanted so much to walk around the back and for Mother to scold me for the bloody graze on my shin and blisters on my hands where I had held the swinging rope in the quarry. I wanted Dad to be there, his stockinged feet up on the fender, steam rising as the damp evaporated.

Wait! The front door was opening. We never use that door! Hurriedly I slipped down next to the hedge, I didn't want to be seen. People around here don't take to strangers staring at their houses.

Hearsay

A young girl ran out, plaited hair flying behind, her chuckles reaching my ears and I smiled. She wore a coat of petrol-blue and a beret of mustard-yellow. She skipped towards the gate, humming a tune.

Another figure, in a camel-brown coat and matching hat came to the door. A stern expression which softened as she watched the girl, before closing the door behind her. Myrtle… my Myrtle.

So, they had stayed. Of course, they would have been left the farm and all the debts and difficulties that came with it. Dad had never been good with the books. Mum tried her best, but her head was in the clouds most of the time. Walking the fields with her dowsing rods or checking the wheat for mysterious circles that formed every few years.

The two of them took a left turn with happy chatter wisping towards me on the breeze. Something about a cow calving and daddy and saving the day. Of course, good old Bradley. Couldn't do anything wrong. He had now become the perfect farmer and parent. Was I the only one who knew what he was capable of?

I shifted position, my back aching from being bent over under the hedge. The girl, her hair twisted gold like corn dollies, let go of her mother's hand to stoop and pick up a pebble. Her eyes sought mine as she straightened. Then, with a wave of a hand, she was gone skipping after her mother.'

A tentative knock on the door made Maurice pause. 'Yes, come in.' His throat felt dry, and he coughed.

Mimi entered, 'Lunch time!' she called cheerily from the door, lightening the mood. Dressed in a black dress and crisp white apron, Mimi looked like she would be very much at home in a posh tearoom. But that was where the comparison ended. Her purple hair and several ear

Maurice

piercings brought her bang into 1985. The heavy black Doc Marten's just added to the image. 'It is lunch time, monsieur. You need to take a break.'

Maurice nodded, pressing the stop button on the tape recorder. 'What a good idea,' he agreed.

Chapter Fifteen

LUC

Light glowed through every window as Luc and Scott made their way along the tarmac path to the entrance of the church. The earlier momentary shower of hail had left silvery white beads strewn across their path like wedding confetti. The solid square bell tower loomed over them as they came to the main entrance.

Luc lifted the iron handle on the solid dark wood door and pushed it open a crack.

'Come in, come in,' a deep voice boomed out.

The man who stood there bathed in light wore a black cassock and ushered them in.

'Well, that was a bit of a hailstorm, wasn't it?' he said, a broad smile crinkling his eyes. 'You're here to talk about the wedding?' He bustled off towards the main aisle where he paused.

Luc and Scott grinned at each other. 'Er, no. That's not us,' Luc stuttered.

'Definitely not us!' Scott's emphatic reply to the man's suggestion surprised Luc and her grin turned to a frown. Seeing the priest was waiting for them they made their way to him.

Luc

Luc, slightly aggrieved and not knowing why, began to explain. 'No, we're here for a friend. We have a few questions about his family and what might have happened to them after the war. Sorry, were you expecting someone? We can come back another time.'

The man, his warm brown eyes twinkling said, 'Ah, yes. I'm sorry. I am expecting a young couple who wanted to come and see the church and to talk about their banns being read.' He checked his watch and added, 'But until they arrive, I may be able to help you. Please sit.' He gestured for them to come and sit on one of the pews. They duly did so while he sat himself down on the pew in front and turned his body to see them.

'I'm the Rector here. How do you do?'

'We're very well thanks. I'm Luc, Lucretia Stourton-Hurt and this is Scott Smith,' Luc explained. She found herself relaxing and felt she could tell this man anything— all her woes and worries—yet she remained silent.

It was Scott who took up the baton to explain further. 'My grandfather grew up in this village before the First World War. His name was Edmund Cruso.'

'Before my time, young man.' The Rector chuckled.

'We thought there ought to be parish records of births, marriages and deaths. That sort of thing. Is that right?' Scott asked, crossing his legs, and leaning back against the dark wood pew.

Before answering, the Rector paused, his head on one side. 'French, that's it isn't it? Your accent?'

Scott nodded.

'I love France. Such a beautiful country. Yes, we have had many holidays there.'

Scott nodded again. Luc waited for the priest to speak, but his eyes were glazing over.

Leaning forward, she said, 'I'm sorry, but we were

asking about the church records. Do you keep any here?'

'Oh yes of course. I am so sorry. My wife is always telling me to stay focused. Now then. Yes, we do have some recent records, but we don't keep the records from that time as we don't have the storage space.' The man stretched out both hands in an apology.

'What about the thirties and perhaps the fifties?' asked Luc.

'You'll need to go to the Council Offices in Shrewsbury, I'm afraid.'

'How far is that, please?' Scott asked, sighing.

The Rector, seemingly picking up Scott's frustration, nodded sagely. 'It's not far, fifteen miles or so. But they'll be closing at five probably. Can you go tomorrow? Are you staying in the area?' Luc could see he was trying to help; deep down she knew this would be more of a marathon than a sprint trying to rebuild the jigsaw of Maurice's life.

'Thank you. You've been very helpful.'

A loud metallic click came from behind and soft voices entered the church.

'Ah, here they are,' said the Rector, jumping to his feet. He strode over to the man and woman who were now standing gazing up at the high roof. He shook their hands vigorously and motioned for them to walk down the aisle.

Stopping next to the pew where Luc and Scott still sat, he said, 'I'm sorry I can't help you but please feel free to pop in anytime here or the Rectory. We're on High Street. The kettle's always on. My wife makes a lovely lemon drizzle. Won first prize at the village fete last year.' He shook Luc's and then Scott's hand. 'You have made me want to go back for a holiday, perhaps Paris this time, or the Dordogne region.' A surreptitious cough came

Luc

from the engaged couple waiting by the heavily carved wooden screen which separated the chancel from the main body of the church. It brought him back to his senses once again. 'Anyway, I must get on. You know you could explore the churchyard. You might find some graves of the family there. Good luck.'

He strode off towards the couple who were now standing holding hands on the red carpeted step of the chancel. Luc could hear him explain to them that the church was nine hundred years old, and that they must come and see the William Morris window.

'Another dead end,' Scott said.

'No, it's not. It's a window being opened instead of a door that's all. We know where to get the information. I was thinking we could ask at the local library and perhaps see if there's a local newspaper office. Maurice was adamant his mother had died in unusual circumstances. That would have made headline news here surely?'

'Yes, I suppose so. I just wanted to be able to phone Maurice this evening and tell him we'd made some progress.'

'We have.' Luc got to her feet. 'Come on, let's go and look at the graves. Hopefully the sun has come out.' Without waiting for him to haul himself up she walked back to the entrance and went outside. The sun was indeed there just peeping behind pale grey clouds. Glancing up at the porch she saw a sun dial. *Not enough sun for that*, she pondered and checked her watch. 'As a shadow, so is life,' Luc murmured.

Scott appeared in the doorway. 'Sorry, what did you say?'

'The sundial. Look what it says.' She pointed upwards and he joined her.

'Hmm. An interesting sentiment. I wonder what it means?' he mused.

'Perhaps that life is short, and we have to grab it by both hands,' Luc suggested, turning away and strolling along the path.

'Very true,' Scott agreed. 'Seeing all these graves makes you think, doesn't it. That'll be us one day. Food for worms.'

They fell in step together; both pondering on their words and followed a meandering path around the side of the church. Luc scanned the graves for names she recognised: some stones straight and stiff, others drooping as though they were being dragged down into the earth to join the dead. A speckled thrush hopped onto the grass, jabbing its beak into the stalks desperate for food. It stopped and tipping its head to one side, it listened. A distant chirruping within a tree by a gate leading to the old school brought it to take wing and Luc watched as it flapped away.

'Here, come and look at this,' Scott had broken off to tour the graves and was crouching down at a stone slab a few yards from the path. As Luc came towards him, he looked up at her, his hair flopping back. 'Look these are the graves of Maurice's parents—Sidney Cruso and Eirene Field Cruso.'

Luc knelt next to him and examined the stone. 'Together, forever,' she read aloud. 'That's nice, isn't it?'

Scott agreed running a finger over the carving. 'I think this is more interesting, though.' He gestured to a metal vase full of nodding daffodils. Their bright yellow petals fresh and clean. 'They look like they could have been put here this morning. What do you think?'

Luc nodded. 'Someone in the village remembers them.' She rocked back to sit on her heels. 'That's exciting. I was sure there was someone in the farmhouse, earlier. Perhaps they're the ones putting the flowers on the grave.'

Luc

Her heart began to beat faster and instinctively she put her hand into Scott's. 'We're on the right track, I can sense it.'

'What do you want to do now?' Scott whispered.

Luc glanced sideways at the graves and the enormity of the situation hit her. Disengaging her hand, and standing purposefully, she added, 'We have to keep looking. I think we drive over to the farm again now. We don't have time today to get to Shrewsbury to check the records or anything. I think we should check in to the hotel in Ashfield and go visit the library.'

On returning to the farm, Luc parked along the road near to a grey breezeblock building, riotous roots and sinuous stems scrambling across its roof where decay and neglect had eaten away at the iron. Rampant vines and ivy congregated—a tangled mass of nature reclaiming the land. Above them turbulent steel-grey clouds lay heavy, expectant and on the horizon, Luc could see rain breaking free. Thunder rolled around in the distance. Grabbing their waterproof coats and scarves this time, they set off to the farmhouse.

Once again, no one answered their knock and call, and on deciding to brave the weather, they set off to explore the area, using Maurice's badly drawn map. Leaving the car, they walked on away from the farm towards the fields.

They soon stopped by a five-barred gate, once painted white, now cracked and peeling and held into place by a fraying green rope. Scanning the vast field, the loamy brown punctuated at intervals by the curving white commas of gulls' wings, Luc lifted a hand to her brow to observe a dark red tractor labouring along the ruts in the furthest corner. With an escort of gulls hovering and darting behind searching for scraps upturned by the ever-rotating discs, the vehicle seemed to have a billowing bridal train.

Hearsay

'Is this the field?' Luc asked glancing at Scott, a man who seemed to be growing more important in her life and not just because of the old man they had left in Paris. Now he returned her gaze and nodded. He unfolded a yellowing document displaying Maurice's hand-drawn map of Bounds End.

Dabbing a finger on one of the sections, Scott said, 'I'm sure this is Top Field. That's the oak tree right in the centre.' His finger hovered over a rudimentary sketch in green pen of a tree and then pointed to the real one, statuesque and dignified, green shoots pushing out from twisted fingers, the promise of the summer ahead. As one they both followed Scott's arm and Luc marvelled at the myriad of ancient, crooked branches stretching out to catch a touch of sunlight, a drop of rain. A majestic force of nature, a kingly presence, that had watched over centuries of people foraging and farming.

'In No Man's Land, Maurice had to climb inside a hollowed out fake tree, a burnt wreck of an old oak to spy on the enemy in the dead of night,' Scott announced. 'I remember him telling me that as a child and I didn't believe him.'

Luc murmured, almost to herself, 'If war hadn't intervened, then it would have grown to match its brother here now. So much loss, so much despair and yet nature seems to always reclaim a place. When we're all gone this earth will be governed by mother nature once again.' Until, she had met Maurice and Scott, she was unaware of the beauty around her. Growing up in Leeds and now living and working in London she had walked past the green spaces, ignored the hills and valleys of Yorkshire. Now, she gingerly stepped onto the lowest bar of the gate and leaned her elbows on the top.

'It's so lovely here, isn't it?' she said.

Luc

Scott joined her, his height allowing him to just lean on the top bar. 'Yes, very peaceful.'

'I can see why Maurice was so happy here as a child. I had alleyways and streets to play in, but he had this to explore. However, I don't fancy plodding through that sticky mud.' Luc pulled her scarf closer to her neck, as a cold breeze flipped around them.

'Me neither. These cost me a fortune.'

Luc scrutinised his violet suede boots and giggled. 'We didn't think this through, did we?'

Scott agreed, zipping up his thin coat against the breeze.

'What shall we do?' Luc asked.

'We could get married and come and live here and have a whole battalion of children,' Scott suggested with a chuckle.

Luc, taken off guard, forgot she was balanced on a wooden slat. Stepping back, she found herself toppling into a thorn bush until Scott grabbed her, pulling her to him. For a moment their eyes met before Luc twisted out of his embrace.

They stood apart and Scott pushed his glasses back onto the bridge of his nose, a habit that Luc found quite endearing.

'I meant, what shall we do now? This minute… this…' Luc's voice trailed away.

'I know what you meant, Luc and I apologise if I've surprised you. It's the French in me, I suppose.'

Luc interjected, 'You're not French.'

'Well, living in France all my life has given me a romantic nature that the British seem to lack.' Scott smirked, goading Luc.

'Cheek!' Luc exclaimed. 'I can be romantic.' Pausing to think about what he had said, she then added. 'I'm just not sure about you, that's all.'

Hearsay

Scott closed the gap between them and took both her hands in his. 'Seriously, Luc. I know we've not known each other long, but there's a connection between us and it's not just chess pieces and Maurice. There's a connection in here too.' Letting go of her hands he placed his own on his chest.

Luc didn't know what to say. This floppy haired man with a strange penchant for garish-coloured footwear had awoken something deep inside her own heart. In a small voice, she said, 'I feel it too.'

A rumbling engine and screeching of brakes heralded the arrival of the tractor and its wedding procession of black-headed gulls. Luc and Scott stepped away from each other and turned to face the driver of the tractor.

'Bloomin' hell!' The driver yelled turning off the engine.

Thinking he was referring to them, Luc was about to remonstrate with the man, when he added, 'They'll be after the seed soon too, the little blighters!'

Jumping down from his cab, he plodded over to them. His dark green gilet had seen better days, and his brown corduroy cap sported splodges of white paint.

'Folks, I need to get on, ta,' he called.

'Oh, yes, of course,' Scott said moving onto the road. Luc followed him.

Wheezing, the man unfastened the rope loop from the gate and drew it back into the field.

Before he could return to his cab, Luc intervened. 'Excuse me. I wonder if you can help us?'

'You lost or summat?'

'No nothing like that. We need some information about this field.'

The man grunted, scratching his cheek. 'It's just a field, nothing more, nothing less.' He trudged back to the

Luc

tractor and swung himself up. The engine roared ending the conversation, but Luc had come a long way; she wasn't going to be ignored. Stomping through the open gateway, determined to get some answers, she found her angry pace slowing as her feet hit mud.

'Please,' she bellowed trying to rise above the engine. The man ignored her but as she started to clamber onto the step of the vehicle, he turned the key. Coughing, he lifted his cap revealing wisps of greying hair before flipping it back on his head. He took a cigarette packet out from his top pocket and shook one into his mouth. Striking a match against the dashboard, he lit the end and breathed in a lungful of smoke. More coughing ensued.

'All right, lass. What do you want to know? I've got another ten acres to do before I finish tonight.'

'Thank you.' Luc breathed heavily from her ungainly stumble and climb. Glancing back, she saw Scott hadn't moved and was watching her carefully. Clinging to the door frame and an enormous mud guard, she faced the man once again.

'We won't keep you. There was a body found here, just after the war, I believe.'

'Ah, you're wanting to know about that?'

'Do you know where it was? In the field, I mean.'

The man drew on his cigarette while Luc tried to stay calm.

Then he spoke. 'Aye, we had a body here. After the Great War it was. Old Jack knows.'

'Old Jack? Is that you?'

The man suddenly tipped his head back and roared with laughter. 'Nay, lass. That's Old Jack,' He pointed to the oak tree. 'He knows. He saw it all. The body was laying in one of them crop circles. We're always getting them detector folk and them spooks nowadays. A pain in the proverbial.'

'Spooks?' Luc repeated.

'Crackpots with their cameras and funny electrical thingummy bobs. I dunno what they hope to find?'

'Right, I see.' Luc was quickly losing patience. 'We're not spooks or crackpots.'

'The old ways are better. They need to dowse along the ley line.' He stubbed out his cigarette on the mud-encrusted floor. 'If you dowse near Old Jack, he'll help you.'

'The ley line? Where is that? More to the point what is it?'

'Oh aye. It runs through here, through the church and along to Lilleshall Hill and beyond.'

'Is it a path or something?'

'Well, they think that's what they were originally, lass. People using the high points on hills to guide them on a journey. Some folks believe mystical powers run along the ley. Anyway, missy, I gotta get on now so if you can just get down, I'll be on my way.'

Luc could see she wasn't going to get any more from the man. Clambering down from the cab, she found herself facing Scott once again. He had followed her through the mud, his beautiful suede boots caked in thick mud. Taking her hand, he led her back to the road.

The tractor rumbled past them, and the man touched his cap in thanks, and they thanked him in unison.

The man shouted over the racket of the engine. 'Aye. You know there was another one, back in the sixties or early seventies.'

'Another what?' shouted Luc at the retreating back of the tractor, the plough lifted up at a forty-five-degree angle for the road, clods of earth slipping to the ground.

'Another body. In the same place too. Another of them crop circles. Shut the gate, ta.' He waved a hand and

Luc

with that he was gone lumbering away down the lane to another field.

Luc and Scott stared at each other. 'Did he say there was a second body?' queried Scott, pushing his glasses back up his nose.

Luc felt numb. 'That's what he said. That can't be right. Maurice never mentioned another death, did he?'

'No. Perhaps he didn't know about this one. It's probably nothing to do with the death of his mother. Probably a spook or a crackpot imitating the crop circle death.'

'That'll be it,' agreed Luc.

Chapter Sixteen

MAURICE

Maurice, feeling refreshed after lunch and a short nap, settled himself once more at his desk. Clicking the record button, memories instantly came to him.

'With talk of another war, we moved to the countryside, far away from London. We rented out the gallery, shop and the tiny flat above and moved to a small holding near Oswestry. We wanted to protect our children, George and Amy, for as long as possible and with them working on the farm, we were able to do just that.

The gallery was sadly bombed and our little flat was no more, so we remained farming the land until Paris beckoned us once again. Amy married a farmer, and they took on our small holding while George got a job in the Diplomatic Corps and moved to France.

Rose and I built our art business from the ground up, supporting unknown artists alongside buying and selling artwork by more prominent ones. Life was good. Grandchildren were born and grew up, some in the shadow of the Eiffel Tower, others harvesting and feeding the cattle, near Oswestry.

Maurice

We came across this house in the 1960s. I had read about Michel Flaubert and the chess set and we had worked out where his house would have been. We were overjoyed to find it intact but requiring a lot of work and money to make it habitable. We moved in, just living in two rooms to begin with and doing it up as and when we could afford to. And somehow, being here in this house, our life changed for the better. I became an auctioneer for a while, we took on more staff at the gallery and expanded the business. We were wealthy.'

Maurice stopped, pressed the stop button and the whirring of the cassette paused. A single tear slid down his cheek. 'And I would give all of that away in the blink of an eye to spend one more day with my lovely Rose.'

He rose to his feet, a little unsteadily, and went to the French windows. Fumbling with the lock, he opened the door out to the garden and made his way down the steps to a bench. The trickle of water from a small fountain, the glossy leaves of a bay tree, the pale pink candy floss cherry blossom all brought him a sense of calm, a sense of peace. The afternoon sun warmed his limbs while he sat contemplating his life and the people within it, each one playing their part like actors on a stage. But, just like a play never seen before, you didn't know the ending. You could work out the plot, get to know the relationships of the characters but the final act would be after the interval and the audience didn't know the outcome as they sipped their wine or licked their ice cream.

One thing, he was sure of, though, was that one day during the epilogue of his life, he would be re-united in the next world with his beloved Rose. And before that, in this world, he would see Myrtle, his first love, and they would bring the circle to an end.

Chapter Seventeen

LUC

Luc and Scott arrived a little early for the library in Ashfield. They peered through the windows of the box-shaped building and could see a woman scurrying around putting on lights and then finally coming to the door. The sound of bolts being drawn back announced the library was now open.

Luc immediately felt at home. The smell of the paper now filled her senses, bringing back memories and she smiled, remembering a trip with her mother many years ago. As a child, Luc was an avid reader and now as an adult she never seemed to find the time to get her nose into a book. Mum had bought her two books that day, both in the series of The Secret Seven. She had devoured them hungrily and felt rather sad when after only a couple of days the adventures had ended. Those adventures stayed with her though as she played in the school playground with her friends making up stories and acting them out.

Now, they made their way to the reception desk, where a woman in a lemon crimplene suit was studying a pile of correspondence. Looking up at their arrival, she beamed. 'Good morning to you both. Isn't it a beautiful day? How may I help you two early birds?'

Luc

Her joy was catching, and Luc found herself smiling back, even though the subject of their visit was going to be a bit more gruesome.

'Good morning,' Scott said before Luc could say anything. 'We wondered if you might have newspapers dating back to the war years.'

'We have some research to do,' added Luc.

'Oh, yes, my dears. We have hundreds in the back room. They're all catalogued and bound in year books. Follow me.' The woman left her desk and asked them to follow her.

The compact room housed a table and two chairs and a wall of beige-coloured book spines.

'Here we are. You can look through these. I hope they're helpful. Was there anything in particular you were interested in?' She stood playing with a string of pearls at her neck, her eyes bright behind gold-framed glasses.

Luc and Scott had already decided to not tell people what they were looking for in so many words. They didn't want to upset anyone and also in some strange way wanted to stay anonymous until they had looked into things.

'We'll be fine, thank you.' Luc smiled again, hoping the woman wouldn't persist with any further questioning.

'Well, you know where to find me. We're open all day.' With that the woman turned and returned back to the reception desk.

Luc let out a sigh. 'Perhaps we should have asked for some guidance. This looks like a mammoth task.'

'Don't worry. We have some ideas of dates jotted down in Maurice's diary box. He said on the phone last night, he came back in the 1930s and saw the graves then. So that could be a good place to start.'

'I think we need to look at the twenties for the information about his mother's death.'

Hearsay

'You're right. And the dates we found on their graves yesterday were…' Scott opened his rucksack and pulled out the grey shoe box. They had added a notebook to the box, and it lay on the top. Scott flicked it over. '1920 for Sidney, Edmund's father and 1922 for Eirene.'

'Maurice said he came back just after the war so that would make it around 1919 when Sidney Cruso didn't recognise him.'

'That must have been awful for him. You finally get your memory back to find your father has lost his completely.'

'Memory is a funny thing, isn't it?'

'Sure is,' agreed Scott going over to the wall of giant books. 'Okay let's start at 1920 and see what was reported about Sidney's death.' Scott walked along the row until he found the right one and slid out the tall thin book that looked more like a notebook for a giant. The size of a broadsheet newspaper it was cumbersome to manoeuvre around the small room. Laying it out on the table they both took their seats and opened it up.

In the obituaries' column of April 10th, 1920, they soon discovered Sidney. *Not much for a life,* Luc thought. Scott read aloud.

'"Sidney Cruso, died peacefully in his sleep at his home, Three Chimneys Farm of Bounds End, Salop on April 8th 1920. The funeral will be held at St Peter's Church on April 14th."'

'Not much for a life, is it?' Scott added.

Having thought the same thing only moments earlier, Luc felt a tingling go through her. *Is that all we become? A sentence in a newspaper?* She took a moment to pause and think about this man who in many ways had started all of this off. Sidney Cruso was the one who had purchased the chess set in Paris, at The Exposition Universalle. Without

Luc

this one action, she and Maurice would have never met. She and Scott would never have met. Glancing to her left she found him staring at her. Their eyes now met, and a gentle warmth flowed through her veins.

'Luc?' Scott murmured.

'I know,' she whispered. She brushed her index finger on the back of his hand, and he turned it so that their palms lay close together. Luc leaned in and touched his cheek with her lips. He went to kiss her mouth, but the door flew open, and they pulled away coughing. The interruption was a small boy, thumb in mouth, eyes like saucers who just stood there. A brown teddy dragged on the floor beside him.

'Oh, my goodness. I am so sorry,' gasped a young woman coming up behind the child. She scooped him up in her arms, closed the door and they could hear the child complaining as he was carried away.

Scott chuckled. 'We never choose the right time, do we?'

Luc giggled. 'Perhaps we should focus on the job in hand. Let's get on.'

They carried the book back to its place after they made notes of dates and things and returned to the table with 1921. They found nothing there and it wasn't until the next one they finally found what they had been searching for. Luc read aloud,

'"On the morning of Tuesday 18th July 1922, the body of a woman was discovered within a field in the village of Bounds End, Near Ashfield, Salop by a dogwalker. This has been identified as the body of Eirene Field Cruso, wife to the late Sidney Cruso, of Three Chimneys Farm.

The body was lying in a flattened circle of wheat. Another two circles were also flattened, a phenomenon, according to Bradley Hurt,"' that's my grandad,' she

Hearsay

added, goosebumps rose on her forearms as she continued. '"A phenomenon, according to Bradley Hurt, a family friend and no relation to the deceased, which had occurred regularly in the field. Mr Hurt and his wife, Myrtle and daughter, Isobel, had moved in with the Cruso family after the war and been farming the land.

The coroner opened the inquest on Friday 21st July and is to be held on Monday 31st July. Anyone with any information regarding this should contact the Ashfield police immediately."'

'So, it seems that Maurice was correct in his assumption that his mother was found dead in a crop circle.' Luc felt an icy cold slither down her back.

Scott stayed silent as he re-read the passage and then turned a few pages finding the newspaper from just after the inquest. The results of the inquest and post-mortem were clearly set out on page four of the Ashfield Advertiser.

Before reading the report, Scott took Luc's hand in his and they stayed in that position while they read in silence.

'Well now we know the truth,' said Scott. 'It appears to have been suicide.'

Luc let go of his hand abruptly. 'Why would she kill herself? It doesn't make any sense. I know she'd lost her son and husband but there was a young child to care for. What pushed her over the edge?'

'The report does say close friends stated that she never really recovered from losing her husband and her son, Edmund. There doesn't seem to have been much evidence collated though.'

'The coroner said she had taken poison. They believe she collected fly papers and removed the arsenic. What a horrible way to die. She must have been desperate to end it all. So sad.' Luc glanced around the room looking for

Luc

answers in the stale air. The garish strip lighting glared down at her offering nothing but the beginnings of a headache. And checking her watch she could see they had been there for almost an hour and not discovered much in the time.

While Scott swapped the books, a sudden thought came to her. 'So, Bradley Hurt, my grandad, married Myrtle and that means my grandma was Bradley's second wife and yet they named their daughter Isobel just as…' she tailed off. 'Oh God, how can I have been so stupid all this time. My mum was their daughter, wasn't she? Myrtle and Bradley's.'

Scott stopped, the next book in his arms. 'How does that work then? It doesn't make sense.' Placing the book on the table, he flicked hair from his eyes and removed his glasses to rub the bridge of his nose. Luc gazed up at him.

'I think we need to check birth and marriage certificates, like we said yesterday while at the church.'

'The rector suggested we go to Shrewsbury. We can go now if you want to.' Scott waited for a response. Luc furrowed her brow, trying to make sense of it all.

'No, I think we need to just backtrack a little. Spend some time here looking at Maurice's diary. I think we've missed something.'

Scott took his seat once again. The news book took up most of the table and they utilised it as a board to lay out their notes along with the fragments of Maurice's memories.

Placing the information into chronological order helped them to see how some of the information aligned with the dates. Luc continued to jot things down in the spiral bound notebook.

The time flew by. Finally, Luc leaned back in her chair and rolled her tight shoulders. The card chess board had become the centre piece, and some scraps of paper now radiated from this. Above this, across the tabletop, a timeline now stretched while the floor itself had been made into yet another data system, names, places, times.

A gentle knock on the door heralded the librarian. The door opened just a crack. 'I'm afraid I need to close the library for lunch.' Looking around her, she exclaimed, 'Oh my goodness me! What have you been up to in here?'

Luc began to explain and apologise. The woman held up her hand. 'There's no need to apologise. It seems to me your research is growing. How about, if you go and find some lunch, I can lock this room, and it will all be there when you get back in an hour? Would that be all right?'

Luc sighed. 'Thank you. That would be wonderful, wouldn't it Scott?'

Scott, who had been kneeling on the floor during this exchange, nodded.

The door closed softly, and they were alone once more. They found themselves looking at the room as the librarian would have seen it. Like a bomb had exploded showering shrapnel everywhere. Tiptoeing around the collage on the floor they left the room and closed the door.

The woman was waiting for them, wearing her coat and hat now. She shooed them out and reminded them to come back in an hour.

Scott and Luc found themselves on the pavement, the church to their left and what looked like a school on the opposite side of the street.

'Lunch it is then,' said Scott, starting off up a cobbled street. 'Come on, let's see what we can find.' He held out a hand and Luc took it and together they went searching for something to eat.

After grabbing a sandwich, they went exploring and soon found a WH Smiths where they purchased folders,

Luc

glue, dividers and paper. Returning to their paper explosion they sorted and categorised, labelled and stuck and finally had a document they could access easily. It hadn't been until they were ready to go that Luc said, 'The other body. We forgot to check up on that.'

'I don't think it's relevant. It's just a copycat, someone thinking it would be interesting and make the papers.'

'I'm not so sure. We have the papers here. It might not be relevant, but it could be linked, somehow.'

Scott checked his watch. 'We're not going to make Shrewsbury now, it's already four. Okay, just to make you happy. After today, I never want to read another newspaper again.'

Luc agreed. 'What was the date that chap said?'

'I think he said the late sixties.' Scott was already heaving out 1965.

It took a lot longer than expected to go through the newspapers, and the librarian looked in to remind them that she was closing in five minutes. Still nothing and they had only got to 1968.

'We'll have to come back tomorrow. Are you okay for another couple of days?' Scott asked.

Luc nodded. 'What about you?'

'I need to get back to Paris tomorrow evening.'

'Divide and conquer,' Luc said.

'Pardon? Who do we need to conquer?'

'Time. We need to conquer time. I could drive to Shrewsbury tomorrow while you stay here. And if we're short on time you could get the train from here perhaps, so you won't miss your flight. I thought I'd visit my family in Leeds tomorrow evening as it's the weekend, and it will be a bit closer driving from here than from London.'

'Sounds like a plan.'

Chapter Eighteen

MAURICE

Scott and Maurice sat together in the courtyard, the fountain's crystal water dancing to their left and the distant sound of traffic to their right. A bottle of pastis, a jug of water and two glasses holding the cloudy golden liquid sat on a wrought iron table between them. The evening sun flared the sky above the high Parisian buildings surrounding them with burnt orange and rose-petal red. Scott had described what he and Luc had learnt in Shropshire and Maurice had nodded and shaken his head at different sections of the story. A comfortable silence now wove around them as they sipped their drink, both wrapped in their own thoughts.

And then Maurice spoke. His voice, soft like velvet, 'Dad was adamant he bought the chess set at one of the stalls at the exhibition. He had gone to visit The Exposition Universalle. He told me he had been desperate to climb the Eiffel Tower. Dad was never one for big speeches, he kept himself like a closed book and certainly never spent much money on anything crazy, so for me as a youngster, listening to him describing the amazing scenes that he witnessed and the long climb to the top of

Maurice

the tower, it was pure heaven. My father, a boring old farmer had lived a life that I could only imagine. When Rose and I moved to Paris, one of the first things we did was to climb the Eiffel Tower and look down, just like Dad had done, at the roads and buildings spread out. We marvelled at the Sacre Coeur, the Arc de Triomphe and Notre Dame, feeling like we were on a cloud. In fact, it began to snow while we were up there, and it felt like we had become the cloud.

Anyway, one day in the 1920's, while studying some old documents from the 19th century I came across Gabriel Blanchard: a craftsman of chess. His sets were worth having and one book published in 1900 about the Exposition Universalle, had a short article about Blanchard. One story told of a set that had never been played and had then mysteriously vanished. I turned the page to read more and there was a drawing of my chess set—well of some of the pieces anyway. They were the hand-drawn designs by Blanchard from 1818.'

Maurice was silent while he sipped his pastis and then said, 'Back in the twenties, setting up a home in Paris was difficult. My chess set wasn't complete, as you now know—the two pawns were still missing—but it could be worth a few hundred francs and that is exactly what Rose and I needed. And in the back of my mind, a feeling that nothing had gone well when I was in possession of the set made me decide to sell it. Mother and Dad along with Myrtle had gone from my life, I had lost months of my life through losing my memory, but I had been given a chance with a new identity. I needed to invest in our future, so I sold it for the princely sum of fifty francs. Not much, but it helped us with our rent and food for a while.'

'Maurice, I think this is something that will interest you.' Scott handed him the thin leather-bound book, entitled, *L'histoire des Jeux d'echecs Blanchard par M. Flaubert*. 'Luc found it in a bookshop in London. I'm translating it for her.' He held up another book, this one handwritten in blue ink. Scott had painstakingly written out the English version. 'It will surprise you that Blanchard's daughter, Florence had crafted most of the pieces.'

'Really? That is amazing!' Maurice murmured, stroking the cover of the French book. 'Thank you. I will read it tonight.'

While they had been talking, darkness had fallen, and a gentle breeze ruffled the leaves of the jasmine around them; its perfume thickening the air.

Scott stood and stretched his elbows back, yawning. 'I'm off to bed.'

'I think I'll just sit for a while longer.'

'Shall I get you a blanket?'

'Oh, stop fussing, boy. Anyone would think I was old or something!' Maurice chuckled.

Scott raised his hands in acquiescence. 'All right, but don't blame me if your back hurts tomorrow.' He turned and entered the house, leaving Maurice to his memories.

L'HISTOIRE DES JEUX D'ECHECS BLANCHARD PAR M. FLAUBERT.
THE STORY OF THE BLANCHARD CHESS SETS BY M. FLAUBERT

Part 1

Paris 1818

Sitting in the deep shadows, cradling a piece of wood, Florence observed the little knicks and cuts her father made. Every so often he would raise his head, grey hair falling across his weather-worn face, hold it to the light pushing through the thick window glass, grunt and then bend his head to study the piece yet again and scrape the tiniest of slivers to ensure perfection.

This was the final piece to be crafted. The red king.

'Florence? Come here.' Her father's voice was soft, a lullaby of sounds.

Florence stirred herself from her reverie, rose from her stool and went to stand beside her father.

'What do you think, cherie?'

She had to blink a few times to bring her sight in line with the brightness. He was holding his hand aloft, palm out flat with the red king standing between the heart line and that of life.

'Can you bring him to life, with your magic touch?'

Florence swallowed. 'Of course, Papa.'

'My angel,' he murmured. 'Where would I be without you?'

Florence reached for the king and held it between her

thumb and forefinger, the ridges gently caressing her skin. Glancing across to her father, she smiled. A smile that hid so many tears of sadness and regret.

In turn, the corners of his mouth lifted momentarily and for a second or two a light came into his milky blue eyes. Then like an ember dying in a fire it was gone.

'Papa, you must rest. You know you put your heart into each set. This one has taken your soul. This one will be remembered for ever.'

Gabriel Blanchard rose and shuffled to the back room behind the workshop where a daybed lay ready for his aging bones. Florence took his vacant stool, her long skirts settling themselves around her, and took up her polishing cloth. Her hair was already wrapped up in a scarf, but one bronze coloured tendril had managed to escape and now lay against the creamy white skin of her neck. A block of sunlight formed a square on the bench and Florence studied the piece carefully, twisting it to see every side. This one was almost perfect, yet she could see that he had turned the wood too far and the single leg was thin. Leaving it in the light, she rose and glided across to the shelves where the rest of the set stood. She lifted the white king and returned to her perch.

Yes, they were different. This cannot be so. Monsieur Flaubert was expecting perfection. She would have to make another king. She smiled at the irony. Born in the year the king and his beautiful wife, Marie Antoinette, lost their heads, Florence had grown up within an ever-changing Paris. She had become used to the violence and corruption that ran within the very veins of Paris. Rebellion never seemed far away. And now a new king, another Louis sat on the throne of France once again.

It was important to Florence that the set was perfect. They needed to be paid. She would take some francs out

Paris 1818

of her father's pocket—some would be hidden away at the bottom of her wooden casket that held her two other dresses; some would be spent on food for now; while some was spent on food that could keep—herbs and spices, garlic and onions. She would keep them alive for a while, living the life they should be able to experience if it were not for Gabriel's black moods and debauched needs. Good meat—a cut of beef, a leg of lamb. Florence would sweat over the open fire in their tiny kitchen, ladling gravies and stews into their pewter bowls. The smell alone of these meals fit for a king would keep Florence going when the money ran low, and she would have to queue for mutton and tripe. Her mother had taught her, before abandoning them, how to flavour the cheaper cuts.

Her mother, Sisay, had experienced Gabriel's black moods for many years until one day she left the house to go to the market and never returned. Gabriel had started searching for her always ending up on one of his spirals that led him down the twisting warrens of Montmartre into the beds of women.

Now, as she began to set up the wood-turning lathe her father had invented, Florence wondered how her mother had put up with so much for so long. Love is a strange mistress, she thought. It can lead you nowhere and to anywhere and to somewhere.

Florence fitted the spindle of bloodwood into the jaws of the lathe and began to work the treadle with her foot. The light was beginning to fade as the king began to take shape, the ridges and furrows catching the shadows. After placing another log on the dying fire, she took a taper from the pot beside the fireplace and was bending to catch a flame when the door to the street was thrown back against its hinges and a monstrous shape filled the entrance.

Hearsay

'Blanchard!'

The shout echoed around the dusty room. Florence stepped away from the fire, her eyes adjusting until she could make out the features of the man at the door. Thick soot-black eyebrows hung over blazing eyes. A mouth hidden away behind a beard of silver and charcoal.

'Monsieur, how may I help you?' Florence wasn't cowed by this man. She had seen so many of his type come haranguing her father.

'Where's that old sot who calls himself your father? He owes me,' grunted the man.

'He is resting, monsieur. May I help?'

The man roared at Florence. 'Get him now or…'

Florence stood her ground. 'Or what? You will beat me black and blue? You don't scare me, you ugly brute.'

The man swung a fist at Florence, but she was too nimble for him. She dodged to one side, and he lost his balance almost falling into the fireplace. This made him angrier, and he bellowed like the bulls at the marketplace.

'I'll have you, bitch.' He ran at Florence. This time she was trapped between the workbench and the shelves where the tools of their trade lay ready, and blocks of wood were piled neatly like the bricks of a wall. Florence felt behind her, her fingers grasping at the metal files and pliers and finally choosing a tool they knew well.

'STOP!' Her father's voice came from the kitchen door. 'Leave my daughter alone, bastard.'

For a second or two, Florence smelt the odious breath of the man as he reached her. She saw his deathly dark eyes flare. His lip curled and he hurled spit into her face before turning away towards the interrupting voice.

'You owe me, Blanchard. Where's my money?'

'You will get it tomorrow, Henri, as I promised. I will sell my best set ever tomorrow and you will have your

Paris 1818

thirty pieces of silver.'

'Your best set? You say that every time,' Henri snarled.

'It is true, this time. This is a set that will be remembered for all time.'

'If the money is not with me by midnight tomorrow you and your bitch of a daughter will be dead.' The man lumbered towards the door. As he passed the workbench, he paused. 'Your stupid little bits of wood had better make you some francs.' At this, he lifted a red pawn and a white pawn in his great paws. They looked so vulnerable and tiny Florence held her breath. The man suddenly gasped, dropping the two pieces. They fell to the stone floor, both snapping in half. Florence froze.

Henri groaned and pressed both hands to his right side and then righted himself. 'I need a drink. This pain in my stomach never leaves me.' He stood at the doorway. 'You cause my pain. You need to bring my money to La Figaro before midnight tomorrow or I will cause you even more pain.' He lurched away down the cobbled street beyond, into the dark of the night.

Gabriel Blanchard knelt picking up the broken pawns with such tenderness, Florence felt the sharp prick of tears come. *I will not give in to weeping. I have to be strong for my papa.*

Looking down, Florence realised she was still gripping the bradawl. Placing it on the workbench, she paused and breathed out some of her suppressed frustration. A few breaths calmed her before helping Gabriel to his chair near the fire. She left the workshop and slipped into the back room which served as kitchen and parlour, where she poured two glasses of ruby wine.

On her return she saw the man she loved and hated in equal measure, bent over, mewing like a cat at the red and white pieces in his cupped hands. 'Henri Placquette will be the death of me, of you. There is no time to make these again.' He started to rock, and the pathetic mewing became groans of anguish. 'The great Almighty is against us. He is punishing us for all my wrongs. I am so sorry, ma petite. I have failed.'

Florence wasn't going to give in to this self-absorption. She threw some wine down her throat and then thrust the other glass under his nose. He took the proffered glass—wine in one hand, wood in the other.

'Blanchards never give in. Give me the pieces. I will work on them tonight and they will be ready in the morning.'

'You don't know how. You can only polish. They have to be made by the hand of the great Gabriel Blanchard.' At this bold statement he began to cry—great ugly sobs, sucking up air and snorting like a horse at the trough.

Florence placed her glass down on a wooden side table. She crouched in front of her father. And there with the flames burning her fair skin, she told him the truth. For the last year or so, she had been repairing his pieces, improving them when he made mistakes, remaking them when they were imperfect.

When she finished telling her story, her father remained silent. He tipped the wine down his throat in one swift stroke. And then he held up his other hand meekly to his beloved daughter offering the broken chess pieces. Florence leaned over and kissed his cheek. She rose, her knees complaining as she stood, and took the pieces to the workbench. She returned and once again took a taper from the pot beside the fireplace and this time, it caught, and the tiny orange flame led her back to the workbench. Precious candles would be needed to see her through this task.

Paris 1818

Florence moved aside some of the tools scattered across the slab of solid oak. Her father had told her the tree had come down in a storm, many years ago, and he and his brother had fashioned it into the bench. Lifting the red pawn to study the break more closely, she was aware her fingers were stained red. Her father had told her of the bloodwood that came all the way to Paris from Madagascar; of the people who cut it down, how they hid the logs under the water of a lagoon where the water ran blood red while waiting for the ships to take it to foreign climes. Yet, the pawns were now bleeding after being broken. How could that be?

She crossed herself. It was magic. The supernatural. Her father said the bloodwood had special powers. The gum, the kino, that bled from the inner rings could heal maladies of the eyes and the stomach.

Working deep into the night, Florence re-fashioned the two pieces, her feet working the treadmill on the lathe, her hands chiselling grooves, chamfering edges, her eyes bright with sharp concentration.

Finally, as the candles' light waned, there on the bench stood the pawns, the proletariat, perfect in every way. Both better than Gabriel had created. The foot soldiers to their kings and queens. Exhausted, Florence stretched out her back and then like the candles, melted onto the oak block, resting her forehead against her forearms.

An angry bellow roused Florence from a dream of a young man, a soldier in his red silks, taking her into his arms and making love with such passion that now awake she could still feel the heat coursing through her blood.

She could hear her father rampaging through the house and shouting, 'Where are MY pawns?'

Florence held her cold palms to her eyes to glimpse

the man of her dreams, but he had vanished just like the night outside the window. The sun had shooed away the moon beckoning in clouds high above the roofs of Paris.

Florence smelt her father before he stumbled into the room. She knew he had spent most of the night drowning himself in ale and absinthe. This was the father she hated. The bully.

'What have you done with them, she-wolf?' Gabriel hollered. He blundered across the flagstone floor. Florence whipped around and at the sight of this shell of a man, tried to hide her disgust at the vomit strewn shirt. Long steel-grey hair lay lank and matted, eyes sunken, bruised with despair.

'I have them here, Papa.' Even to Florence, her voice sounded false. Too light in tone and he would strike with a hand, too sharp and he would use his fists. She waited for the blow, but nothing came.

Gabriel looked as though he was teetering on a tight string, like the entertainers in the city squares. The acrobats looked elegant, like jewels sparkling in the sun. The contrast brought an inward smile to Florence. This was the great Monsieur Blanchard, inventor of the wood-turning lathe for chess pieces, the creator of chess sets that the bourgeoisie sighed over. A true artist in many eyes. *If they only knew the true man, they wouldn't give him one centime for his artistry.*

'Never separate the pieces. NEVER! Do you hear me?'

He had no recollection of the visit from Henri last night, or what his daughter had told him about how she re-made many of his pieces. In his troubled mind, she had stolen the pawns, perhaps to play with like she did as a child.

Florence wanted desperately to shout and scream at

this failure of a father. She wanted to pummel her own fists into his hollow chest and yet, just like every time before, she breathed deeply, then apologised, returning the pawns to the chess set.

'God is watching our every move,' Gabriel muttered, shuffling over to the stool that Florence had vacated moments before. '…and the devil too. He will dance on our graves.' He reached for the chess board and set. 'Never separate them… evil will come and swallow you up.'

For a moment or two, silence filled the room, until a haunting croon started up from Gabriel. Florence needed to act now. They had to take the money tonight to Henri. They must sell the set.

'Papa, would you like me to box it all up and take it to Monsieur Flaubert? I would be happy to help so you can rest after all your hard work carving those last two pieces last night.' The untruths came easily to Florence's lips. She had used them so many times and so many times her father had believed them. She stretched out a hand to take the chess board. Her father was too quick for her. His claw-like fingers dug into the skin of her forearm, and she gasped.

'You're a sly one. You want him all for yourself. You have your eye on him, don't you?' He pushed her arm away.

'No, Papa. He is married to a beautiful woman who is expecting their second child,' Florence protested.

'You seem to know a lot about our benefactor,' Gabriel hissed.

'Only what you have told me.'

'So, you will know that Monsieur Flaubert does not like to be kept waiting.'

Florence nodded, then waited for her father to react

in the usual way. Nothing happened. Instead, he crumpled, his body deflated like one of the sacks after being emptied of the pieces of newly cut wood.

'Henri…' he whispered. 'He was here last night. I must pay him tonight.'

'Yes, we must or…'

Gabriel Blanchard sighed and put a hand to his forehead. 'Will you box it up and come with me to the house of Monsieur Flaubert? I am not feeling too well. I will lie down for a short while.' At this he stood, his body wavering like a tree sapling in the wind and then stumbled to the back room.

Florence looked around her. *I cannot take much more of this! Mother was right to leave. This will be the last time I rescue him, then I will make my own way in the world.*

She went searching for a wooden box and after grubbing around in the cellar, she returned to the chess set with a small crate filled with straw.

The pieces stood ready on the workbench alongside a rectangular box. The lid of the hinged box was the board once opened out flat, inlaid with squares of bloodwood and white oak just like the pieces. The box itself was crafted out of oak, and inside where the pieces would sleep there was a scarlet velvet lining shaped around and into several hollows offering a bed for each. Florence placed each one in the box and before closing the lid she lifted a finger to her lips, kissed it and then stroked first the red king and then the white one.

Florence accompanied her father through the winding thin streets and alleyways. Through the street vendors' cries, past the queues for bread and mutton until they came to the Seine. The grey lifeblood of Paris. Beside this ever-moving, never-sleeping creature stood the solid

Paris 1818

edifice of the Notre Dame; its glorious square towers standing proud and gleaming, its rose window like the eye of God, observant at all times.

They both halted—Florence glad to lay her cargo down for a few moments—mouthed a prayer and crossed themselves. No time to enter and light a candle, but time to pray a brief request. Gabriel took off before Florence could catch her breath and she scurried after him labouring under the wooden crate with the chess set hidden deep beneath the straw.

The main entrance of the house belonging to the Flaubert family was through an iron gate. Gabriel lifted the latch, and it opened smoothly revealing a cool clean courtyard. A pool was situated at the centre, surrounded by smooth white stone. Water danced around a nymph with her hand held high as though to grasp the droplets before they cascaded down her body. Florence was enchanted.

A huge door opened to Gabriel's knock, and they were ushered in by a footman dressed in dark blue velvet. They entered a high-ceilinged entrance hall, white marble tiles led to a sweeping staircase rising to the other floors of the house. Either side of them were closed doors, each wearing a triangular hat of carved marble, each with a different carving. One held grapes and a vine, another wheat and bread.

The footman opened the wine door, to their right, bustled them in, his haughty demeanour unsettling Florence and announced them to what seemed an empty room. A room with walls of turquoise silk, teeming with birds of paradise, peacocks, butterflies and lilies. Tall casement windows looked out to the courtyard they had just left.

They waited.

Hearsay

A plume of silvery smoke trailed up to the ceiling from a chair; its back to them.

Still, they waited.

Florence cleared her throat and tapped her booted foot on the polished wood floor, impatient to hand over the set and to leave. Finally, when Florence had decided she would speak, a voice boomed out from the chair. 'Blanchard, good to see you.'

Florence stifled a snigger. *He can't see us, stupid man.*

'I amuse you Mademoiselle.' Another tendril of smoke twirled upwards.

Beside her, Gabriel hissed. 'Do not react.'

This was too much for Florence. She was a proud woman. She may be the proletariat and this man of the higher echelons of society but there was no need for rudeness. Their time was being wasted by this ignorant man.

'Non, monsieur.' She shifted the crate in her arms. 'May I put this down, sir. It is cumbersome, not heavy.'

'Come into the light. Your voice intrigues me. Your beauty astounds me. Paris is fortunate to be able to look on your radiance.'

Feeling a sudden pinch of her arm, her eyes travelled towards her father. He nodded to her. Florence edged around the chair. An arm gestured for her to place the crate on a table, which she did. While lifting out the box from its bed of straw she was able to peek at their rude benefactor. He wore a jacket of emerald satin, a white silk cravat held by a pin topped with a diamond catching the firelight in its prisms. Above this a chin sliced in the centre, led to thin lips, a hooked nose and penetrating eyes topped by a high forehead reaching to oiled black hair.

The lips parted as a tongue flicked out moistening the skin. Florence was reminded of a lizard she had seen in a painting in The Louvre. Her mother, Sisay, who had taken her as a child would say this was built for Florence as the building had finally opened in the year of her birth—1793. The same year of the death of the monarchy. With death comes life and the circle continues, her mother would say.

Her reverie was broken by Monsieur Flaubert jumping to his feet and taking the chess box from her. Hot breath of smoke caught in her nostrils, and she stepped back. Thankfully he was no longer interested in her; his gaze was on the box. Florence stepped further away noticing the oval looking glass atop a golden stand placed at an angle so he could see whoever entered the room.

The fire cracked and spat. An ormolu clock above held time, a fat cherub sat on the top, his wings pointing out, a golden apple in his hand.

'Exquisite. Your best yet, Gabriel.' Flaubert opened the box revealing the pieces nestled within the soft velvet lining. 'This will bring joy to my wife while she awaits the birth of our second child. This one is causing her trouble even before it enters this world.'

Florence returned to her father's side. *I can smell him,* she thought. *That rancid smell is my own flesh and blood. He disgusts me.*

'Merci, Gabriel. You may go.' Flaubert hadn't looked up from the chess pieces he was cradling in his hand.

'Monsieur?' Beside her, her father faltered.

'Yes, yes, Blanchard. See my footman for your payment. I won't sully my hands with dirty coins.' At this statement, he glanced across to Florence. 'But I will be happy to sully them with you any time, my dear.'

Florence felt bile rising and swallowed it down. 'Come, Papa, we must leave Monsieur Flaubert to his chess.' With all the pride she could muster, she swept out of the room.

The footman was waiting at the door with a small

leather bag. Florence took it before her father could, checked the number of coins nestled inside and nodded. A slight scuffle behind them made her turn back. A small face of a cherub was peeking out between the twisted spindles of the magnificent staircase. *No, not a cherub. A little boy.*

She gave him a little wave and he threw one back, before vanishing and thundering up the stairs to an unknown room.

A chill wind snaked in as the door was opened to the spluttering fountain and Florence and Gabriel left the Flaubert's residence.

Chapter Nineteen

LUC

Luc arrived late at Aunt Alice's house. A Friday night and the 1930s semi was in darkness, a single streetlamp giving enough light for her to squeeze past her uncle's car on the narrow drive. Fumbling to find her key in her bag, Luc cursed under her breath. Her arrival had set the dog off yapping and jumping at the front door. She could hear his claws scraping at the wood through the glass porch. Finally, she found the key and entered the cool hallway. The golden spaniel sniffed her, wagged its tail, decided she was a friend and returned to its basket under the telephone table.

A light came on from above the stairs and a voice called out, 'I'm armed. Go away or I'll call the police.'

Luc dropped her holdall on the floor and gazed upwards. A head of curlers, swathed in a chiffon scarf, was framed by a halo of light, and she giggled. 'Hello Auntie. It's only me.'

'Oh goodness me, Lucretia! What are you doing here? You gave me a proper fright. I thought you were a burglar.' With that the curlers vanished, and a swishing of a dressing gown brought Aunt Alice to the bottom of the stairs, brandishing a paperback.

Luc giggled again. 'Were you going to read them to death? Anyway, where's Uncle Hugh? Shouldn't he be wielding a poker or something at an intruder?'

Aunt Alice chuckled and wrapped her in her arms. 'Hugh? The charge of the light brigade wouldn't wake him. It's the women of this family who have the strength.'

'You might choose a better weapon next time, though. I don't think Jackie Collins will put anyone off.' They laughed again.

'Well, it's lovely to see you. Let's get off to bed and you can explain yourself in the morning. Up the wooden hills, my lass.'

The two of them took the stairs and outside her old room, Luc pecked her aunt's cheek, Pond's cold cream tickling her senses.

Luc woke, feeling refreshed. It was nice to be back in her old bed. This always felt like home. After her mum had abandoned them, her dad couldn't cope bringing up a wilful child. She pondered on the many fallouts they had had over the years. She knew deep down he loved her, but he just didn't understand her. And her mum? *Well, she didn't care about me so why should I care about her. How can a mother walk out on her only child? I wish I could ask her that. Was I not enough for her to stay? And why didn't she take me with her?*

Thoughts like these always came to her, swirling around her mind like boats bobbing on a stormy sea and none more so than when she was here in Leeds, in this very room. This morning was different though. Now there were even more questions to ask, more cans to open and more worms to fling out.

Throwing back the blankets she quickly dressed, pulling on jeans, a navy T shirt and striped jumper. The

Luc

smell of bacon and a scrawled note on the table met her on entering the kitchen. *Gone shopping, see you later. Breakfast in the oven xx*

Carrying a fully laden plate and a coffee, Luc took herself into the sitting room, where she took a place at the table. Her aunt had laid it ready for her and the Daily Express sat folded on a side plate. The headlines of Gorbachev becoming leader of the Soviet Union didn't interest her, but she dutifully glanced through the rest of the paper while shovelling dried up egg, burnt fried bread, beans and bacon into her mouth.

The house was silent, her uncle had probably taken the dog out and she allowed her thoughts to return. So much had happened since she had been here at Christmas, and she needed to make sense of it all. She had met Adam then and consequently she had learned from their brief relationship that she needed to stand up for herself, to be true to oneself and to not date a banker!

Her thoughts quickly shifted to the last few days spent in Shropshire with Scott and some of the things that had come to light. Her grandfather, Bradley Hurt; her mother, Isobel; two deaths in crop circles; the daffodils at the graveside—the list went on and on in her head. And the underlying emotions of becoming closer to Scott throughout. *Where is that all going to lead to*? she wondered.

Luc was brought into the present by the front door slamming and a mass of golden-brown fur hurling itself at her knees. 'Hello you.' Luc made a fuss of the spaniel, its large brown eyes looking hungrily at the bacon fat she had left on her plate.

'Good morning, Lucretia. Alice said you were here.' A deep voice boomed from the hallway. 'Don't give Scamp anything. He doesn't deserve a treat, he's a little beggar. Ran off across the park.'

Hearsay

Too late, thought Luc. The bacon fat had been polished off and Scamp was now eyeing the toast.

'Hello, my lovely girl.' Uncle Hugh cut quite a figure in the doorway. Cherry red jumper and yellow checked trousers, he reminded her of Rupert the Bear. 'Meeting the chaps at the golf course, so must get on. I'm late already thanks to you.' He pointed at Scamp who barked happily while his fringy tail waved frantically. With a shake of his head, Hugh Sydenham left Luc to return to her thoughts but the front door slamming again heralded Aunt Alice, who called out.

'Cooee! Hugh, can you help me with these bags, darling? Before you disappear, please.'

Luc cleared the table and on entering the kitchen found her aunt stuffing food into every crevice.

'Hello, love. I forgot to say we've got a dinner party here this evening. Just some friends, nothing fancy but they do like their food.' Aunt Alice held up two bottles of wine, 'and they like a glass or three.' She bustled about, opening cupboard doors and the fridge. 'You're very welcome to stay. That nice Adam you met at Christmas might be coming too.'

Luc rolled her eyes. That was someone she didn't want to see. 'Don't worry about me, Auntie. I thought I might go and see Dad.'

Alice stopped dead in her tracks. 'Your dad? You want to see your father? Oh, but that's marvellous. He'll be made up seeing you. He's been a bit low since Christmas. Not very good in the winter months, since…'

Luc saw this as an opportunity and waded straight in. 'Aunt Alice, have you got time to sit down for a chat before you start cooking? There's something I want to ask you.'

'Oh, that sounds ominous, love. But I could do with a coffee before tackling this joint of beef. There's a dear—

Luc

you find the Nescafe and I'll take the weight off these old pins of mine in the front room.' She fluttered off down the hall and Luc filled the kettle, her heart thumping hard.

Luc placed a mug in front of her aunt and then taking her place on the armchair opposite, she found her hands were trembling.

'Are you in a spot of bother, sweetie?' Aunt Alice asked, her tone gentle. 'You can tell me.'

'No, nothing like that.' Luc took a sip of coffee and gasped as the heat scalded her lips. Her finger slipped in the handle and the burning liquid cascaded over her lap.

'Oh, shit. Sorry… I'll get a cloth… sorry!' Luc exclaimed, jumping up and dashing to the kitchen.

Dabbing at the velour fabric seemed to make it worse and before she knew it, Luc was on her knees, tears splashing and mingling with the dark stain.

'Luc, just leave it. Come over here and tell me what is going on with you. You're getting me worried now.' Alice patted the seat beside her. Luc did as she was told and sat stiffly on the sofa. 'You're not pregnant, are you?'

In her confused mind, Luc thought that might be easier than everything else she was dealing with. Shaking her head, she sniffed loudly. A tissue was placed in her hand, and she blew her nose.

'It's just like old times, this, isn't it?' Aunt Alice went on. 'Someone breaking your heart at school or you falling out with one of the girls.'

'Auntie Alice…'

'Yes, dear.'

'I've been to Paris.'

'Yes, I know dear. You told me you were going. Didn't you get the job? Is that it? Don't worry there'll be another opportunity soon, I'm sure. You're a clever girl.'

'There wasn't an interview. It was a ruse to get me to

visit and meet someone there.'

'Oh, my good God. Not the white slavers or those people in orange. I've read about them in the papers. You, poor dear.'

Luc sighed. 'No, nothing like that.' She took a deep breath. 'I met a man called Maurice Smith and his grandson, Scott. They know our family.'

'Really. The names don't ring a bell. We don't know anyone who lives in France.' Alice was now sipping at her coffee and surreptitiously glancing at the clock on the mantelpiece.

'I'm sorry, I know you're busy. This can wait for another time.'

'I tell you what,' Alice said, rising to her feet. 'Why don't you come and sit in the kitchen while I make the pudding. It has to sit in the fridge to set.' She scurried out.

Luc remained just staring at the old gas fire, the artificial coals, thick with dust, offered no warmth to the room. *I shouldn't have come. Alice won't know what I'm talking about. But then neither will Dad.*

Scooping up her soggy tissue, she left the room and went into the kitchen. 'Do you know of someone called Edmund Cruso?'

Checking the measuring scales and pouring in sugar, her aunt didn't respond.

'What about Myrtle?'

'Sorry, love, what did you say?' Alice tipped the sugar in a bowl and then began breaking eggs.

Luc sensed her aunt wasn't going to be a lot of help, but she needed to know. 'Please look at me, Auntie.'

Turquoise shadowed eyes turned towards her. 'Sorry, dear. Ask me again? Maurice someone you said?'

'Yes, Maurice Smith and Edmund Cruso… and Myrtle Hurt.'

Luc

'Hurt? Well, that's your family name. Your mum was a Hurt before she married your dad. Don't know Cruso though. Come to think of it, there was a suitcase or something your dad put in our loft when your mum left. Some of Granny Elspeth's things. There might be something in there.'

Another piece to the puzzle, perhaps, thought Luc, hopefully. Aloud, she asked if she was able to go up and have a look, and Aunt Alice nodded, reminding her to get the stepladder from the shed and a torch.

Half an hour later, after phoning her dad and arranging to meet later, with some trepidation, Luc unfastened the loft hatch, allowing it to swing free. Peering into the gloom, dark shapes materialised as her eyes grew accustomed to the darkness. Scrambling up into the void, she just missed banging her head on one of the roof joists before almost straightening up. The torch flickered into life and Luc scanned the inside, a dolls house, wooden tennis racquets in tightly sprung frames, an old television and dozens and dozens of boxes appeared in the circle of light. *Aunt Alice had said a suitcase,* Luc thought as she attempted to clamber over and around the stuff once loved and now forgotten.

Two battered old suitcases sat on end butted up against a large cardboard box. A dusty old footstool peeped out from under a plastic pineapple and a Christmas wreath; moving these carefully to one side she sat down to study the suitcases more closely.

The catches of the first case were rusted and it took some time and force to finally get the lid open.

Empty, apart from two tin soldiers and a hand stitched heart, decorated with tiny seed pearls pinned to create a circular pattern around embroidered letters spelling out the word LOVE. *A Valentine's gift, perhaps,* thought Luc. *Long forgotten.*

The second proved more enticing. Better quality and the locks opened smoothly with a satisfying click to magically reveal a treasure trove of cards, ribbons, toys, tins and small gift boxes.

Using the first case to decant any item looked at and rejected, Luc explored everything with care. This had obviously been her grandmother's things. Elspeth Hurt loved to fill their house in Chapel Allerton, with so much crap and tat and this case was bursting with it. Luc winced at the photos of herself as a baby on a fluffy rug and in school uniform with a toothy grin and hair in bunches.

She had almost reached the bottom of the case, having removed stuff she never wanted to see again or to her mind, should ever be returned to the world due to its bad taste or ugliness. She had loved her granny, but never liked her taste in decor. The final item, however, was a large brown envelope. This could be important, she thought to herself. Luc's heart was in her mouth as she slid it onto her lap The flap was held together by a piece of string looped though two holes. With shaking fingers, Luc pulled at the knot. It was too tightly tied; she would need scissors or tear the paper. She decided to go with the latter.

Ripping the flap off, Luc dived in. Her fingers grasping at the documents inside told her these were important; the paper felt smooth and expensive. Taking out the contents and laying them in her lap, she found a solitary wedding card to Elspeth and Bradley and tucked inside that—a wedding certificate.

Holding her breath, Luc unfolded the long rectangular paper, green with copper plate handwriting in black ink. Bradley Hurt and Elspeth Gould married on 4th February 1917, Leeds.

Luc gasped. That couldn't be so. She had seen the

Luc

wedding certificate for Bradley and Myrtle only the day before in Shrewsbury and that had been in 1919. Did they divorce and remarry? And what about Isobel? Luc felt around in the envelope, had she missed something? Tipping it up, a lock of blond hair, tied in a neat blue bow, fell to the floor and a black edged card.

Luc took the two delicate items and read *Julian Hurt born 18th July 1917, died 25th July 1917. A son to Bradley and Elspeth, R.I.P.*

Chapter Twenty

LUC

One dusty 40-watt bulb offered very little light to Luc in the attic. She felt sick to the stomach. None of it made any sense. *According to Maurice, Grandad had married Myrtle and had children while all the time he had been married to Granny Elspeth. Bradley Hurt was a bigamist. And not only that, Isobel, my Mum, might not be aware of all of this.*

Bradley Hurt: the man she remembered as kind and loving; always there for her with a comic and a paper bag of dusty white bonbons for her; taking time to take her to the park and push her high on the swing. Luc craved that feeling of flying so much her body ached. When life was simple and stress-free. That moment when you're high in the sky with the birds and the clouds before being snatched back by the chains of life, returning you to Earth to look down, down on the very dirt of existence before up and up again to join the skylarks and swallows.

Adulthood isn't all it's cracked up to be, she thought. *Being a child…* at this her mind returned to the lock of hair and the death card. A boy, born and dead within a week, a tiny coffin buried somewhere. They must have been

Luc

traumatised by losing their child. Mum never spoke of her half-brother. Had they spoken to her about him? My mum grew up thinking she was an only child and that's what she had become.

Taking the envelope and leaving behind the remnants of Elspeth's life, Lucretia made her way carefully back down the ladder and into the warmth of the house. *I will talk to Dad this evening and he might be able to help me with another jigsaw piece,* she pondered as she leant the ladder against the banisters ready to take it downstairs and then made her way back to her room. *The trouble is I still don't have a picture to work from, there are just bits of odd-shaped information; nothing joins together. A chess board with scribbles, an incomplete chess set and suspicious deaths.*

Later that day, Luc sat nursing a glass of flat lemonade. She had decided their local was neutral ground to meet her dad. He couldn't make a scene, and she might get him to finally open up to her. The door opened and her father came in stamping his feet and rubbing his hands. A smile came to his lips when he saw Luc, and he strode across to her table. She stood and folded her arms around him, he returned with a one-armed hug.

'This is a nice surprise,' he said pulling away. 'Lovely to see you, Lucretia.' He sounded wary, as though he was worried about what she was going to say.

'Likewise, Dad. What can I get you?'

'Just a pint of bitter. Thanks.' He removed his coat and sat down.

Luc made her way to the bar and ordered the drinks. While she waited for the barman, she glanced back at her father. He was looking old, his face thin, eyes rheumy, mouth downturned. *I ought to spend more time with him,* she thought.

'That'll be £1.12 please, love.'

Paying the man, she carried the two glasses back, one with a brimming head of froth, the other, golden and light.

'How are you, Dad?' she asked taking her seat opposite him.

'So-so, you know. I'm all right. Nothing to complain about. How about you?' Ralph slurped his beer.

The conversation drifted to jobs, health, houses, anything apart from what she'd come for. Finally, Luc placed her half empty glass down. 'Dad, I have some questions to ask you… about… Mum.'

His head shot up and sad eyes glared at her.

Luc wasn't going to be deterred. She held up both palms, in abject apology. 'I don't want to upset you. I don't want us to argue. A lot of stuff has happened to me recently and I just want to know more about my mum.'

Her father made a strange harumphing noise. Then to Luc's consternation he began to cry. Pulling a handkerchief from a pocket, Ralph rubbed at his eyes, blew his nose, and took a deep breath.

'We met at a dance hall. I was terrified of dancing, but my sister, your Aunt Alice, said I would enjoy it, so I went. Isobel, your mum, was just standing there at the edge of the wooden square that housed several gyrating couples. She too looked as though she wanted to run away—a rabbit caught in headlights. That was it. She glanced at me and those eyes… I wanted to drown in those eyes—the deepest blue.' He paused to take a sip of his beer.

Luc shifted, uncomfortable hearing how her parents had fallen in love, but she waited, and he continued.

'She had lived in Leeds all her life, attended school here and had done a secretarial course as many young women did at that time. Yet she always yearned for more. After the war, as you might know, we stayed here, working

Luc

all hours. We both so wanted a child, but it wasn't meant to be. Isobel suffered so many miscarriages; it pulled us apart. Further away each time, like ripping a plaster too slowly so when you finally came along neither of us believed you were real. A changeling, a figment of our imagination. But no, there you were—a tiny screaming scrap of life. The irony was that all the others had stolen our hearts, and we had little love left and the war, of course. That had changed me in so many ways.' He drained his glass this time.

'You were a prisoner, weren't you?' Luc whispered, not wanting to break the spell or her father's train of thought.

He nodded slowly. 'That story will have to wait to be told another day. I can't think of that as well as your mum.' He looked across the table, his eyes pleading.

'Dad, that can wait. But one day when you're strong enough I would like to hear about that.'

He patted her hand and stood. 'I need the gents.' Ralph placed a five-pound note on the table. 'Get another round in. And some ready salted please, Luc. And whatever you want.'

He turned and left. A tingling came to her—he had called her, Luc. He always insisted on calling her by her full name—that of an aging aunt, long gone now. *It's a start*, she thought as she bought more drinks and took her seat once again.

On Ralph's return, he asked. 'Now where were we?'

'Me arriving and disrupting everything,' Luc answered with a grin.

'Ah yes. A baby brings so much.' He glanced at her, his eyes suddenly twinkling. 'Your mum and I fell in love with you the day you came into the world. And we have never stopped loving you. Never forget that, Lucretia.'

Hearsay

The name's back, thought Luc, *but now it's wrapped in love.*
'You said you didn't have any love left when I was born?' she asked.

'What? No, you misunderstand. We had bags of love left for you, but not for each other. We had robbed ourselves of that. I'm so sorry. We both let you down.'

Luc shook her head sadly. 'You haven't let me down, Dad, but Mum on the other hand…'

'Your mum never wanted to hurt you, but she couldn't take you with her. She was in a dark place herself. She said she had to discover her true self. She thought I would cope without her. I couldn't. I fell apart. Hence you going to live with your Aunt Alice. She came to my rescue.

Isobel, your mum, always wanted to paint, to be creative. She said I stifled her. I wanted something different in life and it wasn't daubing paint onto canvas. She had a bit of a breakdown.'

Luc suddenly felt a huge weight, lifting from her shoulders. *Mum hadn't left because of me. She loved me but couldn't cope with everything life threw at her.* It was a revelation.

'Dad, why have you never told me this before?'

Mournful, red-rimmed eyes met hers. 'Because I didn't know how. I felt a failure in your eyes. You were better off without me. Your aunt and uncle have looked after you so well. Better than I could ever have done.' After supping more beer, he continued. 'I am so proud of you, Lucretia, I want you to know that. Watching you become the beautiful, independent, clever woman I see today makes me so proud. None of that is down to me… it's all down to…'

Luc stopped him. Placing her hand on his. 'It's because of you, Dad. I've strived to make you notice me, for the right reasons. To make you proud of me.'

They stared at each other, both now with eyes

Luc

glistening with tears. Luc felt a smile tugging at her mouth and grinned. 'So, no more secrets, no more arguments?'

'Agreed,' her father said emphatically.

Luc looked up to see a young couple approaching. They were obviously making for the table beyond. She shuffled her chair across to allow them space and they muttered a thanks.

'What else do you want to know, love?'

Luc glanced at her dad, his face had softened and now seemed to glow. *He has been carrying all of this with him too,* she thought. He looked a lot younger all of a sudden.

'Where is she, Dad? Where's Mum?'

'To be honest, love. I don't know.'

Placing her hands together on the table, Luc found her fingers automatically going tip to tip, steepling and then sliding down to entwine. Turning them over, her father murmured, 'And there's all the people.' Luc glanced up and saw his hands were doing the same. A childhood rhyme they had both enjoyed. Their eyes met and soon they were chuckling together.

'I'm sorry, love. All I know is that she was in Shropshire, in the village of Bounds End when I saw her last.'

'But she can't be. Scott and I were there only a few weeks ago.'

Ralph flinched as though he had touched a flame.

'You've been there?'

'Yes, but the place was deserted. It looked derelict. We knocked and called out several times. It is the Three Chimneys Farm, isn't it?'

'Yes, that's the place. Well, it's a while since I was there. 1970s, something like that. She was living there with her mum, Myrtle Hurt.'

The images of the newspaper report and the marriage

Hearsay

certificates scratched at her thoughts and for a moment the hubbub of the busy bar stilled as though an angel had entered and made time stand still. It was just a comma, just a second and life returned. Music emanated from the vintage jukebox and normal life was resumed.

'Okay, Dad. I've never been good at maths, but Granny and Grandad are her parents. Mum was born in Leeds.'

Ralph shook his head sadly. 'Another untruth, I'm afraid. That's what your mum believed… what she had always been told.'

'Dad, when does hearsay become the truth?'

'I don't know. I suppose in a court of law they strive to discover the truth. We never truly know what happened in the past. It's the perceptions, the memories of those who were there. And each one can remember a different thing. It's like a very bad jigsaw puzzle.'

Luc laughed. 'Yes, it is. All of this is the worst puzzle ever. And it all started with a bit of wood.' Pulling out her pendant she dangled the red pawn for her dad to see. 'This bit of wood and its white twin.'

'Where did you get that? That's your mother's.'

'She gave it to me before she left.'

'Your Mum believed there was magic in that.'

Luc shifted in her seat. 'I don't know about magic, but it's brought a whole load of problems.' She returned the pendant to below her top. Then she explained everything that had happened since meeting Maurice. Her father listened patiently throughout, and she ended by telling him about the lock of hair and the black-edged card she found up in the loft. Luc sat back, exhausted as though she had been running for miles.

'You think this Maurice Smith is Edmund Cruso?' Ralph asked.

Luc

'That's what he says.'

'There's one way of finding out.'

'Really? What do you suggest?'

'If your mum is with Myrtle and they're both still alive—she would know if he's Edmund or if he's stringing you along. But...' Ralph paused.

'Yes?' Luc urged.

'Why would he make all of this up? What's in it for him?'

'The chess set is worth thousands if it's complete. But I don't think he needs the money, he's a very wealthy man.'

'Ah, I see.' Ralph chewed at his thumb, deep in thought. Then he said, 'Have you found the white one?'

'No, Eirene buried it in a metal soap tin in a crop circle—Top Field, near the farm—during the first world war.'

At this, all of the colour leeched from Ralph's face.

'Dad, are you all right?'

He shook himself from his reverie. 'Yes, I'm fine. Buried, you say?'

Luc explained what she knew about Eirene and her belief in the mysticism of crop circles. 'Unfortunately, magic didn't save her. She was found dead in the same field after the war within another circle. The tragic thing is there was a copycat murder after that—another body set up in the same way, years later...'

Ralph seemed to shrink and fade before her eyes as he stammered. 'A body? Really?' Then he seemed to shake off his strange melancholy and downed his beer in one glug.

Luc, unsure of what was going on in her father's mind but knowing he had seen a lot of death in the second war and could still be affected deeply, understood his reaction.

Hearsay

She had seen him behave like this in the past when there were mass shootings in America; the horrors seemed to stay with him for several days.

'Sorry Dad. All this talk of death. The war and stuff. I didn't think. I don't mean to upset you.'

Ralph shook his head. 'It all comes back to me, you know?'

Luc nodded. 'Anyway, we don't know who it was. Scott was going to do some more research.'

'Scott? Tell me about him.' Ralph had switched the subject neatly putting her on the spot.

'Oh he's…' She could feel her cheeks burning. 'He's very nice. He's been very helpful in all of this. He has a little girl.'

'He's married?'

'No, divorced…' Luc hesitated.

'Hmmm,' said Ralph.

'Anyway, he's not important. What is important is… I've decided to go and see Mum… in Shropshire… if she's still there.' She stared across the table at her father. 'If that's all right with you?'

'Yes, you must go. For your sake and mine. It's all best out in the open. You deserve to have your mum in your life.'

Luc jumped up and went to her father wrapping her arms around him. 'Thank you, Dad.' She stood and grabbed her coat. 'And now I'm going to phone for a taxi. I don't think you should drive. I'll pick up your car tomorrow!'

Chapter Twenty-One

MAURICE

Maurice shuffled into the study while Scott set up the cassette recorder on the desk. They had talked over breakfast about the recordings that Maurice had done so far. 'Your recordings are really helping Luc and I with our research,' Scott was saying. 'Luc is keen to know more about her grandfather, Bradley Hurt. If you're okay to talk about him, that is?'

Maurice grunted.

Scott nodded, distracted with setting up the recording. 'I think we'll try it with the separate mic this time rather than the built-in one—it might be clearer.'

The old man took his seat at the chesterfield desk, dark green leather embossed with gold curlicues stretched out before him. A large silver picture frame stood centre stage, an elderly woman, elegantly dressed in a Chanel two-piece suit with cherry blossom surrounding her and pale pink petals floating in the air like confetti. It was Maurice's favourite photo of Rose, and he glanced at it with fondness now.

'Okay, you're all set. Here's the mic,' Scott said

offering the microphone to his grandfather.

'Testing, testing. 1… 2… 3,' Maurice said, smiling.

Scott grinned back, checked everything again and then went to the door. 'Right, I'll leave you to it. When you've finished, just press stop. I'll sort it all out when I get back. Okay?'

Maurice nodded and gave a little wave. He waited as Scott carefully closed the door behind him. Then, sighing, he pressed the record button and began.

'I had always suspected Bradley Hurt was not what he always appeared. There was just something about him; like a Will-o'-the-Wisp he made you imagine things that weren't really there. A magician pulling a rabbit from a top hat, smoke and mirrors.

One night, at a tavern while on day leave, he let his guard down and just for a moment I saw the real Bradley Hurt. The local beer had loosened his tongue and when one of our comrades had made fun of his ability to charm the ladies, he pounced. Literally. Like a leopard attacks an antelope, Brad was on him, pulling Art up by his collar and pushing his reddened face into the Welshman's pale one. His voice was low, menacing.

With spittle flying he snarled, 'Never make fun of me. Never! Do you hear me?' Then he ripped into him, punching, scratching his face. It took two of us to pull him off.

We all sat, our chests heaving, Art with blood oozing from one eye. 'You, stupid bastard,' he cried. 'It was a joke. Can't you take a joke, Hurt, for fuck's sake?' He wiped his eye with his fist, smearing redness across his face.

Brad jumped up and I thought he was going in for more, but he turned sharply and shot out of the door.

'Stupid sod,' said Crabbe, passing across a grimy hankie.

I stood and said, 'I'll get in another round, lads.

Maurice

Whisky?'

They both nodded, Art dabbing at his face while Crabbe finished his beer in one long draught.

The barman glared at me as I came to the bar. A torrent of French poured out, arms gesticulating. I let it wash over me, apologised and asked for a bottle of Scotch. Then he was all smiles, reaching down behind the bar and bringing out a bottle of French cognac. 'Whisky?' He shook his head. 'Cognac.' He slowly nodded his head and winked.

'Oui, merci,' I answered scooping up the bottle and fingering three glasses.

I placed my haul on the brass topped table to a round of applause and poured large measures into each glass. I sipped while Art threw his back and asked for more.

'How's the eye?' I asked.

'I'll mend. I've had worse out there.' He gestured with his thumb towards the door and grunted.

'We all have mate,' slurred Crabbe. 'Yet we're still here. Cheers lads!'

We all held our glasses aloft and drank deeply. That made us all quiet for a time, thinking of those who weren't here. Sitting there had made us forget for just a short while, made us imagine we were in our respective local pub—The Lamb for me—but those mud holes beckoned. Too soon we would be back there.

'Let's enjoy our time while we can, chaps,' urged Crabbe. 'Who knows what tomorrow will bring?'

We soon found out.

There'd been a torrential bombardment the night before, while we were getting drunk on fine French Cognac, and we spent the day shoring up trenches that had given way and removing the injured and dying, and the night removing the dead. Exhaustion is an easy word

Hearsay

to say and nowhere near how we felt for those 24 hours. Home felt like a distant dream, even the spicy, warmth of the brandy that had burned its way deep into our souls had vanished.

It wasn't until a few days later I had a chance to speak with Bradley. He had been keeping out of our way, helping the quartermaster with provisions. And then, one evening, I was sitting down for a smoke; there was an eerie silence across the fields as though no one wanted to start up again. No one did, the Hun and us. If it had been up to us soldiers, us pawns, we would have finished the game a long time ago; decided on a draw, shook hands and shared a fag. But no, we still had orders to push on.

I was clutching the chess set, a physical, solid thing from home, created by who knew when and thinking of the trees that had died to become this beautiful thing. The oak and the bloodwood. The same family but such a different species. Where one is the King of Summer and abundant in the forests of England, the other is prized by many to make it illegal and attractive to a thief. One stands strong and tall, magnificent over its domain, a symbol of protection and loyalty while the other one? The other one, the bloodwood has had men killed for its luscious red wood, the colour of blood. Through the death of those trees came life, I thought. These pieces will be here long after I have left this Earth. That thought drew me for a second and I murmured a little prayer. 'But not tonight, please God.'

'What's that you say?' The voice came from behind.

Whirling around I was face to face with Brad. I must have looked shocked or something because he said, 'Don't worry, I'm not going to fight you. Learnt my lesson, didn't I?' He perched on an empty wooden case.

I remained silent.

Maurice

'Do you fancy a game?' He nodded at the box I was hugging to my chest. 'I had a good teacher, you know?' Brad grinned then and his blue eyes lit up.

I grunted. 'Yeah, all right. Do you remember the rules? We do have to follow rules.'

Brad nodded. We set up the board together, the two fake pawns taking their places in front of the kings. I was white so went first.

It felt good to be lost in a game again. I loved the strategic play as well as the feel of the actual pieces in my fingers engrained with oil and earth. I allowed Brad to win, moving my pieces so that it led to his success.

After the game, we each lit a fag and sat enjoying the smoke drawing into our lungs. No words necessary. Just two friends sitting in comradeship.

It didn't last.

When I got my corporal's stripe, Brad went back to being a miserable bugger. He was tolerated by the other men, but there was tension, and I was the one to sort it out. Sergeant Frost was a good man, a good leader and he wanted me to learn from him. He would talk to me as an equal but gave me the unpleasant job of punishing Brad for any misdemeanours.

It had been another hard night; hit by a barrage of gunfire. There were several casualties, and I was put in charge of organising the notification of names of the dead, checking their ID with our list. The stretcher bearers did an amazing job, back and forth, plodding through all sorts of debris.

I discovered Brad, searching through the discs on my little folding table. I stood at the entrance of the dugout for a few seconds and then barked, 'Private Hurt. What are you doing?'

He spun around, standing to attention but when he saw it was me, he just said, 'Oh, Cruso me ole mate. It's

Hearsay

only you. Thought it was the sarge.'

I could smell alcohol and could see his glazed eyes in the flickering lamplight.

'You're drunk, private. That's a serious offence.'

'That's a serious offence,' he mimicked. 'Come on, we're comrades at arms, chums, bosom buddies.' He swayed a little as he extended his arms out towards me.

It takes a lot to make me angry, but something just twisted in my gut that day. Perhaps it was having just removed an ID disc from a young lad who had only been with us for a week. Perhaps I was tired, no sleep, little food. Perhaps I was just fed up with this cretin of a man who stood before me. We had suspected he was the one who had been pilfering from the stores and now here was the evidence. No one was given more than their ration of rum. No one could be drunk here of all places. They were a danger to the whole battalion.

I bellowed at him. 'Private, out NOW! Quick march!'

He looked as shocked as I felt about this loudness pouring from my mouth; blood draining from his face. At that moment, Sergeant Frost appeared at my elbow.

And Bradley Hurt marched from the dugout.

Standing to attention on the wooden duckboards, a wall of sandbags behind and the sun on his face, Brad finally looked like he had met his match. I barked at him, spittle flying in the wind, 'You are on latrine duty, until we can speak to the captain about your behaviour. Now, get out of my sight.'

Brad scarpered.

I turned to the sergeant, my chest heaving. 'What was all that about, Cruso?' he asked.

Through my explanation the man nodded and shook his head, his hands deep in the pockets of his greatcoat.

I began to worry that I had gone too far, but Sarge

Maurice

clapped me on the back. 'Well done, Cruso. We'll make a sergeant out of you, yet. I'll pass on the information to the captain, and he can decide whether to take it further.' He tugged at his moustache, smoothing it down either side of his upper lip. 'Heaven knows, we need all the men we can get, after last night.'

At this, the image of young Donald, the lad whose ID disc I still held in my palm, a shy retiring young man who now lay lifeless, a single bullet having ripped that life from him and with it the lives of those back home, flared in my mind. A son who would never become a father, a man who was really just a boy. Tears pricked my eyes, and I rubbed at them with the heel of my empty hand.

Sensing my discomfort, Frost said, 'Let's get a brew on and we'll make a start on these discs.' He ducked his head as he entered the dugout, leaving me there to my thoughts. I opened my fingers, like a flower's petals on a sunny day. How could one disc weigh so heavy, I asked myself. The smell of camp coffee emanated through the makeshift entrance, and I too ducked down and took my place at the wooden table.'

Maurice paused and pressed stop. He was back in his study, Rose smiling at him from her silver frame, sunshine streaming through the tall window, and he bowed his head and wept.

THE STORY OF THE BLANCHARD CHESS SETS BY M. FLAUBERT

Part 2

PARIS 1823

Clutching the letter that had been delivered that morning, Florence climbed the steps to the Flaubert's residence. The same house and yet different. The same fountain and yet no water playing.

Before lifting the knocker as her father had done before, she smoothed down her dress, arranged her linen shawl around her shoulders and hung her dainty drawstring bag over her arm. The crack of metal on metal echoed as though the house was empty and it was a few minutes before the door was opened. The same footman with hair of steel now and dark circles beneath watery eyes.

Florence was shown into a room, the same room as five long years ago. It wasn't Monsieur Flaubert who stood to greet her, it was a boy of around twelve years. She was startled by the resemblance to the man she had met before. A cleft chin and hooked nose were there, family traits. But the eyes were softer, the skin smoother, the lips gentle.

'Where is Gabriel Blanchard?' His voice rose high to the carved ceiling. 'I must see Monsieur Blanchard. It is a matter of life or death.'

'My father…' she began, not knowing what to say to this child who was obviously agitated.

Paris 1823

The boy suddenly lunged at her grabbing the stark white paper from her hand. Florence was his inferior, but she would not stand for rudeness. She spoke sharply. 'My name is Florence Blanchard. My father, Gabriel is unavailable to come today. If you need a chess set, then he can design and craft one for you.'

In the seconds before he replied, Florence glanced at the clock on the mantle. It had stopped at quarter past the hour of eleven.

Sensing her distraction, he said. 'He stopped it. When she passed, he stopped all the clocks.' He didn't elaborate further but took a small package from a side table.

'I am Michel Flaubert. It is imperative that my father does not learn of your attendance here today.'

Florence acquiesced bobbing her head at this manchild who was now unwrapping the package. He unfolded a lace handkerchief on the palm of his hand and there lay the bloodwood queen broken in two.

'What happened?' Florence asked taking the pieces and fitting them together to become whole again. A sliver of wood was missing leaving a gash in the side of the piece.

'The chess set, commissioned by my father, created by your father… it was an accident. It wasn't meant to happen. Can you… make it better?'

'I think so,' ventured Florence.

The boy became hysterical. 'But you must. I beg of you. It was my mother's, but she never played it, never even touched it. She… she…' Michel finally succumbed to sobbing. Through his tears he whispered, 'My little sister killed her.'

Florence couldn't comprehend what the boy was saying. *His sister is a murderer. Surely, he is making up stories to shock me into helping him.*

The ugly sobs subsided. Michel rubbed at his face

Hearsay

with the handkerchief he still held.

'She didn't mean to. It was when Mama was birthing her. They both died.' He stumbled to a chair. 'I miss my mama so much.'

Forgetting about rules, Florence sat in the opposite seat. Her heart went out to this child. She too had lost her mother. She knew the pain would never leave him.

'Why must your father not know about this?'

'He won't let anyone touch the chess set, not since…'

'I see.'

'He will be so angry if he finds out. I can't bear…'

'Of course. I understand.' She still held the pain from the anger of her own father and recognised the haunted look of the boy as if it was her own. 'I will return it this evening, restored to her former beauty.'

'You promise. You can do this?'

'I made some of the original pieces unbeknown to your father. He never guessed that two pairs of hands created the set. He won't know this has been repaired once I've finished with it.'

Rising, Florence placed the pieces into her bag, pulled the ribbon tightly and hooked it on her wrist. She patted it for good measure and then went to the door.

'Where is Monsieur Flaubert now?'

'He is out; he won't be back until tomorrow. Please hurry.' Michel remained slumped in his chair as Florence let herself out through the main door to the once verdant garden, past the sleeping fountain and out onto the main thoroughfare to return home.

Back in the workshop, having changed into her more comfortable cotton work dress and apron, and swapping elegant shoes for leather boots, Florence sat herself on her work stool before the battered old bench. The midday sun was high in the heavens high enough to peep over the tall

Paris 1823

buildings opposite and to light her workspace. *It will save on candles*, she thought removing the pieces of the queen and laying them down.

Life had been difficult since she had last worked on the set. That last night when Henri had come calling and they had delivered the chess set to the Flaubert residence, now came to her mind. Vivid as though it had happened yesterday.

'Father, we must go and pay that man,' Florence had said, when they had left the Flaubert house.

'There is no rush. We have time to celebrate the sale of my best-ever chess set. It will be played by people of wealth, people who will treasure it for all time. Come we will go and eat a meal and drink their health.' His eyes gleamed and his face creased into raptures as he counted the coins.

Before she could say anything, Gabriel shot off down the road; he had the energy of a young man and Florence struggled to keep up with him. Her skirt hampered her progress, so she resorted to shout at his back disappearing into the melee of people and horses. He didn't respond to her calls. Fortunately, she knew where he was heading.

Florence ducked into a side street, the buildings either side towering above her. Ahead of her she glimpsed her father disappearing to his right. She was panting with exertion by the time she too turned right and entered the tavern. Gloomy after the bright Parisian sun, it took her a few moments to scan the many mournful faces greeting her. An alcove to her left held a table and two benches and there sat Gabriel. A glass already lifted to his lips.

Making her way across, she found herself the topic of discussion by two young workmen sitting at a round table in the centre.

'I'd like a go at her sometime,' one said.

'What, Florence? No, she's too good for the likes of you.'

'I'll fight you for her.'

'Get off. You'd lose hands down. She's mine aren't you, cherie?' With this the man stood and took her by the shoulders, he pawed at her breasts before pulling her to him. Florence kicked hard at his shins, spat in his face and swore.

'Get your hands off me!' she shrieked, pulling herself from his grip and stumbling over to her father. Gabriel, oblivious of the commotion behind him, had drained his glass and was now filling it from a bottle.

'Father,' Florence sighed. 'Can't this wait. We need to pay our dues.'

'Rest, my little one. Savour life for a moment. Here…' He poured her a glass of ruby red wine. 'Life is too short to fight.' He nudged the glass towards her, with fingers capable of such finesse and such pain.

Florence knew she wouldn't win. She sipped from her glass and bided her time.

Food was brought to them. Platters of goose in a rich sauce. Florence hadn't eaten such delicious food for a long time and relished this opportunity. At the back of her mind, though, the image of Henri haunted her. He was dangerous and would do as he had promised. Mopping up the gravy with a piece of bread, she contemplated how she was going to get her father out of this place to make the rendezvous before midnight. They were only a short distance from the meeting-place. Gabriel, however looked like he was settled in for the evening. Perhaps she could get him to agree to just her going.

'This is good, yes?' Goose fat dripped from his mouth, and he used the back of his hand to wipe it away. When she didn't reply, he repeated his question. Gouts of meat shot from his mouth as he accentuated his words.

Paris 1823

'Yes, father,' agreed Florence. 'Yes, it is very good.' Having finished her food, she laced her fingers together and laid them in her lap.

She listened to the talk around them. The monarchy, the price of food and coal, the winners of a recent dog fight. Nothing of importance until she heard the name Henri Placquette. Turning her head slightly to absorb more of the words, her heart began to beat quicker.

The man, who had pawed at her earlier, was speaking. 'They found him just before sunset. Dead drunk they thought. Dead, he was.'

'Where was the corpse?'

'On the north bank near Notre Dame. He'd been stabbed... in his side, I think they said. Blood everywhere by all accounts.'

'Well, I won't be crying for that cur. I owed him and now he's gone, my debts are paid.' The men raised their goblets and drank greedily, belching in unison.

Florence smiled inwardly. *Our debts are paid too. Thank the Lord.* She crossed herself. Someone somewhere had listened to her prayer and got rid of this monster. She too raised a glass and drank down the red liquid.

Now, sitting at her workbench repairing the red queen, she silently thanked that stranger who changed her life that night. No more debts. No more terrifying encounters of that man, Henri Placquette.

Since then, Florence had continued to remodel the chess sets her father crafted. More and more he remained at home, morose and miserable, while she visited the elegant houses of their clients. He continued his nightly rampages, only returning in a drunken stupor, sometimes violent but more often becoming pathetic and wheedling, feeble and woeful. And then one night he never returned. She had gone searching all of his regular haunts but returned home without him. Every night for a week she searched desperately for him, but he had disappeared into the darkness. Finally, she realised she was finally free.

The queen was in two pieces. Florence contemplated remodelling another one, but there was little time for that. She set up the pot of gum, basted each edge and held the pieces together briefly before setting them in a vice attached to the bench. Once the glue had dried, she could sand and polish the piece restoring it back to its former beauty and elegance.

While she waited, she busied herself around the house. With the money from the sale of chess sets she had been able to keep up with the rent and to replace some of the furniture. She wasn't rich but she was comfortable. For the first time in her life, she felt a sense of pride in her lodgings and in herself. Commissions for chess sets continued—she would visit the homes of the bourgeoisie, taking their order for her father to craft a set, never telling anyone of his demise and of her own skill. She was not indebted to anyone but herself. There was no man to answer to at all hours of the day and night, yet she knew if anyone found out these sets were made by a woman, however exquisite they were, she would get no more work, turned out of her lodgings and be on the streets.

She had found it surprisingly easy to pretend, her father had always been a man of the night, and no one cared who came and went to brothels and alehouses. If there was a surprise visitor to the house, she would lie about her father resting in the back room.

The glue dry, Florence took her seat once again and sanded and polished the piece. The crack was no more—yes, the fracture was still beneath—from the outside it was restored.

'I am here to see Michel Flaubert,' she announced

Paris 1823

later that evening, after the heavy door swung open.

A maid gestured for her to enter and to wait in the hallway.

'Ah, Florence. We meet again.' The words came from a tall, imposing figure descending the grand staircase.

Florence swallowed and placed a false smile to her lips. 'Monsieur Flaubert. Bon soir.' She curtsied.

Chapter Twenty-Two

LUC

Luc knocked at the cherry red door, paint peeling off onto her knuckles and at her touch the door swung loose exposing a hallway of red and black chequered tiles. Calling out, she stepped onto a worn door mat, only the *we* and *me* of the word *welcome* visible.

Still no reply and with her heart in her mouth, Luc took another step. The hall was dark, all doors closed. She froze at a sudden scrabbling and scratching from the door at the far end. Then it stopped. She called out again and the noise began in earnest. Tiptoeing along the hall, she listened and raised her hand to the latch. A clatter and a crash from beyond the door brought a heavy thump from the floor above and her hand flew to her mouth.

'Hello,' she called out, her voice now shaking.

Thumping came again and was now at the top of the stairs. She couldn't move. Whoever was up there would be coming down any minute. *I wish Scott was here*, she thought. A flurry of fur barrelled down the stairs and skidded to a stop in front of Luce. Two black, soulful eyes gazed at her.

Luc

A brown and white terrier sat, its pink tongue lolling below a conker-coloured nose. Luc's heart was trying to fly out of her ribs, and she took a minute to catch her breath. Finally, she said, 'Hello. Are you a friendly guard dog?' She stretched out tentative fingers and was greeted by a lick. A throaty bark added to the mix, and she shushed him.

The dog scrabbled at the door and Luc lifted the latch. A stripy cat was lying on a wooden kitchen table and fragments of what could have once been a plate were spread across red quarry tiles. The dog bowled past Luc to a metal dish and was soon downing great gulps of water.

There appeared to be no human beings in the house and Luc could see on wandering around the room someone had obviously been here. The remains of breakfast lay on the table alongside the cat who stared at her with yellow eyes that seemed to see into her soul.

Light flooded in through a large plate glass window above a sink and Luc realised that even though the kitchen fittings were old and chipped there was colour everywhere. A scarlet tea towel hung on the silver bar of an aga, a blind at the window sported large crimson carnations and an array of spotty and stripy mugs, plates and dishes filled a large dresser. Luc took all of this in within seconds and then her eyes rested on something incongruous to this scene, something that shouldn't be there but answered a question she had held for so long.

A large painting hung in the centre of a bare wall. Colour poured from every inch, thickly daubed paint, texture from thick brushes. *It's me*, she thought. Her younger self gazed out from the picture, mousy hair held back by a blue band, freckles adorning a small nose. For a moment the Earth stopped spinning as she stepped towards this celebration of herself. *This might mean Mum is here, and that she did care for me after all,* she pondered, tracing her finger across the rough surface of the canvas. *She must have asked someone to paint this from a photograph.*

The dog began to howl, bringing her out of her reverie. He had taken his place by the back door, waiting patiently. Luc, not really knowing what to do, automatically opened the door and followed the terrier outside. A low wall surrounded a tangled mass of shrubs and flowers, and a well-trodden path led down to a gate.

Leaving the dog in the garden, she stepped out onto a concrete-covered yard surrounded by various buildings. On the far side was a large, red-bricked barn with decorative open brickwork under the apex of the roof. Drawn to the building she made her way across the yard and gingerly pushed open a stable door. Inside was chaos and colour, the vibrant melody of David Bowie's Space Oddity rose above the mess and madness while a whirling dervish of a woman, in a flowing kaftan and sandals, threw paint at a canvas astride an easel. A musty, oily smell pervaded her senses—a smell that reminded her of 'painting by numbers' as a child. A large table near to the easel was covered with trays overflowing with squeezed paint tubes, brushes upended in jars, and propped up against every wall there were hundreds of canvases, some clean, some painted; some tiny, some gigantic.

Luc was aware the woman was totally in the zone, unaware of her presence. Then a loud expletive and the paintbrush was flung away until it skittered to a stop next to a table with a coffee machine and kettle.

'Crap! This is just crap! Caffeine! I need caffeine!'

Luc felt her heart tighten. 'Mum?' Her voice hesitant, unsure. This vision couldn't be her mother.

The woman whirled round, chestnut-coloured hair

Luc

cascading around her face, her mouth grim, eyes sharp. Luc's heart sank, she'd been wrong. Then as night becomes day a light returned to the artist's eyes. 'Lucretia? It can't be. Oh my god, Luc, you're here.'

The voice flooded Luc's memory cells—the voice that would read to her at night, the voice that sang her to sleep, the mouth that kissed her cheek every night until… until she went away. A stirring of anger and joy, of love and hate hit her and she was stuck, she couldn't move.

Her mother stumbled towards her. 'Luc, my darling girl. How did you… why are you…?'

Luc didn't know what to say until she was crushed in her mother's arms and smothered with Rive Gauche cologne and then all those lost years melted away. Tears flooded from her, and she sobbed and sobbed into her mother's shoulder. Isobel, in turn wept into Luc's shoulder.

They pulled away, gazing at each other. Isobel said, 'Look at you, you are a beautiful young woman.'

And now the questions came to Luc's lips. 'Please tell me—why did you leave? What is going on? What is all this?' Luc circled her arms around to encompass the enormous space.

Isobel took her hand and led her to an area in front of a wall of glass, with views across the fields, where there were two easy chairs and a low table. 'Let's sit for a while. We have a lot of catching up, and a lot of apologising on my part. Coffee?'

Luc nodded and sat back against soft cushions, while Isobel busied herself with the coffee machine and mugs. A kitchenette in the corner of the room was modern and streamlined, a complete contrast with the kitchen in the farmhouse. Luc found herself observing this woman who was a stranger to her and yet part of her existence. Luc's recollection of her mother was of beige drabness, of monosyllabic sentences, a mouse of a woman. This being was the antithesis—hair with cobalt blue streaks, coloured bangles adorning each arm, a necklace of conch shells and pebbles. She had been an ugly duckling who had become a peacock.

Isobel took her seat after placing a tray with coffee and biscuits on the table between them. 'Moo-Cow biscuits,' Luc murmured as she grabbed a mug.

'What was that?' her mother asked.

'We used to call them Moo-Cow biscuits when I was little.'

'Yes, we did.' Isobel smiled.

Luc felt raw, a hollowed-out husk. *This is so absurd, sitting here talking about biscuits with the woman who cares nothing for me*, she thought. *And after all this time I don't know what to say to her.*

Isobel began, 'I have so much to say to you, my lovely girl. Sorry is not enough, Luc, for abandoning you when you were eight. Believe me though, when I say, I am so dreadfully sorry. I thought I was leaving you in good hands, and I was right. Your aunt and uncle brought you up to be an amazing young woman.'

And that was it. All the hurt, locked away in the depths of her mind, Luc now spewed out. 'How do you know I'm amazing? You don't know anything about me. My dad hates me, my mother obviously hates me. I have no boyfriend, no life, nothing amazing at all.' Luc stared across the space that was becoming a chasm between them, her breath now coming in short tight bursts.

'I fully deserve that.' Her mother's voice was surprisingly calm.

Luc leaned forward, narrowing her eyes and fired a final barrage of statements at her mother, 'And then, I find

Luc

out from two strangers that Grandad was a thief and a murderer. And I can't ask him or Granny because they're both dead.'

'What? Who told you Grandad was a thief and a murderer?'

Taking a deep breath, Luc replied, 'I met a man called Maurice Smith and his grandson, Scott, in Paris. Maurice was in the First World War with Grandad apparently. And he seems to think he tried to kill him.' After regurgitating long-held pain and confusion, Luc's mind was an abyss. She felt drained, empty of all emotion.

Still very calm, Isobel said, 'I'm sorry I don't know a Maurice Smith. However, I'm afraid to say he was right and wrong about your grandfather. My dad, Bradley Hurt, was a bully, a thief and a liar, but not a murderer. I'm sure he killed his share of the enemy during the war, just like so many others.' Isobel sipped her coffee and then placing the mug down, seemingly quite composed she added. 'There's a lot you don't know about him.'

Luc sat back in her chair. 'I think you need to tell me about him and why you left, why you couldn't bring me with you.' She waited, like she had done every night over the past sixteen years or so, to find out the truth. No more hearsay from other people, just the stark reality, however much it hurt.

Isobel took a deep breath as though steeling herself and then began. 'I don't know what your dad or Auntie Alice and Uncle Hugh have told you, and your Gran for that matter. I don't know where to start. The start is right back in the 1920s. That's where it all began.

I think though, for now I will explain my reason for leaving. Your dad and I, we had grown apart by the time you came along. He had suffered dreadfully in the German POW camps back in 1945 and would wake up

Hearsay

screaming and shouting in the night. Me? I had my own problems. Having witnessed my father bully my mum, mentally as well as physically, I built a wall around myself preventing me from showing my true emotions.

I had grown up always doing what my parents told me to do. To go to secretarial college so I could get a good job until I got married. Life was hard for everyone back in the fifties and so I did as I was told. Secretly, I yearned for adventure and wanted to attend art college. When I met your father, I thought he was going to help me with my dreams, but he was coping with his own nightmares. I felt stuck. We tried for a baby. So many miscarriages, so much hope and then agony. My life was put on hold as each month I waited for the dreaded red spots of blood to appear and when they did, I hated my body for its betrayal. Finally, I fell pregnant, suffering dreadful morning-sickness as a result but I held onto you. I promised I would never let you go; I would never give up on you.' Isobel broke off and gazed out of the window.

Luc leaned forward in her chair, anxious for her mum to continue. 'Mum?'

Isobel's eyes rested on Luc, once more. 'I am so sorry—I tried to be a good mother, I tried so hard, but I couldn't take any more—my mind and body were weakened. I suffered dreadful depression. Your father was suffering too. We grew apart. I wanted to leave…' Isobel's eyes filled with more tears. 'I am so sorry I let you down. I wrote to you and sent birthday and Christmas cards and occasionally I would get a letter from Alice.'

'Letters? Cards! I haven't been given anything from you. You're lying—you never cared then, and you don't care now!' Luc jumped up. Isobel cringed as though she was scared Luc was going to strike her.

'I'm not going to hit you. Why would you think that?

Luc

I'm not the baddie here.'

'Neither am I,' said Isobel, rising to her feet. 'I don't know why you didn't get anything from me—someone must have hidden them from you. Oh God, Luc, no wonder you hate me. You really think I abandoned you.' Isobel took Luc's hands in hers and scrutinised her daughter's face. 'Luc, I loved you from the moment I knew I was carrying you. I think of you every day. I love you. I paint because of you. I wasn't running away from you, but I couldn't take you with me. Please sit down and let me tell you more about what happened.'

Luc allowed herself to be led back to the chair and she sat once again.

'My dad, your grandad was a real mixture of good and bad, just like every human being is, I suppose. He was extreme though. One minute he would be pushing me on a swing, the next he would be locking me in the cellar for chewing too loudly at dinner time. He blamed the war, the whisky, the weather, the news, the government. Of course, it was never his fault.

That was why marrying your dad was a lifeline. I really did love him you know. Your dad was a good man, but he was socially and emotionally inept and was unaware of how to support me when I suffered from post-natal depression.

Anyway, my father, Bradley Hurt, had been drinking at The Dog one day. Autumn of 1968, it was. Won something on the horses, I think. I was visiting Mum; you were at home with your dad. Mum and I were having tea and a slab of bread pudding in their kitchen. He came in, drunk and Mum and I knew what that would mean so we were careful in how we handled him. I remarked on how nice my mum looked that day and that's when he told me. I had been part of his deception for all these years and that this woman, Elspeth Hurt was not my real mother.'

Luc gasped. What she had suspected after finding the stuff in the loft was true. She waited for Isobel to continue.

Isobel began pacing up and down the room. The hem of her kaftan softly swishing on the floor. She seemed to be verbally reliving that moment from all those years ago.

'What do you mean, Dad?' I asked, trying to stay calm.

'What I say, girl. Your mother didn't want you, so I brought you to Elspeth, my first love.' He smirked and winked luridly at Mother.

'Are you my real dad?'

''course I am. You don't think I'd bring up another man's brat, do you?' He lit a cigarette and puffed smoke into my face.

'Who is she? Who's my real mum? You owe me that at least. I want to see her.'

'I don't owe you anything,' he shouted grabbing and twisting my wrist, so his face was right up against mine. 'In fact, you owe me for bringing you up.' His beery breath was hot and stale. 'You're married, aren't you? Got a kid of your own. What else is there for a woman to do?' He threw me across the kitchen then.

My chest heaved as I lay there, dazed from the fall and what he had said. Pulling myself to sitting, I asked my mum then if she could corroborate all this. And she did. And in that kitchen that day, where I'd played with my doll, drew pictures of happy families on scraps of paper, where I had dipped my finger into sweet cake mixture when mum wasn't looking, my life changed forever. My heart broke there and then.

I remember stumbling out of the house, slamming the front door not knowing what to do or where to go.'

Luc

Abruptly, Isobel stopped mid-pace. 'That's why I left, Luc. I had to find out where I really belonged, where I had come from.'

Luc gaped at her mother. Then as an afterthought, she asked, 'You were shattered back then just as I am now with all of this information. Please help me understand.'

Isobel threw herself to her knees in front of Lucretia. 'Oh, my darling, girl. Granny Elspeth was Bradley Hurt's first wife, but not my mum. They never divorced; they lost a child I believe during the First World War and that pushed them both over the precipice of reality. He was a bigamist.'

'Is Myrtle Hurt your real mum?' Luc ventured.

Isobel blinked hard. 'You know Myrtle? How? When? She's never said…'

'No, I haven't met her, unfortunately. The man I mentioned before, Maurice Smith, knew her before the war.'

Isobel shook her head. 'As I said before, I don't know of anyone of that name.'

'How about Edmund Cruso?'

'Edmund Cruso? He's dead.' Isobel's face had drained of all colour, her eyes huge and staring.

Luc continued. 'Well, that's what everyone thought. They believed he'd died in the war.'

'No, no! You don't understand. Edmund Cruso came back here in the 1960s. He was discovered dead in a crop circle in Top Field.'

Chapter Twenty-Three

MAURICE

Scott and Maurice took their seats towards the back of the grand ballroom where the auction was to take place. Each had a catalogue—Maurice's was well-thumbed having had it for a while, but Scott's was still pristine, having just been handed it on entering.

'I wish Luc could have been here for this,' Scott whispered.

'Yes, it is a shame, but she had to go to see her mother. She deserves to know the truth. When will you see her again? There is still much to do.'

'I'm not sure, hopefully in the next few days.'

'You two are becoming fond of each other, yes?' Maurice nudged Scott's elbow.

Scott nodded. 'I think so but I'm not sure if she feels the same way about me. She didn't phone me last night and I can't get hold of her while she's in Shropshire. I keep saying the wrong thing or acting in the wrong way. She seemed very quiet when I spoke to her last.' He sighed and began to flick through the catalogue on his knee.

Maurice grunted. 'I'm sure it will all turn out right in

Maurice

the end.' Scott didn't reply and Maurice gazed around him, realising he wasn't going to get any further with his grandson. The gold mouldings of the Baroque ceiling soared above him, while striped vermillion and ivory wallpaper separated each of the long casement windows. There was a buzz of excitement rippling through the audience as the auctioneer took her place at a rostrum at the front of the room. She was dressed in a lilac silk dress layered with grey and pink chiffon. Her striking silver hair was pinned into a French pleat, and she stood appraising the audience, a slight smile coming to her pink lips.

Silence fell.

The woman introduced herself as Genevieve Dumont, talked a little about some of the lots and then began. There were several items before the chess set and it was warm in the ballroom of the Ritz hotel, Parisian sunshine pouring through the glass and Maurice found his eyes becoming heavy. Rubbing his face to bring life back, he noticed Scott was doodling on a page in the catalogue. Genivieve's lilting voice and the rhythmical bidding finally brought Maurice's eyes to close, and his thoughts went straight to chess. He saw his mother kneeling within a golden circle of barley, a small metal soap tin in her hand. She was lifting the lid and placing the white pawn on a bed of cotton wool. Then he was sitting at the scrubbed kitchen table opposite his father, pondering on his next move and lifting the king and whispering, check. His father, young, no grey hair or wrinkles, his memory intact, smiled and did a thumbs up. Myrtle's face, pink cheeks, ruby-red lips and dark hair curling to her shoulders shot into view. Her smile turned to anger as she hurled the red pawn into the bracken below the trees in the woods. Her face suddenly melted into that of Bradley Hurt, sneering and taunting him; Mrytle doesn't want you, you're a useless specimen, she deserves a real man, not a child. The voices of each of them shouting, whispering, screaming at him were suffocating. He pulled away, feeling someone strike him, he flinched, and his eyes sprang open.

'Are you okay?' Scott was asking, his voice full of concern.

'Yes. Just a bit warm. Must have nodded off,' he replied, stretching out his back.

'Yes, you were mumbling to yourself.'

'I was not!' Maurice, his voice sharp, indignant at Scott's remark. 'Get me a glass of water, please?'

Scott, at the end of the row, rose to his feet and slipped out to the bar in the other room. He returned soon after with two glasses of mineral water, ice jostling with lemon slices.

'We're on after this one,' Maurice said, taking the proffered glass. The icy water shook him awake and the thought of finally owning his chess set invigorated him. And then, in a flash, he could hear Rose's velvet tones saying, 'You must live, my love. Live in the light and when there is no light and only darkness then you must burn a candle flame. Find what you have missed from your previous life. You were fortunate to have had two lives, not many have that chance. Once I'm gone you must search out that first life and complete the circle. Bits of wood don't matter, expensive art is not important, it is family and friendship, encircled with love and trust that is. Find out the truth—complete the circle.'

Maurice found himself nodding and, in his head, he replied to the woman who had given him all of these. 'Yes, my love, you are right, as always. But this is more than a work of art, an object of my wealth. This brings us all back together to complete the circle.' From nowhere, a white feather fluttered down and landed on the back of his hand,

Maurice

and he smiled. 'I love you, Rosemary.'

A gentle nudge to his arm, brought him back to the present once again. It was Scott. 'It's show time!'

Maurice looked towards the auctioneer and there to her left stood a man in a dark suit holding up the chess set. *My chess set*, he thought.

'An incomplete set, believed to have been crafted by Gabriel Blanchard in 1818, but now through rigorous testing discovered to have been made by his daughter, Florence Blanchard. I would like to start the bidding at one thousand francs.

Maurice caught her eye and nodded.

'Thank you, Monsieur Smith. We have our first bid.'

A voice came from the front of the audience. '1200.'

Maurice threw back, '1500!'

The bidding continued until the other bidder suddenly shouted out, '6000 francs.'

Maurice was incensed. Who else wants my chess set? '8000!' he called, pulling at the collar of his shirt, its tightness too much to bear.

No reply came. People shifted and sighed and fell silent.

Once again, the auctioneer asked the stranger. Maurice clutched at Scott's hand as they both held their breath. The other bidder must have shaken their head as the gavel crashed down on the mahogany lectern.

And suddenly, Scott was hugging him. He went to rise from his seat, but the floor began pitching from side to side—he staggered to right himself and just as a wave hits a ship, he hit the deck. The lights were extinguished all around him as he fought to breathe—*is this drowning?*

Then all was dark. And still.

Maurice found himself gazing at a woman, hair swathed within a turquoise silk scarf, her figure hugged

Hearsay

within a sheath dress of blues and gold, her face showing a slight frown to the forehead. She was holding up her left hand, fingers splayed to warn him of something. A single gold band encircled her ring finger, catching the sunlight.

'Return to the light, my love. The circle must be complete, then you can join me. Go back, my love, go back into the light.' The woman's voice was tender, full of concern and love.

Maurice, stretching out an arm, sighed. 'I miss you so much, Rose. You were my life and now I don't know how to keep going without you.'

'You must tell the story. Our story and that of Florence. Her story must come to light.'

'You always knew best, Rose.'

'Not always.' The woman smiled. 'But I do know this is not your time.' She began to retreat, the image fading.

'Rose, my love. Rose…'

Another voice came from his right. 'Maurice, it's Luc. I'm here.' A small cool hand took his. Opening his eyes, shadows materialised into objects and, on turning his head, into Lucretia.

'Where am I?' His voice sounded dry and gritty.

Another deeper voice came from far away and he screwed up his eyes to clear the images before him. There was Scott, his face pale, eyes pink and strained. 'You're in hospital. How are you feeling? You gave us quite a turn collapsing like that.'

Before answering, Maurice tested himself by shifting until he was more upright. Luc plumped up the pillows as he did so. Just this small change of position made him feel weary and he leaned back and closed his eyes. *What day is it?* He thought. *What happened?*

'Would you like some water?' Luc asked. His eyelids slowly lifted, and he nodded. The coldness of the glass

Maurice

against his lips soothed him and the water refreshed him. *How did he get here? Where was Rose?* He thought to himself. And then the realness engulfed him. She was no longer with him, no longer by his side. Tears spilled over and he wept.

Luc patted his hand and gently wiped his face. 'Don't worry, you're going to be okay. You've been here for a few days. A mild heart attack.'

'You can come home soon, Maurice,' Scott added. 'With strict instructions about your diet. Fresh fruit and vegetables, no cake and no alcohol.'

Maurice frowned. 'That doesn't sound much fun,' he muttered, and Luc and Scott chuckled.

A shaft of moonlight came through the windows, draping itself across the bed covers, like someone settling themselves down to listen. A memory tugged at his mind, yarn unthreading from the hem of a jumper, just like his mother would do to his old ones to enable her to add more rows. And just like wool unhooking itself and being re-connected his mind began to piece things back together again: squares of a chessboard interlocking, circles spiralling, light flickering and a hammer falling.

'The chess set!' Maurice exclaimed. 'What happened? Scott, what happened?' Maurice's voice grew in strength and urgency.

Scott skirted the end of the bed and lifted a wooden box onto his grandfather's lap. 'It's yours once more,' he whispered before pulling up a chair and seating himself next to the bed.

Maurice cradled the box before smoothing his fingers across the surface of bloodwood red squares and white oak squares. He felt as though he was finally home, a feeling he should have had on his return to the farm all those years ago. His hand shook as he lifted the lid and there within their own shallow velvet graves lay the soldiers, bar two, the horses, the bishops, the castles and the monarchy. Maurice traced the two empty spaces with a forefinger.

'You seem to be missing two pawns. Perhaps this will fit,' Luc said placing the red pawn, which she had worn as a pendant, into its little bed.

'A perfect fit,' said Maurice grinning up at her and then at Scott.

'We know where the white pawn is,' Luc announced.

His head shot back, and he gaped at her, unblinking. 'Really? Was it buried in the field?'

'Not anymore.' Luc smiled and patted his hand.

'It's a bit of a story and we'll let the keeper of the pawn tell you. But for that you must travel to England, to a little village in Shropshire.'

Maurice grabbed at the blanket to toss it from his legs, but Scott intervened. 'Once you have fully recovered, of course. There's no rush. The pawn is safe. After all, you have waited a long time for this, a few more days won't hurt.'

Maurice fell back against the pillows, while Luc tucked the blanket around him once more, saying, 'The doctor says you must rest. I will go and ask the nurse about your medication. Now behave yourself while I'm gone.' With that, she left the room.

He knew he was beaten and grumbled at her retreating back. Scott had taken his seat once again and was studying the chess pieces.

'Just think back in 1818, here in Paris, Florence Blanchard made these pieces and only a few people believed a woman could create such beauty.'

Maurice nodded. 'Rose wants me to tell her story to the world. What do you think? I have read the book. Poor Florence. Such a waste.'

Maurice

Scott nodded. 'Yes, it is a sad story. I'm going to give the translation to Luc this evening. What did you have in mind?'

'Perhaps an exhibition. Now, I think I will sleep.'

Scott helped Maurice with the chess box, placing it on the bedside table. He rose from his seat, closing curtains and straightening the bed covers. Maurice closed his eyes and was soon asleep and walking through wheatfields with his mother on one side and his beloved Rose on the other.

Chapter Twenty-Four

LUC

The taxi drive from the hospital seemed to take forever. Luc kept looking across at Scott whose focus was through his own window. They hadn't spoken since leaving Maurice and now for some reason there was an atmosphere so thick that Luc couldn't cut through to get to this man, who she loved. *Yes, I love him*, she finally admitted to herself.

Tentatively, she said, 'Are you okay?'

Scott turned to her. 'Yes, I'm fine. Just… just… a bit shaken up. I thought I'd lost him. At that moment of him finally getting it back too. It seemed so unfair, so cruel after everything he's been through. And then, you…' His voice petered out and he turned back to his window.

'Me? What have I done?' Even to Luc, her voice sounded spiky. She rounded the edges and tried again. 'Please, Scott, tell me.'

Before he could say anything, the taxi pulled up outside the iron gates leading to the house. Just a solitary light above the front door shone into the darkness of the night. They climbed out, Scott paid, Luc heaved her bag out of the boot, and they soon found themselves in the hallway.

'I'm going to bed,' Scott announced and began

Luc

making his way to the stairs. 'The spare room is made up for you.'

Luc trailed after him, dragging her bag behind her. *I can't take this*, she thought, *I have to know what I've done.* 'Scott, I have to know. What is wrong? Please?'

Scott was heading towards his own room but paused at the door. Slowly, he turned. 'You haven't phoned me for days and when you do you seem distant, and I don't mean literally. And why didn't you tell me about the white pawn? I thought we were a team. I thought we...' he trailed off, chewing his lip.

Luc remained silent for a moment mulling over his accusations. 'Scott, I haven't had chance. I came straight to the hospital from the airport. I was so scared that Maurice might die before knowing about the pawn.' Dumping her bag, she came towards Scott and stopped a few feet away. 'And...' She swallowed. 'I was ashamed.' She looked away and gazed blankly at the carved dado rail on the wall beyond.

'Ashamed? Of me? Why?' His questions penetrated her sub-conscious.

'No! Not of you. No, myself, my family.' Sighing, she added in a small voice. 'My grandfather was... a... a... bigamist and a bully. Everything I remembered was a sham. He was married to two women, kidnapped his daughter, and he physically and mentally abused them all.'

Scott shifted his posture, pushed his glasses back onto the bridge of his nose and said, 'Luc, you have nothing to be ashamed of. This was him, not you. You're not like him. I'm sorry your family have suffered so much. I'm sorry I wasn't there for you when you found all of this out. A stupid chess set is nothing compared to family, to trust and to love.' He took a tentative step towards her.

'I have so much to tell you. So much has happened.

But I was worried about Maurice and for you. I care so much about you both. I don't know what I would do without you in my life…' She looked down at her feet, squirming inside.

'I'm sorry, Luc. I'm so sorry. I've been beside myself with worry about the old man. Since reading Florence's story, I wanted to put everything right.' Another step forward closing the gap between them, he added, his voice soft. 'My darling Luc, I missed you so much.'

Luc looked up into Scott's face, his eyes, framed by glasses, seemed even larger, soulful, and her heart skipped several beats. 'Me too. I haven't seen the pawn yet. I just know where it is. I…' And suddenly, Scott's mouth was on hers. An urgency, a physical need took over and she clung to him. They pulled apart, their eyes locked.

'Luc,' Scott whispered, his hand stroked her hair, cupped her chin and then another kiss. Gentle, tender, savoured this time. For Luc, it was like she had finally come home. This was the man she wanted to be with for the rest of her life, but… she pulled away.

'I have to know,' she murmured.

In answer, Scott pushed the door open and led her inside. Moonlight glanced through the windows, its silvery beam caressing the floor.

'Luc, I love you. I want to be by your side for all eternity.' Scott took her hands in his. 'I have to know too.'

In answer she gently kissed his lips. 'I love you, Scott. You are everything to me…' His lips stopped any further words. She tugged at his jacket, and he shrugged it to the floor. In turn, he pulled her jumper over her head and dropped it. Clothes soon piled around them and the touch of bare skin brought another torrent of emotions through Luc's body. Falling on the bed, they remained entwined, exploring, touching, stroking.

Luc

'You're so beautiful,' Scott whispered, his voice husky. All she could manage was a moan as his fingers stroked her breast and a yearning deep within her brought heat and a need for more.

The night was full of satiated desire, love and tenderness, passion and hunger. And Luc woke to the sunlight with Scott's arms wrapped around her. She stirred. Scott rolled over onto his back, a soft snore made Luc smile, and she traced a finger across his chest. A few golden hairs dusted the surface and lazily she wrapped one around her little finger.

Scott flinched. She smiled before dropping her face to nuzzle his chest. 'That's the best way to be woken up,' Scott sighed.

Luc rested her chin on him. 'Good morning.'

'Hello you,' Scott said. 'How did you sleep?'

'Well to be honest I didn't get a lot of sleep. Someone kept waking me up.' She grinned.

Scott chuckled. 'Funny, I thought it was you waking me up.' They kissed and snuggled down under the duvet. A knock on the door made them pull apart.

It was Mimi, the housekeeper. Her voice came through the door. 'I'm sorry to bother you, Scott, but the hospital is on the phone. They say they need to speak to you, now.'

Scott threw off the covers and grabbing a robe, went to the door. Mimi stood there, wringing her hands. 'I'm so sorry. Please can you come now.'

Scott disappeared off with Mimi, leaving Luc curled up hoping and praying to a god she didn't really believe in, that Maurice was all right.

Having dressed hurriedly, throwing on jeans and a jumper, Luc entered the kitchen where she found Scott's daughter, Sophia, sitting at the table dipping a pain au chocolat into a bowl. A book lay open beside her. She was in another world. She only looked up at Luc's greeting and Luc was met with a beaming smile. 'Bonjour, Luc.'

'Ah, Luc,' said a voice. 'What can I get you for breakfast?' Mimi's English was perfect. A good thing, Luc thought as her own schoolgirl French was pitiful. *Well, I did manage CSE Grade 1,* she pondered taking a seat next to Sophia.

'Good morning, Mimi. I will have what Sophia is having, thank you. Merci.'

Mimi, this morning dressed in black jeans, an orange top and spiky hair of turquoise and pink grinned back at her. 'Okay, no problem.' Luc watched the young woman smoothly take things from the fridge, the cupboards and wondered, not for the first time, why she did this job.

'Sorry about that.' A deep voice from the open-door heralded Scott's approach. Luc looked up and their eyes met, a sudden heat brushed her cheeks as she remembered the night before. He in turn, just grinned at her.

'Is everything okay at the hospital?' Mimi asked. Luc, felt guilty, she should have been the one to ask that.

Scott helped himself to a coffee and said, 'Everything's fine, but they want Maurice to stay in for a few more days for some tests and things.'

'Is Grand-Pere going to be okay?' Sophia asked. 'He promised to take me to the zoo next week.'

Scott hugged his daughter. 'He's going to be fine, but he's very old and his heart has had a bit of…' He paused, looking across at Luc for help.

Luc pitched in. 'As your dad says, he's an old man, but he's also very strong. His heart just needs to be looked after and then he'll be as good as new. And then he will be able to take you to see the animals.'

'Come along, now, sweetie,' said Scott. 'Why don't

Luc

you go and do some of your colouring. You could make a get-well card for Grand-Pere.'

Sophia, jumping off the stool, whooped. 'Yes, I will do that, Papa.' And she was gone, leaving crumbs and chocolate slicks in her wake.

Scott came across to Luc and slid his arms around her. 'Thank you.' He kissed her fully on the mouth.

A polite cough brought them apart. Mimi was holding a plate with pastries on the other side of the counter. 'And may I say,' she added. 'It's about time. Though I now owe Maurice, ten francs, as I said it would be next month before…' She broke off, grinning.

Scott looked at her in amazement, Luc just giggled. 'Mimi, you are incorrigible. And Maurice—you two devious…' And then he too was laughing.

Later, sitting in the lounge, Luc felt a contentment she had never known before. Scott loved her. Maurice was getting better. And her mother was back in her life. Scott had presented her with the translated story of Florence Blanchard, and she had already read some of it, enthralled with the story of a woman who had to fight to be heard. He now sat opposite her, sorting through a pile of papers and post; every so often pausing to remove his glasses to peer at something. Smiling to herself, she opened the book in her lap, turned to p three and began to read.

THE STORY OF THE BLANCHARD CHESS SETS BY M. FLAUBERT

Part 3

Paris 1823

Florence felt as though she was going to be sick seeing the master of the house. She swallowed the rising bile. She had to think fast. Michel had asked her to not tell his father about the breakage and the repair of the queen.

'Y-y-your secretary,' she stammered. 'It was your secretary who asked me to attend.'

Flaubert gestured for her to enter the salon, the room she had visited with her father five years ago.

The man sat himself in the armchair near the fireplace, crossing his legs. His thick lips played with a smirk, becoming a rather sardonic smile. Florence sensed the man was playing with her, enjoying her discomfort.

'My secretary? What for, may I ask?' He reached for a pipe, tamped down the tobacco before lighting it with a spill lit by the fire. Smoke rose, as he sucked greedily on the mouthpiece.

'I don't know, monsieur. He didn't explain.'

'How curious? I shall ring for him.' Flaubert moved his hand nonchalantly to the embroidered bell pull that hung near the mantlepiece. His eyes never leaving Florence's face.

'No!' Her voice was strident with panic.

Flaubert slowly closed his eyes, and then opening

Paris 1823

them, with the pupils reacting to the light, his face took on a sinister stare. His lip curled. 'Excuse me?' he thundered.

'Pardon, Monsieur. There has perhaps been a mistake. I won't take up any more of your time. I am so sorry.' Florence dropping her eyes to the floor, she curtsied and turned to leave and on doing so, her eyes rested on the chess set. Cobwebs and dust clothed each piece, the squares indistinguishable apart from one. A dust free circle where the queen should have stood. The same queen that nestled within her bag.

Flaubert was now on his feet. Any moment now he would see what she was seeing. He was walking towards her, his eyes dropping to her bosom.

'You play games with me, I think, cherie? I like to play with young women like you.'

Think, Florence. What must I do? Then a sudden thought came to her rescue. A small sigh escaped from her lips, and she put her hand to her forehead, turning her back to the chess and Michel's secret.

'Forgive me, sir, but I feel a little faint. Perhaps I could have a little wine or ale, please.'

Flaubert stopped in motion; Florence hoped it was his gentlemanly conscience taking over. *The bourgeoisie,* thought Florence, *are steeped in tradition. Perhaps this will work.*

The man frowned, turned on his heel and strode to a sideboard. Before he returned, Florence took the red queen from her pocket and placed it back on its square, delicately stretching a cobweb for a veil before straightening herself. Flaubert was making his way towards her, a crystal glass of amber liquid in each hand. He held one out to her.

Florence took a sip, and the fiery cognac slipped

down her throat, warming her neck and breast. She felt heat rise to her cheeks.

'Yes, a drink will help, I'm sure,' Flaubert said, tipping his glass and glugging a drink that would have set Florence back a year's salary. She sipped again and nodded her thanks.

'Now, where were we? I believe you came to see me,' the man said taking a step towards her. His hot breath seared her cheek as he leaned in to kiss her. Florence knew how to keep away from men, bourgeoisie or proletariat, gentlemen or beggars. She nimbly stepped to one side, as though dancing the cotillion, gathered her thoughts and murmured, 'Do you play?'

Flaubert lunged at her. 'What do you want to play? I am very good at games.' He leered and licked his lips.

She sidestepped and pirouetted away from him until the chess board was between them. 'How about chess?'

The man's eyes darkened, and he snarled, 'No one will ever play this, no one will ever touch this. My beautiful wife was taken from me; never touching it in her lifetime. It remains there, just as it did when I gave it to her. I lost my child that day too, a daughter. All I have now is my useless son.' His voice had risen to a shout and the door flew open.

'Pardon, monsieur. Are you well? Shall I call for the doctor?' The servant, who stood there with one arm behind his back, waited for his master to reply, but Flaubert just crumpled to the ground.

'Get out. GET OUT!' Flaubert screamed at Florence.

Florence slipped out into the hallway, followed by the footman, who closed the door behind him.

'You were lucky, mademoiselle. He usually throws things too.' To almost underline this statement, the sound of shattering glass came from the salon.

'Thank you,' sighed Florence. Shaken, she stepped gingerly towards the door. A loud hiss came from behind her.

'Florence… oh, Florence.'

Whipping around, thinking it was Flaubert, she was gratified to see Michel Flaubert standing on the lowest stair. His nightgown came to below his knees and his bare feet looked blue with cold.

'Is it returned?' he whispered, eyes shining bright as the candle flames in the decadent chandelier above them.

'Oui, monsieur. It is all returned.'

Joy sprang to the boy's features. 'Merci beaucoup, Florence Blanchard. I will never forget you. You have saved my life this night.'

Florence smiled at the boy. 'My pleasure, ma petit.'

The front door opened, and she went out into the night, hoping she would never have to return.

Paris 1824

Florence, in deep concentration, her eyes focused on the knight clamped to the work bench, didn't hear the tap at the door. Reaching for the sanding block to shape the edges smooth, she paused, her senses heightened, listening. No sound came. She resumed.

The knock that came next jerked her upwards. A sharp rat-a-tat-tat; a business knock. Before she could rise, the door swung open and a man entered followed closely by a bent old woman gesticulating at Florence, a torrent of words flooded into the room, her mouth moving continuously to a crescendo.

'Madame.' The man was addressing the woman who Florence now recognised as Collette, one of her neighbours. 'Please, enough of your prattling. Enough, I say.' He had raised his hand, and the torrent dried to a drip, drip of monosyllabic mutterings. The woman's eyes darted around, her fingers twisting, spittle dripping from her whiskery chin.

Florence was now standing, smoothed her apron and asked if she could help him in some way.

The man, barrel-chested, clad in purple-black reminded Florence of a strutting crow. His beady eyes fixed on hers and he cocked his head to one side as though listening.

'This woman says your father is missing. Is this true?'

A shudder went through Florence's body, but she stood her ground. 'What do you mean, gone missing? Who are you to ask me this?'

'I am with the police. Just answer the question,' came the blunt reply.

Florence swallowed before answering. 'My father is well. He is always going off around the whore houses and public houses. I don't know where he is.' She lifted her chin and folded her arms across her chest.

'She's killed him, she has,' the old crone shrieked.

The policeman laid a placatory hand on her arm. 'Enough, woman,' he barked. But the woman wasn't going to give in without a fight.

'She's done him in.' And with that she began to hunt around the room and then disappeared into the back room.

The man shook his head and grunted. 'When do you expect him back?'

'As I said, I never know where he is these days. Since he's taken to drinking it can be days before he comes home. I will tell him you were looking for him.' Florence held her stance, there was nothing to find here.

Suddenly a shrill scream came from the other room

Paris 1824

and the man shot off towards the noise with Florence following close behind. A wooden linen chest, crafted only recently by Florence, lay open with sheets and shirts, bloomers and aprons strewn around, like the guts of a dead animal. The old woman was kneeling in the centre clutching an embroidered cloth.

Florence crossed the room and grabbed at the cloth. 'Get off my things, you old hag. This was my mother's. Get your filthy hands off it!' The woman wouldn't let go. Florence slapped her—the loud thwack echoed through the room and the woman fell to one side. Florence pushed her away and began to bundle everything to her, scooping things to her chest. The old woman crawled across snatching at fabric, her cheek a blazing scarlet. She reared up in front of Florence, her clawed fingers ready to attack.

'Ladies. ENOUGH!' the man yelled, and the women froze, chests heaving, breath labouring.

'You,' he said pointing at the old woman. 'Out now. You're mad and I will lock you up in the Salpêtrière Hospital if you're not careful. And you…' He turned to Florence. 'Sort your things out. I will return next week, if I can be bothered, to meet with your father.' He strode towards the door to leave but not before the old woman shrieked once again pouncing onto a man's shirt.

'Blood! There's blood on this. She's killed him, I say, and she hid him in this box.'

Florence sat back on her heels and stared at the white cotton shirt, one of her father's, with droplets of something like rust. The man paused, held out his hand for the item and then sniffed the fabric. He looked back at Florence. 'This is blood.'

Florence slowly got to her feet and stumbled over to the policeman. 'That, sir, is not blood. It is the sap from the bloodwood tree. We use the wood for our chess pieces. It stains easily. Let me show you.' Florence led them back into the workshop and took the red knight from the vice and handed it to the policeman. He studied it carefully and then throwing his head back, roared with laughter.

'You said "we use the wood". Surely you, a mere woman cannot make these pieces of art.'

Florence mumbled that yes, she did make the pieces just like her father. He took up another piece from the table, the king. 'This is magnificent, the artistry. It is enchanting.' He returned the pieces to the workbench and laid the shirt on the back of a chair. 'Come, hag, be off with you. This woman is not a murderer, just a very bad liar. Her father is still very much alive and making these. He just has a large appetite for wine, women and song and who doesn't.' He leered at Florence at this. 'No pathetic woman could craft such beauty, such elegance.'

As the old woman shuffled towards the door, she hissed, 'I'm watching you, my girl.'

'Leave me be,' murmured Florence.

The two interlopers took their leave, and Florence bolted the door behind them. She almost fell into the chair by the fire. Exhaustion fell upon her like a Paris fog, and she wept.

Chapter Twenty-Five

LUC

Now, Luc, sitting in a comfortable chair surrounded by expensive furnishings and artwork, dipped her head and she too wept for Florence Blanchard.

Her weeping brought Scott to her side. 'You're reading about Florence?'

She nodded. 'She had such a tough life.' She pulled a tissue out and blew her nose. 'Why didn't they acknowledge her talent, her creativity? Women were governed by men, owned by their husbands and punished if they went against the norm. Even now in the twentieth century, women must fight for men to see them as equals. The women in my family were all seen as unimportant. It is so unfair.'

Scott agreed. Crouching beside her, he added. 'Maurice has suggested we set up an exhibition to celebrate the life and art of Florence Blanchard.' Taking her hands in his, he stared up at her. 'The rest of the story is important to Maurice: our story, the story of your grandfather, of Myrtle and Isobel, of his parents and of Edmund Cruso, but this also seems to be important to him.'

Hearsay

'Then that is what we must do. I have experience in setting up exhibitions, I can finally use my degree. I have some contacts back in London.' An image of her mother's paintings nudged into her mind. 'Perhaps a celebration of female artists from different eras.' A thrill of excitement rushed through her at the prospect of this turn of events. 'I can do this, we can do this, can't we?'

Scott smiled. 'I always knew you were the right woman for the job.'

'Well, it took you a while,' Luc mocked, grinning.

In answer, Scott stood and pulled her to her feet, kissed her and said, 'Right, we have work to do. We have other things to attend to first before we can start planning an exhibition. Can we go through all the stuff we've found out so far? I want to finish the jigsaw before we embark on the next project.'

Luc nodded and found herself being led along the hall to a room at the back of the house. Magnificent windows overlooked a lawn with sculptures set around it, shrubs and trees surrounding it, leaves unfurling, dots of colour daubed here and there: cherry blossom, clematis and azalea showing off their petals like fondant icing. The room had high ceilings that looked down on a huge table of white oak, the surface showing the knots and whorls where once branches and twigs had reached out to the sunshine. Piled on the polished wood were the folders they had put together in the library in Ashfield. The grey shoebox sat on top of the chessboard; scrawled words peeping out.

'Before we get started, I need to tell you something my mum told me.' Luc fiddled with a biro she had found lying next to the folders. Scott had taken his seat and looked up at her, waiting.

'She was there when the second body was discovered in the field. And she says it was…'

Luc

'Edmund Cruso,' Scott ended her sentence. 'Yes, I know. I read that when I went back to check the newspapers.'

'Why didn't you tell me?' Luc asked.

Scott pushed another chair away from the table and gestured for her to sit. She did so regarding his face. 'I didn't know what to think when I read it. There are so many loose ends to all of this. I know Maurice is telling the truth, that he is Edmund… was Edmund. Yet, I'm not sure what to make of it all. I haven't told him, by the way.'

Luc exhaled. 'Okay, so let's look back at our notes. I think we need to go further back to make sense of this other body. Why was it identified as Edmund?' She shook her head trying to make sense of it all.

'I don't know. Let's start with Eirene, Maurice's mother.' Scott opened one of the folders for clarity. 'Her death was suicide. We checked the newspapers and the registers, dates and so on. Yes, the death was recorded as a suicide. It seems she took herself off to the field when another circle appeared within the crop. According to Myrtle Hurt, who gave evidence at the inquest, Eirene, firmly believed in the magic of this phenomenon. She said it gave her strength. Apparently, this time she didn't come back, and Myrtle went looking for her. Luc, can you find the transcript?'

Luc nodded and said, 'You also need to know Myrtle Hurt is my grandmother,' before pulling across another folder, turning to a section and unclipping a sheet.

'Really? How?'

'Like I said last night, my grandfather was a bigamist. But let's do this in order. Here you are,' she said handing him the copied sheet.

Scott read aloud.

'"Her body stretched out across the circle—hands

and toes reaching to touch the upright cornstalks. I thought she was sleeping. As I called her name, I could see bright red lipstick had been drawn around her lips. Eirene rarely wore make up and this was unlike her. I touched her open palm, and it was ice cold. Her eyes glared at the sky. I remember trying to wake her, screaming for my husband, Brad, to come and help. I ran to the telephone box on the corner, we had no phone at the farm and dialled 999. The police and an ambulance came soon after and Bradley and I gave them all the information they asked for."'

'Now we also found out she had been collecting fly paper and soaking off the arsenic, according to Bradley Hurt's transcript.' Luc had turned to another sheet of paper and now read from this.

'"I arrived in Bounds End after the war. I met Eirene then. A strong woman, looking after a farm and a husband with dementia. She was concerned about her son, Edmund, who hadn't returned from the war. The authorities had said he was 'missing in action'. The last I remember we were in a mud hole, explosions going off all directions. We shouldn't have been there. The sergeant sent us out to bring back a corpse. Corporal Cruso was a friend and a loyal soldier, but his father thought he was a deserter and wouldn't waver from this idea.

They kindly took me in. I had no family. I helped on the farm and fell in love with a woman called Myrtle. She and Edmund had been sweethearts before the war. I looked after her in her grief at losing Edmund. Eirene never got over losing Edmund and her husband who passed away in his sleep not long after Myrtle and I were wed. I believe she killed herself with arsenic from flypapers. A tragic waste, in my opinion."'

'Something doesn't add up,' Scott muttered. 'I've

Luc

listened to Maurice's recordings about Bradley Hurt, and with all due respect, Luc, he sounds like a complete madman, violent and bitter. He seems to just lie all the time, even to the authorities.'

Luc nodded. 'I know. I'm beginning to get to know the real Bradley Hurt and not just hearsay from other people. He was a bully, maybe even a sociopath. He walked out on Myrtle leaving her destitute at a farm where she couldn't cope. He took their only child and went back to his first wife in Leeds, and they brought her up as theirs.' She paused. 'In some ways I feel sympathy for Elspeth, my granny in Leeds. She had lost a baby while her husband was in France fighting and she discovered she couldn't have any more children as the birth had complications. His answer to that, to allay his own pain of losing a son, was to infiltrate another man's home, take his girlfriend's trust, marry her and then walk out on taking his prize of a new baby back to Elspeth.'

They both fell silent, both pondering on this. Luc drummed her fingers on the table and then said. 'I have checked birth and marriage certificates, and they all prove it. In the eyes of the law, Myrtle was never married to Bradley because he was married to Elspeth.' She rose to her feet and went to the window, looking out across the lawn. 'And the frustrating thing of all of this is that I can't ask my grandfather any of this because I don't know where he is.'

Scott appeared next to her. 'I thought he'd died when you were young.'

Turning to him, she whispered. 'I thought so too. But no. According to my mum, he left Granny back in the sixties. He walked out on her, just like he had done with Myrtle all those years ago. She was so ashamed she pretended he'd died.'

Hearsay

'Are you thinking what I'm thinking, Luc?' Scott asked.

Luc looked at him. 'I think, the body in the crop circle was Bradley Hurt and Myrtle lied about who it was.'

'I think so too, but how can that be? None of this makes any sense.'

Luc scanned Scott's face for an answer, an explanation, anything. 'No, that's just ridiculous. Perhaps Myrtle was traumatised at finding another body, perhaps…'

'Let's have a break and think things through. I want to visit Maurice this afternoon, take him something to read.'

'May I come with you?'

Scott nodded, then he pulled her to him and held her tight. 'Whatever we find out, I am here for you,' he whispered into her hair. 'Always.'

THE STORY OF THE BLANCHARD CHESS SETS BY M. FLAUBERT

Part 4

Paris 1833

Florence had slept fitfully, her mattress hard and lumpy and woke to the red dawn brushing the city with a warm glow after a cold, monochrome night.

Removing her nightshift and placing it carefully on a wooden chair, she dressed quickly. Today she was summoned once again to the Flaubert house. Ten years previously, she had hoped she would never have to return. The intervening years had been a struggle for Florence. Not only because of so many rebellions in her beloved city bringing many to their knees and others to their untimely deaths, but she had been forced to tell the world her father had perished, for she knew not where he was, and now the sets she sold went for a lot less than before.

Entering the house, Florence could see little had changed, yet there was a different atmosphere, an essence of something she did not recognise and then the salon door flew open, revealing a man; the same chiselled face, but this was of a younger man with eyes bright with joy. She smiled. Michel, a grown man, a handsome man, thought Florence, blushing. He was half her age and a different class, yet she found herself self-consciously straightening her clothes and smoothing back her hair.

'Mademoiselle Blanchard. Welcome. Please come in,' Michel said, standing back for her to enter the room.

Hearsay

And here also was the change. Paintings had been moved about, the wallpaper was a soft pink and gold. The furniture was of the fashion, elegant but comfortable. Florence stood waiting.

'Please, sit down. Perhaps a drink or a sweetmeat? You have come a long way. You are looking well.' Michel seemed nervous, his fingers interlocking and twisting alongside his words.

Florence bowed her head and then looking up her eyes reached his; deep green, like the ocean she had only glimpsed within paintings in the galleries she attended with her mother.

'Thank you, you are very kind. Will your father be joining us?' At this the door opened and her heart strummed faster ready to face the monster, but it was a servant bearing a tray with a crystal decanter and goblets. After placing this on a side table, with gold leaf mouldings running down each bowed leg, he began to pour red wine and handed a glass first to Florence and then to his master. He stood aside, linking his arms behind his very straight back and waited. Michel nodded and the footman was gone, like a ghost slipping away.

Michel cleared his throat and announced. 'My father is dead. Santè!' They both sipped as the clock on the mantel suddenly struck the hour, three tinny dings filled the room. Time no longer stood still in this house. And that was the essence Florence had picked up. Life had returned.

'It is time to pay you for helping me all those years ago, Florence. May I call you Florence?'

Nodding slowly, she placed her glass on another side table, the marquetry pattern adorning the top, of trees and foliage seemed to encircle the swirling red liquid. 'You don't owe me anything, Monsieur Flaubert.'

Michel rose from his seat and moved across the room

Paris 1833

towards a stunning round mirror with plumes of golden feathers above and round the base, and above this a majestic eagle with its wings wide, ready to take off. Below the mirror stood a polished mahogany cabinet with yet more gold leaf, intricately carved cherubs, lions' heads and sunbursts. From where she sat, and from her own experience, Florence could appreciate the hours that craftsmen needed to create such beautiful furniture. Michel turned with a flourish. And in his hands lay the chess set. Returning to her side he placed it reverently on the table by her chair. Cobwebs and dust no longer remained. This was polished until each piece shone, the deep bloodwood contrasting with the white oak. This was cared for; a set ready for playing.

Returning to his seat, Michel explained, 'When my father passed away, he left strict instructions in his will to have this set buried with him and Mama in the family crypt. I, however, after a lifetime of following his instructions and living in the shadows with the ghosts of my family, rejected this idea. This is a piece of art that should be cherished.'

Florence stayed silent and reached a tentative hand to the red queen she had once repaired. It glowed dark red in the palm of her hand. No one would ever know it had been put back together, the fracture remained hidden within its outer shell.

'Would you teach me how to play, Monsieur Flaubert?' she whispered.

Michel shook his head sadly. 'I can't, Florence.'

Florence returned the queen to stand between the king and the bishop. 'I understand. It is not my place to ask. Forgive me.'

'No, you don't understand… I… I… I don't know how to play.'

Hearsay

Florence gazed at him, this sensitive, beautiful young man and found her lips twitch into a smile. In turn, Michel, with eyes sparkling, grinned and they laughed in unison at the irony of their situation.

Chapter Twenty-Six

LUC

On the plane home, Luc had tried to finish the translation of the book about Florence Blanchard, whose life seemed to be improving, but her thoughts kept returning to Scott and Maurice. She had stayed for a few days while Maurice was made comfortable in his own home. Mimi made up a bed in his study which he was not happy about, but eventually seeing sense he settled in, especially when Scott moved a television in there.

Having arranged to visit her mum in Shropshire again, Luc was keen to see her and to find out more about the family. Saying goodbye to Scott, this time, was hard and they held each other tightly before letting go. They promised to call each other regularly and once Maurice was a bit stronger; Scott would come and visit.

In some ways, the need to discover their past was becoming less urgent and the need to plan their future became more uppermost in their minds. Unearthing a needle of truth amongst a haystack of lies was getting easier, but each time they found one needle another glinted from the past. Their late-night-into-the-morning discussions had become more about love and what that meant to them.

Hearsay

They wanted to learn from past mistakes on their own part but also of the people who had preceded them.

Now, Luc was following behind her mother along a pleasant, carpeted corridor. The Chetwynd Firs Care Home in Ashfield, where Myrtle Hurt now lived, was a block of Georgian splendour. It had been adapted sympathetically for modern living and for residents over seventy to reside comfortably. Isobel stopped outside a cream-coloured door, knocked and went in, ushering Luc before her.

Even though the room was bright with sunshine streaming through a large window, Luc had a sense of being hemmed in. Every surface was smothered in either ceramic ornaments: birds, fish, butterflies, dogs and cats or potted plants with leaves of every hue and size. Within all of this, a dainty white-haired elderly lady sat in a pink chenille armchair knitting. The click clacks of the needles kept in time with the enormous clock to her left. Bars of an electric fire glowed red and a black cat lay stretched out on the multi-coloured rug. Pointed ears twitched and turned and bronze eyes blinked open observing the intruders.

Isobel shimmied around the sofa and bent to whisper to the woman. The clacking stopped and Luc found herself being under intense scrutiny by both her mother and this stranger. Isobel straightened. 'Let me introduce you to your grandmother, Myrtle Hurt. Myrtle, this is Lucretia.'

The elderly woman beamed. 'Oh, Lucretia, how lovely to finally meet you. Isobel has told me so much about you.' She patted the sofa. 'Come and sit down.'

Luc did as she was told, perching on the edge of an over-stuffed sofa piled high with velvet cushions. Myrtle went on. 'I always have a sherry around now. Would you

Luc

like one, my dear? It might bring some colour back to those pale cheeks. Izzie, love, do the honours please.'

The cat was nowhere to be seen as Luc was handed a glass of amber liquid. Taking a sip and swallowing down the taste of Christmas, Luc felt more in charge of her faculties to speak. 'It's very nice to finally meet you, Myrtle.'

'I understand from Isobel that you have been doing a bit of detective work.'

Luc nodded, aware her mother had sat down, and she glanced sideways to this vision of colour who was not like the mother she had grown up with.

Myrtle continued, 'A lot of things in life get forgotten or adapted, moulded into our memories.'

'Sometimes, I feel like I'm in Bladerunner. Discovering new identities of human beings,' Luc said.

'Charming!' spluttered Isobel.

'Sorry. No, I didn't mean... you know... I...' Luc trailed off.

A warm hand patted her own cool one. It was Myrtle. 'I know what you're going through, my dear. Imagine discovering your own daughter on your doorstep after... what was it, Izzie?'

'Almost fifty years, Mum,' Isobel responded. 'It was just as much of a shock for me. I thought my mother was Elspeth Hurt.'

Luc flinched as the cat sprang from nowhere onto the back of the sofa.

'Jones, get down from there. Lucretia doesn't need you bothering her,' Myrtle said.

'I'm fine. He's fine. It just made me jump, that's all,' Luc remonstrated.

'She's a girl. And just like you, I like a bit of Harrison Ford too. Very handsome in Bladerunner. I loved him in

The Empire Strikes Back and of course, Raiders of the Lost Ark. I love going to the pictures, do you?' Myrtle's eyes were shining above her sherry glass, and she chuckled. 'You think I'm too old for that sort of thing. It's not just for you youngsters, you know.'

Luc felt she was now slipping into another dimension but continued in the same vein. 'I love going to the cinema, Myrtle.'

'Perhaps, Izzie could take us to see the new one coming out. What do you think?'

Before, she fell into a vortex of total disbelief, Luc apologised. 'Look, I'm really sorry. I would love to come to the cinema with you but please can you both just explain the stories.'

'Oh, yes. Well, in The Empire Strikes…'

Luc held up her hand to stop Myrtle giving a synopsis of a film she had seen herself three times. 'No, I mean your story. Please can you tell me what happened, from the beginning.'

'Oh, I see. Yes, of course. Oh Izzie, dear, I don't seem to have any more sherry. Be a dear, won't you?'

In answer, Isobel, swished off into the miniscule kitchen saying, 'I think tea might be better, Mum.'

Myrtle harumphed. 'She's no fun. She's probably right though.' Sitting back in her armchair, she sighed. 'Where shall I start?'

'How about the beginning?' Luc said, her voice gentle.

'The beginning was a long time ago, but I'll try. Bradley was the one who broke my heart and patched it up to only smash it into tiny pieces. When he came and told us Edmund was dead, my whole world fell apart. Edmund hadn't replied to my letters but had corresponded with his mother, Eirene. She and I used to

Luc

pour over those flimsy sheets, reading every word a thousand times and every word that lay under the surface was a topic of discussion.'

Myrtle paused while sherry glasses were swapped with teacups, steam swirling from a milky brew. Laying the cup and saucer down, she continued.

'We had a bond. The two of us were given a pawn each. Me the red one and Eirene the white. She used her dowsing rods to find mine in the leaves of the forest. I thought then that Edmund would come back to me. He would forgive my silly outburst over me wanting a diamond ring and we would marry and be together. I took to helping on the farm. Eirene and I believed Edmund would return, and that knowledge kept us both warm on those chilly early mornings getting the cows in for milking.'

She shifted in her seat. 'Bradley handed me Edmund's identity tag. A red one. I found out later that he left the green one on his… the body. That's what they did, you know, to keep count of all the dead.' Her voice cracked and she took a taste of her tea. Luc turned her eyes to the clock, hoping the woman wouldn't think her rude. Her movement had been noted.

Myrtle continued, 'Anyway, to cut a long story short, Eirene invited Brad to stay. We needed help on the farm. We got to know each other, and he proposed. Not many young men came back from the war, you know. I didn't want to be an old maid, so I said yes. He was very dashing then, very charming. Izzie came along soon after and everything was fine, until Eirene passed away. That was tough. I was fond of her and Sidney. He had died in his sleep in the previous November. Towards the end he began to say that Edmund had been to the house and was sure he was alive. He said Edmund had taken the chess set which Brad had returned to the family on his first arrival. Brad got very angry with him. It was awful—they used to argue and shout at each other. The chess set couldn't be found, and we all thought Sidney had hidden it somewhere. He had no memory of things he did during the day. Anyway, it was forgotten by Brad and Sidney. Chess wasn't important to them or me come to think of it, but I kept the red pawn in my jewellery box along with Edmund's red tag. It was a memory of Edmund, of happier times before a war which left so much hardship and pain.

Eirene would go off dowsing in the fields and looking for crop circles. She would come in late at night covered in mud after digging in the field trying to find the tin holding the white pawn. She began to say things like Edmund wasn't dead, that she had seen him. She had seen him at the train station with his kit bag after the war. She said she hadn't been sure at the time but as she became older, she seemed to become more and more reluctant to let go. She wanted Brad to help contact the authorities to check. He told her as a deserter he was unimportant, that it wouldn't be worth it.'

'We thought he was missing in action,' interceded Luc. 'Was that not the case?'

'That's what Brad had originally told us. Then one day just before Sidney passed, he told us that Edmund Cruso had been a coward, that he'd given his tags to Brad and that he'd run off. Of course, Eirene thought he might still be alive, but in the end, she couldn't cope with the not-knowing. She took her own life in one of her beloved crop circles.' Myrtle again put down her cup. 'And then, Brad stole away in the dead of night with my darling baby girl. She was only two. Given to another woman to bring her up. He left a note, warning me not to follow him. Izzie

Luc

knew nothing of this until her father told her in 1968 and that was when she appeared on the doorstep at the farm.'

A single tear trickled down a cheek, criss-crossed with the lines of life. Luc knelt next to the old woman. 'I'm sorry. I didn't mean to upset you.' Taking one of her hands, she added. 'I can come back another time. You look tired. After all we have a lot of catching up to do.'

Myrtle pulled out a lacy hankie, embroidered with a lone M and wiped her eyes. The tears were spilling over now. 'No, I'm sorry. I'm sorry for not looking for your mother. It was just after the war and the farm needed my attention and…' Luc patted her hand.

Luc closed her eyes, trying to soak up all this new information. Such a lot to process, but now was not the time. She felt a hand on her shoulder and looked up to see her mother leaning towards her. 'She'll be all right, love. Let's get off back to the farm. We can talk another time.'

Before standing, Luc slipped her arms around Myrtle's shoulders saying, 'We have a lot to talk about. We'll be back tomorrow. If that's okay with you?'

Red-rimmed eyes crinkled at the edges and Myrtle smiled. 'We have a date, don't we? The pictures remember?'

Luc grinned. 'We have a date.' She went to the door and almost missed Myrtle's final remark.

'I gave it to Izzie.'

'What did you give me, Mum?' Isobel asked, hovering by the open door.

'The red pawn. I hid it in a woollen cardigan when her father took her away. He probably chucked it away.' The old lady sighed and shook her head sadly.

Luc rushed around the sofa and dropped to her knees by Myrtle once again. 'She gave it to me. Look.' She lifted her pendant out from under her jumper. 'I wear it always.'

And just as Maurice had done, Myrtle reached out to

Hearsay

touch the wooden pawn. 'Oh,' she said in wonderment. 'Will you look at that? Bradley must have kept it after all.'

Isobel sat down heavily next to her mother and daughter. 'No, my mum… Elspeth, gave it to me when I was eight. She had hidden it from my father since that first day I arrived. She was a good woman, you know.' She sniffed loudly. 'A wronged woman in so many ways. She took the bruises and the cuts to protect me.'

Luc found herself on the sofa holding her mother while she sobbed away the hurt from her childhood. Myrtle patted Isobel's back and then rose unsteadily to her feet. 'I think another sherry is in order, don't you?' Then almost as an afterthought, she said, 'You'll find the white pawn on the mantlepiece. Well, I think it is. My cleaner may have moved it.'

With everything else going on, Luc had quite forgotten her mum had said Myrtle might have the white pawn. *And just like that*, Luc thought to herself, *without fanfare or fireworks we finally find the missing piece.*

Leaving her mum on the sofa, Luc went to the wood-effect fireplace. The whole surface of the shelf above the gas fire was smothered in knick-knacks—Wade animals, gonks, silver pots, a ceramic figurine. *It's like a Bring and Buy sale,* Luc thought, *just like Elspeth's house, full of dust-catchers.* And there, tucked in between a miniature cup and saucer and a little pot with Greetings from Tenby stood the white pawn.

Luc took it and held it in her palm. A tiny piece of wood that had opened up so many stories: of the war, of the 19th century, of her own life. This was it. *How can such a tiny thing link so many of us together?* 'So, Eirene found it after all,' she murmured.

'No, she didn't,' said Myrtle, coming over to her. 'She died having never found it.'

Luc

'So, how did it get here?'

Myrtle chuckled. 'Life happens in mysterious ways. Come and sit down. I'll let your mum tell you that story.'

Chapter Twenty-Seven

MAURICE

Maurice was sitting in his favourite chair next to the fireplace. He looked sadly down at the tray in his lap, a plate of fruit stared back at him. Mimi had strict instructions to keep him on a healthy diet and as a joke had laid the strawberries as eyes, peach slices as a mouth. But even this didn't entice him to eat it.

He looked across at his grandson who was speaking animatedly into the phone. Scott placed the receiver on its cradle and wandered over to sit opposite him.

'Well?' Maurice asked, raising his eyebrows.

'Well,' Scott began. 'What would you like to know first?'

'How is Lucretia? Is she well? Has she seen Myrtle?' He felt like a child again, waiting in anticipation for Christmas morning to arrive, not that there were ever many gifts then, but like now he was optimistic. Then he always hoped mum would have bought him a catapult or even a train set, now, he just wanted one tiny piece of wood, because that would bring his story to a close. Now as an adult, he went through the polite questions asking

Maurice

after people first when all he wanted was to be that child once again.

Scott, seeming to sense Maurice's excitement, answered quickly. 'Luc is well. She has met Myrtle…'

'And how is she? Is she well? Does she remember me?' It wasn't the bit of wood that mattered after all, it was his first love that he wanted to know about. The chess wasn't important, not at this moment, anyway.

'Luc says Myrtle is very well, living in a posh care home in Ashfield. They chatted for a long time. And they have the white pawn. You'll never guess how they found it.'

Maurice wasn't interested in that. 'Don't worry about that now. But she remembers me?'

Scott grinned. 'Yes of course she does. She wants to see you as soon as you are better.'

'Really?' Maurice felt like all of his Christmases had finally come. Then, looking down at himself, he added. 'I'm just an old man now. What will she think of me?'

Scott laughed. 'She's an old lady, with white hair now. Luc said they're going to the cinema together and then out to a wine bar in Ashfield.'

Maurice chuckled. 'Can we fly there tomorrow? I'd like to do that too.'

'No. You have to eat up your fruit and get well. Mimi will be here in a minute, and she won't be happy if it's not all gone.' Scott stood and stretched. 'And if you do that you can have a small coffee.'

Maurice knew he was beaten. Myrtle wouldn't be interested in an old sick man. He polished off the fruit and was duly rewarded with an espresso.

Settling back in his chair, happier than he'd been for a long time he said, 'Now, you can tell me all about the white pawn.'

Hearsay

Scott re-told the story that Lucretia had just revealed on the phone. A story of a sleepy village Summer Fete and a little girl and her father bringing her Sindy doll and its clothes and bits of toy furniture to sell at a stall. 'Luc called it a White Elephant stall. I don't know what that is, I'm afraid,' Scott added.

Maurice looked up and chuckled. 'I do. It's when you bring things to sell that you don't want, because they are too costly to look after, for example having to look after an elephant, or things you don't want anymore. Go on.'

Scott continued. 'The little girl had helped Myrtle to set up the stall and she was displaying her doll with various accessories. Myrtle noticed a little wooden ornament on the doll's table and thought it resembled the red chess piece she used to have. The little girl saw her holding it up and explained that her daddy had found it in a field, with his metal detector. It was buried treasure in a battered metal tin and so she had used it as a candlestick for her little table.'

'Well, I never!' exclaimed Maurice. 'How extraordinary!'

'It really is,' agreed Scott. 'So, Myrtle paid the little girl and kept the pawn. Luc said it was hidden amongst lots of things on Myrtle's mantlepiece.'

'I need to get well quickly, so I can visit Myrtle and re-unite the chess pieces.'

'Well, Luc has said she will arrange for you to speak with Myrtle on the phone very soon.'

Maurice felt tears prick his eyes. 'She wants to speak with me. After all this time. Yet, I let her down. I was the coward. I should have gone to her after the war, but I was so scared. Scared of being turned away again, terrified my family didn't want me.' He rubbed at his eyes with the back of his hand.

Maurice

'No.' Scott was adamant. 'You were never a coward. You were wronged by a man who you trusted. The war took away your identity when Bradley Hurt took away your identity tags. You have lived your life with grandma and our family, and I admire and love you for the life you have given me.'

Tears returned to Maurice's eyes, listening to his grandson speak. 'Your parents are so proud of you, Scott.'

'I know and I need to phone them very soon. They've been travelling in the Andes, so I haven't been able to speak with them. They return to California in the next few months, I think. I will have to take Luc out there to meet them. Tell them, I want to marry her.'

Maurice gazed across at Scott and smiled. 'Really? That's marvellous. When did you propose?'

'I haven't yet. Perhaps when we go to the UK.'

Maurice struggled to sit more upright. 'Finally, some good news.' He waved away Scott's words about Myrtle and the chess set. 'A new chapter begins, a new generation. I'm so pleased for you. I had better get well. Go and get me some of that delicious fruit, I need to be well and strong for you all.'

Scott laughed at this. 'Mimi will be very happy. I'll go and see her and see what she can do.' He went off to the kitchen leaving Maurice with his thoughts of the future and the past. The far distant past came to him as he looked once again at the chess board set up on a small, elegant table beside him. *Now, we need to put right the worst wrong in this tale. Florence needs to be acknowledged as the true creator,* he perused.

THE STORY OF THE BLANCHARD CHESS SETS BY M. FLAUBERT

Part 5

PARIS 1833

Florence swept along the pavement, above the cobbled street where the filth of the city lay. People of note enjoyed walking around showing off the fashions of the day and today was no different. Florence had already seen many people adorned with extravagant hats, velvet and brocade coats, dresses and suits of rich silks and satin, yet in many areas of Paris, the squalor and filth still piled up. But there was a change in the air, a more positive air. The city had lived through so much, the recent revolution in June 1832 had changed so much and yet very little, depending on where you lived and who you were. There was a new monarch on the throne of France, perhaps Louis-Philippe would bring calm and order after so much rebellion. For Florence, life was constant. She worked, she ate, she slept. There was little time for entertainment, yet she would always find time to visit an art gallery or to walk in one of the parks and appreciate nature.

A chilly spring wind ruffled at Florence's hair loosening a ringlet from her tightly fitting bonnet. Her coat and dress were simple compared to the richness she had passed by, but she walked with her head held high, proud of what she had achieved. With the help of Michel Flaubert, she had made two sales. The bourgeois

Paris 1833

households took her in on the merit of her father. They believed her explanations that these were sets he had crafted before he had died. They never supposed that she, Florence Blanchard had designed and made the chess sets they now played in their sumptuous salons or their decadent dining rooms.

Another sale that day and she now could feel the comfortable weight of coins within the drawstring bag swinging at her elbow. Another set crafted by her but not crafted by her for she was a weak woman, weak and uneducated. How could she make such things of elegance and beauty? She smiled inwardly at this thought. If they only knew.

Yet, she still remembered the policeman and that mad, old crone from down the street searching through her things trying to find her father. Thinking the stains from the bloodwood were of blood. Suggesting that Florence had killed Gabriel. She turned into another street with high buildings, the windows staring down at her, challenging her with the lies she had told over the years. *I am the one going mad,* she thought. *Will the police return? I have nothing to hide and yet I don't feel safe. That drunken sot of a father: he must be dead by now, surely. One day the two worlds I exist between will collide and then where will I be?*

Deep in thought as she arrived at the end of her own street, it took her a moment to realise that outside her front door stood two horses and a carriage, all three polished to a glossy shine. Drawing herself back into an alleyway, she watched and listened. The horses shook their magnificent coal-black heads, snorting smoke like dragons, their bridle and brasses clinking and rattling.

It could be a new client, her heart whispered. *It could be the police*, replied her head. It could mean a commission, or it could mean prison. She wasn't a fearful woman, yet perhaps the past was now catching up with her, perhaps it was time to come clean. It was not just what had happened to Gabriel but also the other matter she had held to her heart all this time; the timely death of Henri Placquette.

With no time to think on that matter, she collected herself, with her heart in her mouth, Florence decided to continue her walk down the street and pretend she didn't live there. She pulled her bag close to her heart and glided towards the carriage; the rich smell of the horse leather mixing with the odour of manure as she passed. She set her face forwards, her bonnet hiding her from either side.

'Florence!'

A shout from within the carriage caused her to pause briefly but she continued. Friend or foe, she was unsure, yet she continued her way.

The shout came again; this time punctuated by the clatter of boots on the cobbles. Whipping around, she saw the figure was one she knew. Michel Flaubert. The relief must have reflected in her face as he darted towards her grabbing her arm. With her head spinning she held onto him.

'Are you quite well, Florence? Here let me help you.' His voice, tender, his expression showing concern, she allowed herself to be escorted to her door. In a daze, she handed him the key, a plain rusted affair with a ribbon and wooden toggle dangling from it.

Taking the key, he bent to unlock the door. Pushing it open he led her to the wooden settle beside the open fire, embers just glowing behind a metal framed screen.

'Do you have any wine or ale?' Michel asked.

Florence nodded and gestured to the back room. He disappeared while she found her breathing return and discovered she was clinging to her draw-string bag. He soon returned and offered a glass of wine, which she took

Paris 1833

and swallowed in one draft. Warmth from this and the fire seemed to bring her to her senses. Michel had seated himself on the chair opposite, that of her father's, observing her over the rim of his glass and she felt her skin colouring.

'Oh Monsieur, I am so sorry. You must think me so silly.' She went to rise, her legs not responding, and she thought better of it and sank back down again.

'Florence, you don't need to apologise. I am glad I was here to help you. Are you unwell? Have you eaten today?'

His questions and another mouthful of wine brought her to ponder on the situation. Yes, she had eaten, no, she wasn't unwell. And then the memory of the police and the old crone returned alongside the ghost of her father, and she found the pain of tears scratching her eyes and she sobbed.

A lace-edged handkerchief was thrust at her. Dabbing her face and blowing her nose gave her time to realise the burden she had carried for so long, the pretence and the hiding in the shadows. The man sitting opposite her now, she knew she could trust. The man whom she had seen as a child devoid of his father's love, a boy who had lost his mother and so she told him her tale. The visit by the police, of the neighbours wanting to see her father, how he had disappeared into the night and had never returned, how she had searched for him night after night and how, for a while, she had continued to make the chess sets and pretend her father had made them.

Silence met the ending of her story; she held her breath. Had she been right in opening up to this man she hardly knew?

When he spoke, his voice was strained, and he coughed to clear the words. 'Florence, you are safe now. I will take care of you. You can continue to work for me making your chess pieces. You do not need to hide behind your father anymore. We will tell the world that you are the true artist.'

'It is not just that. I think I killed a man…'

Michel stared at her, his eyes narrowing. 'What do you mean? Who? When?'

Florence's voice sounded high and tight to her own ears. 'It was in self-defence. A man who attacked me many years ago. Henri Placquette was his name.'

'Tell me what happened, Florence,' Michel urged. 'Why do you think you killed him?'

'He attacked me, and I was holding a bradawl to defend myself.' She stood, her head still swimming, and went to her workbench. 'One of these.' She held up a metal tool. 'I discovered later on he had been found on the banks of the Seine, bleeding from a cut in his side. I had thought the red on my hand was just the sap of the bloodwood, the wood I use for the pieces. I was so thankful my father wouldn't owe him so much money I did nothing about it.' Florence fell into her seat, the weight she had carried for so long, now seemed to float above her head, between her and this young man who had been so kind to her.

Michel leaned forward, 'Florence, I am sure if what you say is true about this man, he had many enemies. It may not have been your cut that killed him. There has been so much bloodshed in this city in the name of revolution and it is time for you to stop worrying about this man. Life needs to move on for you, for Paris, just like it has for me.'

A banging at the door, a shout and a flurry of blackness surged into the room and Florence and Michel stood as one at the interruption. Two men—one being the coachman—were remonstrating with each other, 'You cannot enter, sir.'

The other shouting, 'Unhand me, get out of my way. I am an officer of the law.'

'What is the meaning of this intrusion, Gilbert?' Michel asked, his voice thick with anger.

The coachman answered quickly. 'Monsieur Flaubert, a thousand apologies. I tried to stop him, but he was adamant he must see Mademoiselle Blanchard immediately.'

'Mademoiselle Blanchard,' the policeman announced. 'I am here to tell you a body has been found, well what is left of what was once a man.'

A coldness crawled across Florence's skin.

The man continued, 'We believe it is your father.'

Florence raised one hand to her open mouth, a gasp escaping as she fell back into her seat, heat now sweeping over her. Above her, the voices continued.

'A stab wound punctures the heart. Rocks were in the pockets, holding it down in the Seine. I am here to arrest this woman as we believe she has killed her father.'

'NO! That is not true!' Florence screamed. 'My father walked out. I searched for him. I searched for weeks.'

'You have been pretending all this time that your father deserted you.' The policeman grabbed her wrist, yanked her hard out of her chair and tried to drag her to the door.

Florence clung to Michel, and he held her tight. She stared up into his face. 'This is all lies. Please, Monsieur Flaubert, Michel, I beg of you, please don't believe all of what he says.' The policeman pulled her away, his strength unmatched by either Florence or Michel.

'Unhand her, sir.' Michel was shouting. 'She is innocent until proven guilty. You cannot take her.'

Hearsay

Florence was bundled out of the door, digging her heels in, scratching at the man's face. Michel's voice rang in her ears, 'I will get the best lawyer in Paris, Florence. Where are you taking her, sir?'

'The Salpêtrière Hospital for the criminally insane,' came the reply. 'Until she goes to court, she will be held there.'

Florence squealed with pain as she was thrown into the back of a covered cart, a barred door clanged shut and a key rasped in a lock. Pulling herself to the door, she could see Michel Flaubert and Gilbert, his coachman, standing together while a horde of by-standers gawked at her. A missile of rotten cabbage hit the bars, while the crowd shouted obscenities, and she ducked down to protect herself. The cart lurched and moved away from the crowd, away from her saviour, Michel Flaubert and away from the curiosity of strangers.

Pulling herself into a tight ball, Florence's mind raced with thoughts and images of where she was going. She had seen the women in the hospital grounds raving as she passed. *I am not mad, I am just a woman*, her heart shouted. *Just like them*, her head replied.

Chapter Twenty-Eight

LUC

Luc sat back on her heels and wiped the sweat off her forehead. A hot summer's day was not a time for painting a kitchen, she thought. Across the room she could hear her mum humming to herself, as she too slapped paint on a wall and Luc smiled to herself. Luc had booked some days off work, and she had offered to help with some decorating at the farm. The kitchen had been stripped and new fitted cabinets now adorned the walls; their stark whiteness standing out against the mustard yellow.

The two women worked on for another hour or so finally stopping for a sandwich which they took out to the back garden with a jug of lemonade and a bowl of strawberries.

Bees buzzed lazily in the large pink daisies while a pale blue butterfly fluttered from one lavender bush to another. In the distance the sound of a combine harvester biting through the wheatfields, cutting the stalks, separating the grain brought new noises to Luc's ears. Growing up in the middle of Leeds, she had spent the occasional day out in the countryside or on the moors and had been stuck behind farm machinery on narrow lanes, but she had never really listened to the clanking, droning of the giant beasts chomping through the waving wheat and barley to leave sharp, spiky stubble.

Scott was due to visit in a few days' time, and they wanted to get the decorating finished before then. There was a lot to do. Isobel hadn't done very much to the house, just focused her time on her studio and her art. Luc spent many evenings talking late into the night with her mum, drinking in all the things she had missed about her mum's life and in turn Isobel gorged herself on Luc's life and what she had missed.

Returning to the kitchen, both Luc and Isobel paused to admire their work. 'We're nearly there, I think, Luc. That extra coat was certainly necessary. Even your father would be impressed.'

Luc grinned. 'I like it. Brings in the sunshine. It was so dark in here before.'

They got back to work, now with the radio on— Radio 1 playing summer songs and they sang along to Kate Bush and Madonna, their voices rising together.

Later that evening, the two of them sat once again in the garden side by side on stripy deckchairs, this time toasting their painting success with a glass of chilled rose. Conversation turned as always to their life apart, but Luc wanted to lead it further back.

'Mum, why do you think Myrtle didn't come looking for you?'

Isobel glanced across and sighed. 'From what she has told me, I don't think she was able to. She had discovered she was pregnant just before Dad and I left. She had been waiting for the right time to tell him and so he never knew. The shock of losing me brought on a miscarriage and she was very poorly for a while. It was just after the war, she didn't have much money, so couldn't afford to travel to

Luc

Leeds. They didn't have a phone then and I think she just gave up. She lost so many people she loved; all of the fight went out of her.'

'How did she manage the farm by herself? Were there farmworkers here to help?'

'As you know, Luc, a lot of young men didn't return from the trenches. The farm was rented; Myrtle thought she would be thrown out. The owner came to her rescue. He was recently widowed and had one daughter. He asked Myrtle to stay on as housekeeper and nanny and he moved into the farm. He kept it going and the farm was flourishing. Apparently, he was very good with the livestock, looking after the calves and suchlike.'

Luc gasped. 'Maurice came back in the 1930's. He said he'd seen Myrtle with a little girl skipping along and they'd been talking about how the girl's daddy had helped a cow with a difficult calving. He thought they'd been talking about Brad. He assumed Myrtle was still married to Brad and this was their daughter. That's why he never said anything.'

Isobel sighed. 'What a shame. That's so sad.'

Luc agreed. 'But,' she continued, 'he was married to Rose by then. He couldn't have been with Myrtle. And then of course the Second World War came along.'

'Life is full of 'what ifs',' murmured Isobel.

'Yes, like what if grandad was still alive to explain himself?' Luc asked. 'He would have several of us clamouring to know why he behaved the way he did.'

'I think I would be first in line,' Isobel muttered under her breath.

'Really, but he doted on you.'

'I think that was the guilt from snatching me from my real mum. He knocked Elspeth around; he bullied me into going to be a secretary when I wanted to go to art college.'

Isobel's voice rose with anger at the memories. 'He was a cruel, manipulative man. I hope he rots in hell.'

Luc bit her lip. While her mum was angry with her grandfather this was the time to ask her. She knew what she was going to ask next might have a catastrophic effect on her relationship with her mum, but she had to know. Taking a deep breath, she said, 'Mum?'

Isobel drained her glass and filled it up quickly. 'Yes, love.' Her words were slurring a little around the edges.

'Mum, why did Myrtle say that the body she found in the crop circle was Edmund Cruso? Was it…' She had to know. 'Was it grandad's body?'

Isobel snorted into her drink. 'Why would you think that? He walked out on Elspeth and God knows where he is now. He's probably dead in a ditch somewhere.'

'But why did Myrtle lie about it?'

'I don't know, love. Perhaps you should ask her. She was probably confused with the shock of another body in the field. She must have been traumatised.'

'Didn't the police question her? There must have been an investigation. We couldn't find out much about it.'

'When was the body found?' asked Isobel.

'1969, I think. July 20th seems to ring a bell. I'll have to check my notes.'

'Well of course there wouldn't be much in the news then. That was the day of the moon landings. I remember it well. A good day to hide a murder, my father would have said. A day when something big happens in the world and the petty thieves and criminals come out like rats in the night.'

'Of course. I hadn't thought of that.' Luc drank her own wine down and deciding not to have another and to get an early night, said, 'I think I'll go to bed. A lot to do

Luc

tomorrow.' At the door, a thought came to her. 'Mum, you would have been here then. In 1969, you were here. Why didn't you identify the body? Did you suspect it might be your father?'

Isobel glared at Luc, her eyes narrowing. 'I wasn't here. I was away seeing friends in Shrewsbury. I found out about it when I got back. It's nothing to do with me, or you for that matter.' Isobel pointed a finger jabbing it at Luc, her voice now harsh. 'Leave it alone, Luc. It doesn't matter anymore. It's not important. It was sixteen years ago for God's sake.' Her hand was shaking now. Luc stared back at her mother.

'I'm sorry. I didn't mean to upset you. I'll get off to bed and see you in the morning.' Luc fled into the house, up the stairs and shut her bedroom door behind her. *I wish Scott was here, he would know what to do, what to say.* Her mind was in turmoil. Was it the drink making her mum so angry or was it something deeper more suspicious than that? What was she hiding?

Luc slept fitfully and woke to another hot summer's day. Pulling on denim shorts and a T shirt she padded downstairs in her bare feet. Isobel was sitting at the kitchen table with a coffee mug and toast, reading a book. She turned at Luc's arrival. 'Luc, I'm so sorry about last night. I don't know what came over me. Please forgive me.'

Sighing, Luc went to her mother and hugged her. 'There's nothing to apologise for. I'm sorry I keep asking you questions.' She went to the kettle and shook it, water sloshed back and forth, and she raised the lid on the range exposing the hotplate. While the kettle boiled, she found cereal and milk and finally sat down opposite her mum.

'I think you're right. It doesn't matter. Not in the great scheme of things.' Luc munched her cornflakes reading the back of the packet. *A free gift of a sunhat was available if you bought 5 boxes of cereal,* she read. *Wow, not exactly free then, is it? Well, nothing in life is free*, she mused. *You think you're getting a bargain but in actual fact it's a rip off. There's always something in the small print that you haven't read. The small print…* Luc's mind turned over and over like a plough slicing through earth. Then another thought came and with it a plan.

'Mum, would it be all right if I go shopping today. I'd like to get a new outfit for when Scott comes over. He's booked a fancy restaurant. I thought I could go over to Shrewsbury.'

Isobel's face brightened. 'Of course, love. What a great idea. We could make a day of it. Mother and daughter shopping together.'

Luc attached a false smile to her face. This was not what she had in mind, but before she could say anything Isobel was continuing. 'Oh no, I'm sorry. I can't today. I need to organise the paintings for my exhibition. We could go tomorrow.'

Luc's heart began to beat again. Relief! 'I think I'll still go today but we could go and have a coffee in Ashfield tomorrow perhaps.'

It was Isobel's turn to smile this time. She leaned across and patted Luc's hand. 'Yes, that's a good idea and we could invite Myrtle. She'd like that.'

'It's a date.' Luc grinned. After putting the breakfast things into the new dishwasher, Luc almost skipped up the stairs. The clothes shopping would be fun, but she also wanted to check something first, at the records office.

Chapter Twenty-Nine

MAURICE

It was late September before Maurice was well enough to fly to London and then to travel up to the village of Bounds End in Shropshire. Scott drove the hire-car along the high street, Maurice could see children searching for conkers below the spreading trees and smiled to himself. Memories of him and Bobby doing the same thing came to his mind's eye and winding down the window he listened to the shouts of glee from those who had been successful in discovering a glossy brown treasure that was destined to be a niner for sure.

They turned right and soon arrived at the farm. Luc's little Hillman Imp was already there, parked up in the farmyard. And as Scott drew up next to it the back door of the house opened, and Luc flew down the path to greet them. She hugged them both and Maurice noticed the autumn sun sparkle off a large diamond on her left hand. His grandson had done the right thing, he mused. A diamond, not a bit of wood, was the way to a woman's heart. But then, he pondered further, none of this would ever have happened without those bits of wood. Fate intervened when it was needed to shape our lives.

Maurice allowed himself to be led into the house and into the kitchen where once his father sat with stockinged feet on the hearth reading the newspaper while his mother scrubbed the wooden table and set out the plates for dinner.

Luc and Isobel had been busy over the summer painting the walls and they were now a mustard-yellow colour. The cupboards had been replaced with more modern fitted units. But the range and the hearth remained, a kettle still sat on top singing merrily and a rough-haired terrier lay splayed out on the rug.

Luc introduced Isobel to Maurice. Scott had met her during the summer when he had come over to meet Luc's family and to then propose. They had travelled up to Leeds, seen Luc's father, aunt and uncle and then back to Shropshire to see Isobel and Myrtle. Maurice took Isobel's hands in his and kissed her on each cheek. 'You look just like your mother,' he said, smiling.

'And you look just like your photo,' Isobel said, reaching up to the mantlepiece where a black and white faded image of a young man in army uniform was surrounded by a gilt frame. Handing it to him, she now smiled. 'I can see why my mother fell in love with you.'

Maurice remembered the day so clearly. Going to the photographers, his mum spitting into her hankie and then wiping his chin while he waved her away full of nerves and embarrassment. The flash and the standing-still, trying not to smile. This was Edmund Cruso before he metamorphosed into Maurice Smith.

'Do you want coffee, Maurice?' Luc asked, breaking into his thoughts.

He nodded, his mind still in 1917.

'Why don't you sit yourself down here?' Scott said,

Maurice

helping him to a comfortable chair next to the hearth. His parents' old chairs were gone, two upright armchairs upholstered with a bright yellow and blue check fabric stood in their place. He suddenly felt weary. Should he have travelled here? Was this the right thing to do to come back? But looking around him seeing Isobel pouring coffee and the rich aroma of recently ground beans tickling his senses; seeing Scott whisper something to Luc and hearing them giggling together brought him into 1985. Life changes, it moves on and if we hang onto the past, we cannot be ready to face our present and future lives. An image of his wife, Rose, came to him then. Their life together had been full of joy, bringing up their adopted children and then having grandchildren was more than he had ever thought possible. A successful art dealer and gallery owner, wealthy and highly respected in the world of art; he hoped his parents were proud of him and they forgave him for not coming home until now.

'Is the coffee to your liking, Maurice?' Isobel asked. 'Luc says you are very particular about flavours. I love coffee too and have tried all sorts of roasts, but this one is my favourite. What do you think?'

Maurice sipped and savoured a mouthful. He slowly nodded. 'Ah, yes. This is wonderful, thank you.'

With the ice broken, Isobel and Maurice started to chat. Luc and Scott occasionally adding a comment and soon they were all laughing together over things they had seen on the television or heard on the radio. Maurice was keen to see Isobel's artwork, so they all wandered over the farmyard to the studio.

'Luc tells me you have an exhibition coming up,' Maurice said as he wandered around the studio.

'Oh, it's nothing really. Just a local show.'

'I'm sure your paintings would be very much

appreciated.' He stopped at a canvas propped against a table. 'This is an interesting one. Two women as one. Who sat for you, may I ask?'

'That's Myrtle. As she is now and as she was as a young woman. I used an old photo and a recent Polaroid I took.'

Maurice looked more closely and there she was, his Myrtle. Smiling into the camera, a memory of a previous life. *I must see her*, he thought.

As though reading his mind, Scott said, 'Luc and I are going to collect Myrtle now. We'll be back very soon.'

'That's fine,' Isobel said. 'We can get to know each other, can't we, Maurice?'

Maurice nodded and sat himself down on one of the chairs in front of the huge window. 'That would be nice. I'm happy just looking out onto the fields and if I'm allowed another coffee, I will be very happy indeed.'

'Coming right up!' answered Isobel.

Left alone, the two of them settled down. A cafetiere and fresh cups, along with a plate of chocolate digestives, now on the low table between them.

Maurice looked out across an open field. 'I remember when this was an old barn and this window, was a door for a giant and within it a little door for someone like me. But I like this very much.' He waved his arm around encompassing the space. 'I like to mix the modern with the old too. You must come to Paris. I would love to take you to my gallery. Perhaps you would be interested in showing some of your work.'

Isobel gasped. 'Really? Do you think my work is good enough? That would be marvellous.' She beamed. 'Thank you, Maurice.'

'I know true talent when I see it. In fact, I would like to talk something over with you regarding women and their art. As you know, I've been trying to re-unite some chess pieces.'

Isobel nodded and sipped her drink.

'To begin with, I wanted something to do after my wife died. She and the family had been so much part of my life that I felt lost without her. I still feel the pain of not seeing her every day, not being able to talk and laugh with her. She had a wicked sense of humour.' Maurice stretched out for his coffee and took a sip. 'She hated coffee though.' He chuckled. 'Loved her tea, especially darjeeling. Anyway, as I said, the chess set was a little project for me. And I thought that along the way I could fill in some gaps about my life, things I had pushed to the back of my mind and my heart. I never thought I would find absolute joy in bringing Scott and Lucretia together and I am so pleased they are now engaged.'

'Me too,' agreed Isobel, raising her cup as a toast to the happy couple. 'I think Scott is a lovely young man and he seems to really love Luc.'

Maurice nodded, 'To be honest, I am feeling quite nervous about meeting Myrtle after all this time.'

'She's nervous too. You are now a very successful gallery owner in Paris. In comparison she feels she didn't do much in her life. Yes, she was rewarded with this house when her landlord and his daughter left for America and selling the farmland made her quite a wealthy woman, but she never found true love. Myrtle did a lot in the village, always busy with committees and clubs and of course working at the local school as a secretary. And when I arrived on her doorstep in 1968, she welcomed me with open arms. I have had the pleasure of spending time with my mum. You will like her—she's an amazing woman.'

'Talking of amazing women,' Maurice said. 'I have read the true story of Florence Blanchard, after Luc discovered the book. It was she who made the chess set. As part of my exhibition in Paris, I want to include her work and other female artists to celebrate the incredible things they have achieved in spite of men pushing them into the background.'

'That sounds wonderful, Maurice.'

'Luc has agreed to organise it all. Scott, with his writer hat on, is going to write an article for the newspapers.'

The sound of a car coming into the yard prevented more discussion. Isobel shot out of her chair. 'I must check the oven. The roast chicken will be burnt to smithereens!' She dashed out of the building, waved at the three people now getting out of the car and disappeared into the kitchen, shouting hello and for Scott and Luc to come and help.

Maurice was on his feet after following her to the door of the barn and there in front of him was a white-haired old lady with eyes sparkling and a cheeky grin under a pert nose. She was dressed in an elegant floral dress with a pale blue jacket, matching handbag and shoes.

'Edmund?'

He stepped gingerly towards her, holding out both hands to grasp hers. 'Myrtle?'

'Well look at us, old farts,' giggled Myrtle. 'Your hair's whiter than mine.'

Maurice chuckled. 'You still look beautiful to me.' They embraced, a little awkward but soon found they seemed to mould into each other's body. The years melted away and there they were in a farmyard with the cows lowing in the field, chickens running stupidly around their feet and the farm cat sunning itself on a wall.

'We have a lot to catch up on, haven't we?' Myrtle murmured, pulling away.

Maurice nodded, taking her hand, and leading her

Maurice

into the art studio. 'Let's sit down and you can tell me all about your life.' He smiled at the woman who was his first love and as he walked through the door, he felt Rose, his second love's presence, giving them her blessing.

Chapter Thirty

LUC

The roast chicken had not been ruined, the lunch was a success and the apple crumble for dessert was polished off very quickly. Luc looked around the table: Scott, her fiancé, his floppy hair and gentle smile; Maurice, silver-haired, wearing a camel-coloured suit with a scarlet tie and a shirt with a fine pink check, his eyes sparkling; Isobel, looking radiant in a flowing kaftan of blue and green and Myrtle, Luc's real grandmother at the head of the table, animated and laughing. Luc caught Myrtle's eye, and the old lady winked at her.

This was not the time or the place to break the news of what she had discovered a few weeks ago. She wanted to finally enjoy this moment when her family were reunited, and yet the spectre of her grandfather, Bradley Hurt seemed to be forever in her thoughts. He had left Leeds in 1969 and not died as she had been led to believe. On visiting the records offices in Shrewsbury and speaking to her aunt and uncle, along with more research, Luc had cross-checked dates and times, and all the dots seem to have joined around 1969, here in Bounds End.

Luc

Yes, he had been a bully and had left Edmund Cruso for dead; yes, he had walked out on Myrtle, and yes, he abused people but was it fair to have been killed? According to news reports from the time, the alleged murder of Edmund Cruso in 1969 remained unsolved and Luc was certain that the body discovered lying in the crop circle was that of Bradley Hurt.

He had wronged so many people in his life, she thought to herself, and yet other people could have made different choices. Edmund could have opened the letter from Myrtle during the war; he could have visited his mother and Myrtle after the war; Myrtle could have followed Brad to Leeds and got her daughter back; Elspeth could have stood up for herself against his bullying and thrown him out. Luc knew, though, people are fallible. We are all flawed, no one is truly good, we all hold secrets. And thankfully, no one can read our minds. She looked again around the table. Everyone was chatting, nobody had noticed she had gone quiet, except Scott. He was gazing at her now, his eyes probing her face. 'Are you okay, Luc?' he asked in a hushed tone.

She nodded.

The room fell silent, the fat walls of the old building keeping out most sounds apart from a lone blackbird chirruping outside the open window. The air around her thickened all of a sudden and for a moment, she felt a little dizzy. Blinking, she realised everyone was looking at her.

'What do you think, Lucretia?' Myrtle asked.

'I'm sorry. I was miles away.' Luc hadn't heard a question.

Scott intervened. 'Yes, Maurice, I think that's a good idea. It's time to re-unite the chess pieces.' He smiled encouragingly at her, and she slowly nodded. Scott rose from his seat, went to a leather holdall and without

Hearsay

ceremony brought out the wooden box. He placed it amongst the mess of pudding bowls, scraped clean while Isobel hurriedly cleared a space.

Maurice opened up the box revealing the red and white pieces cocooned in their little beds of velvet. Luc passed her red pawn across after removing it from its ribbon and loop. Maurice reverently placed it in its rightful space and then looked across at Myrtle. She in turn placed her handbag on the table and lifted out a white handkerchief. Carefully, unrolling the white pawn from its shroud she placed it in Maurice's outstretched hand. And finally, the set was complete. Again, the room fell silent. No blackbird sang this time, just the hum of the fridge and a soft roaring from the range.

Breaking into the quiet, Maurice clapped his hands and announced, 'Finally we are complete.'

And suddenly, Luc was on her feet. 'Is that it? Is that really what we've been searching for? What about Eirene and Sidney? What about Bradley Hurt? And what about Florence Blanchard who started all of this off? Don't they all deserve justice? Putting bits of wood into a box doesn't explain what happened to them, does it?' Her voice had risen, her frustration boiling over.

Everyone glared at her. No one spoke. And then a small voice from the other end of the table said, 'Sit down, Lucretia. You're right. It is time.'

Isobel looked at her mother, all colour draining from her face. 'Mum, you don't have to do this.' She turned and looked back at Luc. 'There's no need for this. She's an old woman. We can move on from this. There's so much to look forward to now. Your wedding, a new life. Stop looking back, look ahead to your future with Scott.' Isobel stared across at Scott who was silently shaking his head.

'Luc is right,' Scott said, his voice strong in the sea of

Luc

anger and accusations. In that moment, Luc knew he would always be there for her. He would stand by her, whatever happened. 'Perhaps we do need to put all the pieces of your lives finally together, not just the chess set. Luc and I were tasked with this, and we still have questions. We cannot move on without knowing.'

Myrtle's voice came again, a calming sound alleviating the heightened pressure of emotions around the table. 'Bradley came here in 1969 intent on seeing Isobel. The shock of seeing him in the kitchen nearly stopped my heart. He just walked in, bold as you like. Still a handsome man, still with eyes you can fall into and never come out. I almost felt sorry for him. I had got my daughter back and he had lost her. I knew how that felt. But, once I had overcome my distress, all of the hate for him came rising up inside me. I threw questions at him, but he dodged them just like he always had. He made himself comfortable in the armchair Edmund's father, Sidney, had always sat and told me to put the kettle on. He asked me to forgive him, I softened just for a second, but I remembered the hurt and the bruises.

I knew he liked to use his fists. He had done so on many occasions. He was good at ensuring that where he hit me, the damage wouldn't show. Anger within me, which I had held onto for so long, surfaced. I mocked him, and said when he left, I had been carrying his child and because he had beaten me so much and then taken my daughter, I suffered a miscarriage. I actually laughed at his expression. Sadness etched itself into his skin, his liquid eyes turned to stone. He finally knew the pain I had suffered.

I shouldn't have laughed. He sneered and then having composed himself he told me he had smothered Sidney in his sleep, because he kept saying Edmund was alive. He said he had poisoned Eirene because she kept saying the same thing and had dragged her body to the crop circle. The lipstick he added to give the woman some colour in her dreary little life, he said. He finished off by saying he had killed Edmund Cruso and left him for dead in a crater in No Man's Land.

I asked him why he hated this family so much? And do you know what he said?' Myrtle looked around, her eyes red-rimmed and strained with the grief of telling her story. 'He said that he was jealous of Edmund Cruso. He used some choice words to describe him, and I won't repeat them here. The hate and envy dripped from his lips. He said, Edmund had everything and he, Bradley Hurt had nothing. He said, "I lost my only son Julian and Cruso handed me the letter informing me of this. He was grinning when he gave it to me. He asked me if this was from my sweetheart as there was a faint smell of perfume. I never told him I was married. I didn't want him to know my business. And then the stupid idiot doesn't even read the letter from his own girl. I did though. I took it from his pocket while we were hidden in the artificial oak tree looking at the Hun. I read every word again and again. She truly loved him, she was sorry about doubting him, she had found the red pawn and kept it under her pillow."' Myrtle paused and looked down into her lap. 'That girl was me, that letter was from me, and you never read it, Edmund. Why didn't you read it?'

Maurice sighed. 'Because I was stupid. I was a coward. I thought you had written to tell me you didn't love me, and I couldn't take any more rejection. The things I saw in those trenches haunted me for years. I mislaid the letter, when I was on duty in the tree watching the enemy camp from the metal branches. Bradley hid below me, on guard. I never knew he'd taken it. Myrtle?'

Luc

he took her hand, 'I am so very sorry for everything.'

Myrtle smiled at him. 'Life is full of twists and turns. If this hadn't happened, then I wouldn't have had Isobel and my beautiful granddaughter, Luc. You wouldn't have met Rose and had your children and, may I say, very handsome, grandson. This generation has learned from our mistakes and are still learning. They will mess up too, we are all imperfect in our own way. Sometimes things happen because they have to.' She removed her hand from Maurice's before continuing. 'And to my eternal shame, I made a huge mistake. I tried to fight Brad. Everything he had divulged threw me into such resentment that I started to pummel his chest. He pushed me off and I fell hard against the range. He stood over me, raving, swearing at me and then began kicking me and…'

'I hit him,' Isobel interrupted. 'It wasn't Myrtle. I had to stop him; he would have killed her.'

A gasp went around the table. She continued. 'I came back to find my father standing over Myrtle, his hands balled into fists, calling her names. I had seen this so many times with Elspeth and so I did something which I should have done long ago. I grabbed a saucepan and swung it hitting the back of his head. I just wanted to stun him, but he dropped like a stone.'

'What happened then, Mum?' Luc wanted to know.

'We both panicked, Myrtle and me. He didn't move. Myrtle wanted to call the police, a doctor, someone, anyone who could put this right again.'

'Eventually we decided not to seek help,' Myrtle added. 'This man was evil; he had killed three people and he was intent on killing me when Izzie came to my rescue. For some crazy reason we decided we wanted revenge, hysteria took over. We waited until darkness fell and then trundled him in a wheelbarrow to Top Field. We created our own crop circle with boards and laid him there.'

Isobel added, 'I found a rock, smeared it with his blood and set him in the circle of barley. We made it look as though he had fallen against the rock. We kept telling ourselves this was revenge for what he had done to Eirene, such a lovely lady and of course to Sidney and Edmund. We've lived with that secret ever since and not told anyone.'

'That's not strictly true, is it?' Luc said. 'You told Elspeth, and you told Dad. When I asked him, he admitted they both knew what had happened.'

Isobel bent her head. 'Yes, we did.'

'And so, they were party to your guilt, telling people Bradley Hurt had died, but not disclosing the dreadful circumstances,' Luc went on.

Isobel looked across the table at Luc. 'Yes, that is right. Luc, he was a cruel, evil man. I know you remember him as good, but he wasn't. He manipulated people. Yes, he suffered when his son, whom he never saw, died after only a few days and that resentment ate away at his heart, leaving him full of cruelty. He had always treated others like his pawns, controlling them, taking advantage of their good nature.'

'And as pawns,' Myrtle said, 'we can overcome difficulties and on reaching the far side of the board we too can become whatever we want. A pawn can even become a queen.' She smiled encouragingly. 'What are you going to do now, Luc?'

Four pairs of eyes turned on Luc and she felt like a judge imposing a sentence. 'I'm not sure. There should be an investigation, but I don't think they would listen to hearsay. What you've said wouldn't stand up in court.'

Scott agreed. 'We have done quite a bit of research, well Luc has. She went to Shrewsbury back in the summer

Luc

and unearthed quite a bit about the case. It's been left as unsolved. No family member has come forward to prove it wasn't Edmund Cruso's body.'

A deep voice joined the conversation. Maurice had been silent throughout and now he said, 'Edmund Cruso is dead. Can we keep this to ourselves? Myrtle is in her eighties, as am I. Isobel, with all due respect, isn't getting any younger either. I now know the truth about my parents' deaths. I had always suspected Bradley, but my life had moved in another direction, and I firmly believed no one cared about me, so I never investigated further. I moved on then and I think we all need to do this now.'

'I don't know if I can,' Luc said. 'People have died. That's not right.' Scott went to her, and she fell into his arms. 'I'm right, aren't I, Scott?'

'It was an accident, Luc. He fell and hit his head in a field, that's all,' Scott muttered.

Luc pushed him away. He was complicit in this cover-up. She stared at all the people around the table, each one of them she had come to love only recently and yet this was her family now. *Yes, I have Dad, but then even he's been lying. He never told me about this, and he's admitted to hiding all of Mum's letters.* 'I'm going for a walk; I need some air,' she announced and went to the door. Scott began to follow her, and she raised her hand gently. 'No, I need some time to myself.'

It was a cool September day, the beginning of Autumn and as she walked down the lane towards the fields, she found herself swooshing through golden and bronze leaves in the roadside. Stopping by the five barred gate leading to Top Field, she decided to enter and go to see Old Jack, the oak tree that stood within the field. The land no longer belonged to them; the crop had been harvested and the stubble remained, so she skirted around along the hedge until she only had a small distance to get to the ancient tree.

A sense of peace and tranquillity came over her as she approached the tree. It was magnificent in all its autumn glory. Orange, yellow and brown treasure adorned the branches high above the ground; leaves shivering in their death throes before floating gently to the ground. A sudden breeze caused a rainfall of golden leaves and for one brief moment the sun popped out its face to glance at the world below. Luc looked down and saw nestled within the gnarled roots an upturned golden brown leaf cupping rainwater like a child begging for more. Beside it a tiny acorn cup sat without a saucer, surrounded by softly smudged leaf mould and the brown earth patterned with remnants of lives gone by.

All around there is decay and death and yet life abounds too, Luc pondered surveying the scene. *The glimmer of sunshine brings hope and warmth and tiny acorns—the promise of new life.*

Luc had grabbed her bag as she walked out of the house, and now she sat and took out the translation of Florence's life. It felt right for her to finish the story here. She turned to the final chapter.

THE STORY OF THE BLANCHARD CHESS SETS BY M. FLAUBERT

Part 6

PARIS 1834

My name is Michel Flaubert. I have penned this book based on what Florence Blanchard has told me. She once saved my life, and I wish to save her too. However, I may be too late to save her soul. She has been incarcerated in the Salpêtrière Hospital for eight long months now. Few people come out of there.

I have written this as a testament to her creativity and determination and to prove her innocence. I have discovered that Henri Placquette, the man who physically attacked her in her home was found to have been stabbed in the chest. A slight wound, possibly caused by the bradawl she used to deter him caused only a slight rupture to the skin. This would not have killed him.

I have also ascertained her father, Gabriel Blanchard died due to an attack while living in a slum in Montmartre. The killer, another itinerant, admitted he weighed the corpse down with rocks to prevent it floating on the waters of the Seine.

Florence Blanchard is only guilty of hearsay. As a single woman she has no rights in this so-called modern city of Paris. To keep her craft, she had to lie. To feed herself, she had to pretend. To live, she had to be like a man. She is not mad. She is saner than any man I know.

Hearsay

Florence Blanchard is an artist of worth. Her art should be celebrated and honoured, and she should be remembered for creating exquisite chess sets.

Michel Flaubert   1834

Luc closed the book. She knew what to do, now. Looking across the field, she could see Scott standing at the gate. *He's wearing orange suede shoes today, he won't venture across the mud,* she thought. Laughing, she waved at him, rose from her earthy seat and made her way across the field back to him and towards her future.

EPILOGUE

PARIS 1986

'Are we going to have enough champagne?' Luc asked Isobel. Her feet were already sore from wearing high heels and her mouth ached from all the smiling.

'There's plenty, stop worrying. Everything is going very well.' Isobel seemed remarkably calm for someone whose artwork was being displayed in a Parisian gallery.

Luc paused and took stock of the situation. Over a hundred guests had been invited and almost all of them had arrived at the same time. Friendly chatter and laughter glided around the vaulted ceiling while people crowded to view each painting and to discuss the subject matter. The clink of glasses punctuated each discussion, the tap-tap-tap of heels echoed on the flagstone floor as another wave moved on.

A thin champagne flute full of bubbling gold was thrust under her nose and Luc blinked. It was Scott, dressed in a black suit and bow tie with his signature suede shoes, a scarlet pair today, adding flair to his ensemble. Taking the glass, she sipped not taking her eyes off the room.

Hearsay

'Are you pleased with how it's going so far, Luc?' he asked.

'Yes, I think so, but I wish Maurice was here to see all of this. It was such a shame after all he has done; he was destined not to make it.'

Scott hugged her. 'I know I miss him very much too. He's here in spirit.' They were both silent contemplating Maurice Smith.

'I like the way you've had the chess set displayed. Let's go and pay homage. Maurice would have liked that,' Scott suggested, taking Luc's hand.

They were stopped so many times by guests marvelling at their achievements and success of the exhibition and asking after Maurice, that it was a full half an hour before they could enter the Atrium. All around the room, display boards stood with information about different women artists from history alongside their artwork—sculpture, oil paintings on canvas, pencil drawings, ceramics and there in the centre under a dome of Perspex was the chess set. It was surprisingly quiet standing there under the glass roof, a pure blue from the sky above; just a few people wandering around the exhibits.

'Thank you, Scott,' Luc said, her voice hushed.

'Why are you thanking me? You've done all the hard work.' He laughed and then bent to kiss her lips. 'I love you, Luc.'

'I love you, too,' she whispered back. 'Thank you for being there for me. I wish I had met Florence Blanchard. She sounds like an amazing woman. When I read she was treated as insane, I knew this was my mission to bring her story to the world, to celebrate her life and her art. This,' she gestured to the chess set, 'will go a little way to right some of those wrongs.'

EPILOGUE – Paris 1986

'We can all go a bit mad at times,' murmured Scott. 'Just like your mum and Myrtle lost their sanity for a moment.'

'Yes, I'm glad that was all sorted out. I'm glad they went to the police too on their own volition and not being forced by me. Suspended sentences for perverting the cause of justice were a fair result. Unlike what happened to Florence. That was cruel and certainly not justice.'

'Maurice managed to bring it all together, but he wouldn't have done it without us. He's been gone for so long now; I'm thinking of selling the house.' Before Luc could answer, several people entered the Atrium. Myrtle, a diamond necklace sparkling at her neck, holding hands with little Sophia, led the group followed by Luc's father, aunt and uncle and finally Isobel. The hugging seemed to go on and on and then parting like the Red Sea to filter around the glass dome housing the chess set, a single figure was revealed, standing alone. A pinstripe suit with a lime green shirt, a tie of navy and green and a pocket handkerchief of green polka dots. Maurice Smith. Luc smiled and rushed to hug him.

'You made it. How was the cruise? We heard you were held up and wouldn't make it in time,' Luc said.

'Well, I thought I'd better get here before my grandson decides to sell my house,' Maurice said winking at Luc.

'I was only joking,' Scott spluttered. 'Well, if you will go off for several months with Myrtle on a world cruise.' He laughed.

'You can never sell that house, Scott. It belonged to the Flaubert family. It is another link to the past. Now, let me see what you have managed to do here.' Maurice slowly walked around the dome. 'Yes, you have done Florence, proud. Well done to you both. And may I say

Isobel's art is fabulous. Lots of orders have been taken so that is wonderful. I will drink to that.' He took a glass of champagne from Myrtle and raised his glass high.

Luc and Scott held each other close as everyone raised their glasses. 'Santé!'

The End

ACKNOWLEDGEMENTS

Seeing a chess set in an antique shop with two pawns missing and a card saying that a soldier had given one pawn to his mother and one to his sweetheart before leaving to go to war set me thinking. If he had returned, why were the pieces still missing? This question led me to write Hearsay.

Thank you to all of the lovely people who kindly agreed to read the novel and for their feedback. I know how much time it takes to do this, and I very much appreciate your support and comments.

Thank you to the Olney Writing Group—you are a tower of strength and are interwoven within my writing journey. Thank you to the authors I have met through the Olney WordFest and for your guidance and advice.

Thank you to my publisher, Deb Griffiths at BAA. You are amazing!

Thank you to all of the incredible women in my life, thank you for your love, support and inspiration.

Thank you to my long-suffering family for supporting me and making me endless cups of tea to sustain the brain!

ABOUT THE AUTHOR

E. M. Tilstone lives in Buckinghamshire with her family. She loves to write and to coach other writers. She enjoys researching the history behind her novels and to bringing their stories to life.

Follow E. M. Tilstone on Instagram @emtilstone_author

And find out more on www.sueupton-author.com

Printed in Great Britain
by Amazon